MISSING

MELISSA

Also by Alretha Thomas

Daughter Denied

Dancing Her Dreams Away

Married in the Nick of Nine

The Baby in the Window

One Harte, Two Loves

Renee's Return

Four Ladies Only

MISSING

MELISSA

A NOVEL

ALRETHA THOMAS

DAC

Diverse Arts Collective

ACKNOWLEDGMENTS

Missing Melissa is my eighth novel. Like its predecessors, its conception and birth came with moments of hilarity and delight as well as waves of sadness and disappointment. I was beyond ecstatic when the idea came to me to write a story about identical twin sisters who are separated at a young age due to the nefarious deeds of an unknown person. Early on, I saw the makings of a good mystery. I have been told by countless readers that my novels cross genres. In my novel, The Baby in the Window, there are strong elements of suspense and crime. However, Missing Melissa would be pure mystery. With that in mind, I knew I would need my beta readers.

After completing my first final draft, I reached out to my team, bracing myself for their suggested revisions. Special thanks to Yolanda Oliver, Vivian A. Baker, Aleksandra August, Alisha M. Simko, and Selatha Simmons. Ladies, I'm indebted to you for your time and honesty. After countless additional drafts, I finally reached a point where I felt comfortable turning my manuscript over to my development editor, Karinya Funsett-Topping, of The Editorial Department. When I received her evaluation, I realized there was more work to be done. Karinya, thank you for digging deep, leaving no stone unturned. Finally, I had a novel I believed could withstand the scrutiny of top literary agents.

Someone once said, "We make plans and God laughs." The later was true in my case, because destiny would have it that I, and not a publisher, would launch Missing Melissa. It took me more than a minute to let go of my plan and let God take over, but I did and I'm thrilled I did. Because of that decision, you're holding this book in your hands today versus the year 2016 or beyond. Maddie's story needed to be told *now*. I thank God for giving me this story. I hope it leaves you believing more, hoping more, and loving more.

Finally, thanks to every book club, friends, and family who have supported me on my literary journey thus far. Much love!

MISSING

MELISSA

This book is dedicated to:

My incredible husband, Audesah L. Thomas.
Thank you for your undying love and faith in me.

Chapter 1

She's not dead.

I sit bolt upright in bed, my heart pounding, and my mind racing with thoughts about my twin. I pull my knees to my chest, wrap my arms around them, and rock back and forth. The movement calms me. When I turn toward my nightstand, my gaze locks onto the clock. *It can't be one-thirty.*

The doorbell rings, followed by muffled voices filtering through my bedroom door, most likely my parents, and whoever's visiting. Curious, I get up, open it, and am nearly knocked to the floor by my mastiff. He greets me with hugs and licks.

"Good afternoon to you, too, Pepper. Mommy loves you. Yes I do, sweetie." He barks and makes a run for my bed. I sit next to him and smooth my hand over his soft coat of thick, shiny tan fur. "I had a dream about Melissa, Pepper." I look into his eyes, wondering if he would have loved my twin as much as he loves me. High heels clicking on the other side of my bedroom door interrupt my thoughts.

"Happy Birthday, Maddie," Ruby says, sashaying her way into my room. "Are you just waking up?"

I feel a flush spreading over my face and neck, surprised she's already here. We hug and so much love oozes out of her I get choked up. There's nothing like a BFF.

Before I can get a word out, Pepper barks. Ruby and I crack up. "Pepper, what are we going to do with this woman?" Ruby asks. He raises his ears and tilts his colossal head. More giggles.

There's always laughter when Ruby comes around. The kind that makes you pee your pants and get raccoon eyes. I step back and stare at her regal face.

"What's wrong with you, Maddie?"

"Nothing's wrong," I say, flopping down onto my bed. "I'm surprised you're here already, and yes, I'm just getting up."

Squinting, she gives me *that look*. It's the one I get when she thinks I'm keeping something from her. Next she'll be planting her hands on her slender hips. I knew it. I swear she could be a model. Five-foot eight, a whole three inches taller than me, almond shaped eyes, legs that go on forever.

"When did you get here?"

"An hour ago," she says, patting her afro.

"An hour ago? I thought that was you ringing the doorbell just now."

"No, I've been here. That was your grandmother. I was downstairs helping your father with his desktop computer and his new Dumbphone."

"Wow, I wish I had known, I would have come down

and saved you."

"No worries. Your mother finally got him to give me a break and then she sent me up here to wake you. Maddie, we all know you like to get your beauty rest, but damn, it's almost two. Your party starts in an hour."

"I know. I didn't sleep at all last night. It was almost six by the time I finally got a little shut-eye."

"I can tell. Your baby blues are red. Have you been crying?" she asks.

"No," I say.

"Then what's going on?"

"I guess I have a lot on my mind. It's June, but it feels like December. You know with graduating last month, the upcoming move, starting my new job in a week. And I feel so *old*."

"Madeline Louise Patterson, you're twenty-two, not ninety-two! Since when is twenty-two old?"

"I know but—"

"We're grown now. We asked for this," she says, towering over me, looking at me with her 'I got your back' smile. "It's all good. Remember when we were in the tenth grade how we used to fantasize about being grown-ass women, being able to stay up all night, screwing good-looking guys, and marrying rich ones?"

"Yep, I sure do," I say, rising. "But…"

"But what?" she asks.

"Melissa's still alive."

"What do you mean, she's still alive?"

"She's alive. I had a dre—"

"Don't do this, Maddie. Not today. Let it go."

"I knew you were going to react like that," I say.

Before she has a chance to go off on me, I run into the

bathroom, lock the door, and slip out of my tattered sweat pants and favorite UCLA jersey. Entering the shower, I turn the faucet on full blast. I ignore Ruby who's now on the other side of the door, probably with her hands on her hips, calling out to me.

"We need to talk, Maddie. Right now. Get out of the shower right now, please."

"I can't hear you," I say, reaching for my favorite shampoo.

"Madeline Louise Patterson, open this door right now."

The water rains down on my head, soaking my hair, and I sing Pharrell's "Happy" because I am happy. Melissa's alive. She's not dead. I know I'm not supposed to believe that. I'm supposed to believe the investigators, the reporters, the naysayers, the nosey neighbors, the psychics, the pundits, all those people nineteen years ago and several years after, that gave up on the little three-year-old-girl who was driven away by the bad guys, never to be seen again. I'm supposed to believe my parents and my best friend that Melissa's dead.

I shut my eyes and concentrate. Why can't I remember the day she was taken? It's always bits and pieces. Like a puzzle. I see my mother's face, her smile, her eyes. She's wearing a coat and so are we. Our matching red and blue jackets with the hoods trimmed in fake fur. I see Melissa's mouth. It's open wide and she's crying. Everything is meshed. Our SUV, our car seats. I press on my head trying to remember, but I can't.

The dream I had last night or I should say this afternoon, wasn't the first dream I've had about my sister, but it's the first time I've dreamed about her being an adult. All the other times she was still three. I used to have other dreams, too — dreams about people coming in and out of our house. Strange men in suits and ties, wearing big guns and badges.

Men and women with cameras and microphones, gawking at me, pointing at me. Sometimes my dreams were nightmares starring my parents. My father falling over drunk, slurring his words, hitting the wall until his fist bled. My mother, comatose, out of it, a bag of bones, hopeless, helpless, barely alive. Everything is jumbled and mixed up, dreams, real life. I can't put it together.

While getting out of the shower and drying off, the silence gives me pause. "Ruby? Pepper?" Wow, I was on one. I totally forgot about Ruby. That's what happens when I start focusing on Melissa. I'm not supposed to focus on Melissa. I'm supposed to take care of myself, my life. That's what I've been told, and believe you me; I have worked hard to do just that. But it hasn't been easy. How can you forget about a part of yourself? It's like asking a leg amputee to forget about his or her legs.

I unlock the bathroom door and step into my empty bedroom. Ruby and Pepper are gone. I hope Ruby's not pissed with me, but I didn't want to get into it with her. I can't stand it when she tells me to not go there. To let it go. To be grateful I'm still here and that God has His reasons.

My eyes lock onto the wall near my bedroom door that's covered in family photos that make me all misty-eyed, especially the baby pictures. The crazy photos I have with Ruby lift my spirits. We took some kick-ass graduation pictures. I laugh out loud at the one where Ruby's pointing to her head and rolling her eyes. COMPUTER GEEK is scrawled across the front of her black cap.

I enter my walk-in closet that's filled to the brim with clothes and shoes. I check out the red dress section. Yep, I'm anal like that when it comes to my wardrobe. I rifle through my favs. I had thought about wearing pants, but Ruby's got a thing about dresses, and I want to get on her good side. I'm going to need an advocate when I tell my parents I want to reopen Melissa's case.

I set the dress to the side, brush my teeth so well, my dad would be proud, blow dry and style my hair, and put on my makeup. By the time I choose the perfect red shoes, and am dressed, it's almost three. Sizing myself up in my standalone mirror, I smooth my hand over my dress and toss my hair over my shoulder. Sighing, I take in my room. I'm going to miss it. I'm going to miss this house.

"Maddie! Where are you? Your guests are arriving."

My face breaks into a huge smile when I hear my mother's voice. I've always loved her voice. It's so melodic. I go to my door, open it, and say, "I'll be down in a minute, Mom. In a minute."

"Okay, hurry. There's someone here who's dying to see you. You're going to be so surprised."

♊

Descending the stairs, I turn my head toward the gust of laughter coming from the family room. So much for Ruby being mad at me. She, and whoever has fallen under her magic spell, seem to be having a blast. Before I reach the bottom step, my mother appears all decked out in her favorite pink Prada dress and to die for matching shoes.

"Maddie, come on. Are you okay? Ruby said you didn't go to sleep until this morning." She reaches for my hand and pulls me forward like she used to when I was little and we had to cross a busy intersection. Then she plants a big, fat, juicy kiss on my cheek.

"I'm fine, Mom," I say, giving her hand a reassuring squeeze. It's warm and soft—stay-at-home-mom soft. Outside of working periodically at my father's dental practice, I don't believe she's ever held down a real job. I've never seen her with the Sunday night blues—the bleakness that hits you when you know the weekend's coming to an end and you have to report to work the next day. I don't think I've ever even heard her say, *Thank God it's Friday*. For her, every day's Friday.

"You should be more than *fine*, young lady. Today's your birthday," she says, rubbing her thumb across my cheek. "Sorry, I got lipstick on you. Anyway, you should be exultant, Maddie." Her eyes widen and she stops in the hallway. I lean against the wall that's decorated with a few of Grandma Patterson's oil paintings. "Red? Why all the red, Maddie? Blue is your color."

"It's for Melissa."

She gives me a smile that struggles to reach her eyes. "Right. For Melissa. Of course."

We step into the family room and are greeted by a rowdy chorus of "SURPRISE!" I curl over, cracking up. Everyone here is certifiably insane. My mother, Grandma Patterson, and Ruby had planned to give me a surprise party, but I found out about it when Pepper nearly choked on the guest list. Ironically, the only part of the list that was legible, after I pulled it out of his mouth, was the part that read *Invitees to Maddie's Surprise Birthday Party*.

"You guys are nuts, but I love you anyway. Thank you." I pull away from my mother and mingle with the other people in the room. Grandma Patterson points to the blue birthday hat with silver tassels she's wearing. She moves her head from side to side, swishing her salt and pepper bob.

"Happy birthday, my darling Maddie," she says, pulling me into a tight embrace. "I love you forever."

I relax in her arms, sucking up all her unconditional love. She smells like she always does—ivory soap mixed with expensive perfume. "I love you more," I say.

"And I love you both more." My father wedges his way

between us and wraps his gangly arms around our shoulders. "What a lucky man I am, surrounded by beautiful women. Beautiful mother, wife, and daughter. And they all have great teeth, thanks to me."

"Alvin, the older you get, the more you remind me of your father," my grandmother says, slipping out of his grasp.

"I'm not sure if that's a compliment or a dig," he says, faking a pout and passing his hand over his thinning, brown curly hair. The white birthday cap with yellow and green dots he's wearing falls to the floor.

"A compliment of course," she says, pointing to his hat.

He picks it up and sticks his chest out like she had told him he was Superman. I guess he's justified because Grandpa Patterson was a saint. Well, almost a saint. He treated my grandmother like a queen and he was a great father and grandfather. Unfortunately he died of a heart attack ten years ago. A blue collar guy who worked on the docks, he was so proud of my father becoming a dentist and having his own practice. He would tell perfect strangers about his son the dentist, whenever given the chance. My grandmother says he was heartbroken when Melissa went missing and he even blamed himself. She believes he never really got over losing Melissa and that he actually died from a broken heart and not a clogged one.

I leave the two of them to each other and make my way through the room, giving shout-outs to the other guests while at the same time admiring all the blue balloons, streamers, and assortment of party favorites. A huge blue and white cake, decorated with the number twenty-two, sits on a table near the sliding glass door that leads to the backyard. I get a momentary kick in my gut when I flash back to the swing set that used to be out back. My mother said Melissa and I loved it so much, we would make our father push us until his arms hurt. My face melts into a smile at the sight of Pepper, wearing a red birthday hat, pressing his nose on the glass door. Poor thing. Whenever we have lots of guests over he has to be put out back. He doesn't do well in crowds.

I focus on the party and perk up when I notice another table covered with a white linen tablecloth and birthday cards, hopefully filled with checks payable to my favorite charity, Children's Hospital, as I had requested. I go to the table feeling blessed to have so many generous family and friends. A gentle tap on my shoulder gets my attention and I turn around. My eyes meet Ruby's narrowed glare.

Chapter 2

"I see you finally finished showering. Why didn't you open the door? I knocked for more than five minutes." She takes a sip of what looks like champagne in the flute she's holding.

"I'm sorry," I say, sending an impish grin her way.

"You better be glad it's your birthday and that you're wearing a dress. We need to talk, Maddie. I heard what you said."

"My—"

Before I can say "my bad," my mother, followed too closely by a twenty-something stranger, approaches. At a closer glance, he looks somewhat familiar. Maybe a fellow Bruin, but then again he doesn't have that collegiate air, or worse, fraternity-hazed look that tends to linger way past graduation.

"Madeline, this is our surprise guest," she says, motioning toward…toward.

"It's me, Ted, Ted Wright."

"Forgive me, Ted. Madeline, this is Ted. Remember Ted, Sarah's younger brother?" my mother asks.

"Way younger brother. We're eleven years apart," he says, thrusting his hand my way. He flashes a goofy toothy grin and winks.

"Teddy. Teddy Wright." I shake his sweaty hand and quickly pull mine away. While he's not looking, I wipe it on the linen tablecloth behind me.

He runs his freckled fingers through his red hair and says, "Right. I go by *Ted now*," apparently way past his 'Teddy' days. He then looks at Ruby and says, "I've been here a while. I really appreciate Ruby making me feel at home. She's a very funny lady. It's not very often funny and beauty intersects."

We all turn toward Ruby who's having a coughing fit. Tears streaming down her face, she grabs the napkin stuck to the bottom of her glass and wipes her eyes.

"I'm sorry," Ted says. "I tend to kinda say what comes to my mind. Sarah says I'm filter-challenged."

My mother and I exchange sly looks and burst out laughing. Soon Ruby and Ted join us. In between giggles, I say, "You left out brains. You should have said beauty, funny, and brains. Ruby was our high school valedictorian and she graduated magna cum laude from UCLA."

Ted reins himself in and says, "I'm intimidated."

"Don't be," Ruby says.

"What's so funny?" my father asks, with Grandma Patterson on his heels, taking gulps of what appears to be wine from a wide mouthed crystal glass.

"Ruby's funny, Mr. Patterson. Funny, beautiful, and smart," Ted adds.

"You're preaching to the choir, Ted. She single-handedly set up my new Smartphone and got the bugs out of my desktop."

Ruby fidgets and gives the room a nervous once-over. Her face lights up and I look over my shoulder to see what or who's upstaging Ted and my father.

"Mom, Dad," Ruby calls out, waving to a middle-aged couple standing near the front door, dressed in matching outfits. "Excuse me, my parents are here. I'll be right back," she says.

Watching Ruby distance herself from Ted, I can't help but think about Clayton, her on-again, off-again, soon-to-be-attorney boyfriend, who attends Harvard. He proposed to her last year, but she told him she needed to think about it. He was crushed, but willing to give her time. She told him she really didn't want to be in a long-distance relationship. Knowing Ruby like I do, I don't think she wants to be in *any* relationship, at least not right now. She says she wants to take her time, do it right, like our parents.

"Millicent, let's go say hi to Greg and Rosalyn. We haven't seen them since Greg did our taxes," my father says to my mother while at the same time nodding to Ruby's father, Greg.

"Sure," my mother says. She takes my father's hand and they leave Ted, Grandma Patterson, and me, sharing awkward glances.

I decide I'll be the one to kill the silence, but before I have a chance to part my lips, my grandmother starts to speak. Relieved, I wait anxiously for her to kick-start the next round of stimulating conversation.

"I'm going to let you two catch up on old times while I get a refill." My grandmother lifts her glass in an imaginary toast and heads to the bar.

"Madeline Patterson," Ted announces like a school teacher taking roll.

"Present," I say, expecting him to get the joke and laugh. But he doesn't. He gives me a blank stare. *I can't believe my grandmother abandoned me.*

"Boy, you have changed. I mean, if I had seen you on the street, I never would have recognized you. You're gorgeous. You always did have bionic blonde hair."

"Bionic?"

"It's another way of saying otherworldly, you know perfect," he says, turning redder than his unruly shock of red hair.

"Perfect? I don't think so, but thanks. It's been a long time," I say.

"I was nine when Sarah used to babysit you and Melissa."

"And we were in our twos. Terrible twos."

"You have a good memory."

"Not really. My grandmother told me all these stories about how we drove Sarah bonkers and how we would fight over these Elmo dolls. I wanted the blue one and Melissa wanted the red one and Sarah couldn't figure it out. By the time she did, we had already driven her crazy. She didn't know Melissa loved everything red and I loved all things blue."

"That explains why Melissa was always grabbing my hair," he says. "Yeah, I remember those Elmo dolls and playing with you guys out back. You used to have a swing set. Sarah would let me push you guys sometimes."

"Right," I say, wistfully.

"I'm sorry. Are you okay?"

"I'm fine. By the way, how's Sarah?"

"Married with three kids. She lives in Vegas. My whole family's there."

"I wondered where you all had moved to. How is it?"

"Great. My dad's making a mint out there with his real estate developments. I work with him at his company. It's a burgeoning operation. Remember that never ending huge redevelopment project not too far from here?"

I shake my head and say, "My father messes around in construction, well, more like home projects, plumbing, that sort of thing."

I'm not sure if it's on purpose, but he ignores me interrupting him and rattles on. "It was an eyesore, cement trucks, caterpillars everywhere...anyway, that was one of our projects. You were probably too young to even notice it."

"I see," I say. "So what brings you back to the neighborhood?"

"I'm tying up some loose ends for my father. We have rental property out here. I came by our old house and I saw the balloons out front and all the cars. So I got curious. I wasn't sure if you all still lived here, but I took a chance and your mother answered the door. She remembered me right away. I guess the red hair is kind of a dead giveaway. By the way, you look like your mother. She hasn't changed much at all. Well, I guess a little, I mean she seems much calmer. I have to admit it was a relief knowing you all were still here."

"I'm glad, but why?"

"You probably don't remember much, but it was like a three-ring circus around here nineteen years ago, when Melissa went missing."

Listening to Ted, I feel a twinge in my belly, but I ignore the sensation and give him my full attention. I want to hear what he has to say. Outside of my grandmother, I can't find anyone who's willing to revisit that dark period in our lives. And over the years, my grandmother has pretty much put it all behind her, and Ruby didn't even live here at the time. She moved into the neighborhood six years later and we met in the fourth grade. When she did find out I was the sister of the twin who went missing, unlike most of the other kids in school, she didn't treat me like I was cursed. Nor did she try to dig, she let me talk about it when I was comfortable doing so.

"You're right, there's a lot I don't remember."

"I guess that's a good thing," he says, thrusting his stubby hands into his pockets.

I notice a tan line on the ring finger of his left hand. Hmm, *divorced, cheating?* "It is and it isn't...I mean, I wish I had been older because I have so many unanswered questions," I say, looking at him pointedly, wanting him to keep it real and speak his mind.

"Well, first off, the media took over the entire neighborhood. They were camped out twenty-four-seven. It was national news, you know with Melissa being so young and pretty. I mean, we had never had anything like that happen in Dancing Hills before. Back then people didn't even lock their doors. What do you expect from a town whose hills dance," he says, chuckling. "Back in the day, Dancing Hills was named the safest city in California— actually, the safest in the country." Ted looks around the room and then he whispers, "The thing that shocked everybody even more than the carjacking was your father being arrested."

"Arrested?" *What the hell.*

"Wow, I'm sorry. You didn't know?"

Shaking my head, I motion for some water.

"Don't move, I'll be right back," he says, sprinting toward the bar.

My eyes scan the room. They lock onto my father chatting up Ruby's parents, while my mother hangs on his every word. Ted returns with a bottle of water. I take a gulp and say, "Thank you."

"I'm talking way too much. It's your birthday for Christ's sake. I shouldn't be talking to you about any of this."

"No, I want to know. I *need* to know. You said my father was arrested."

"Well, I should have been clearer. He wasn't exactly *arrested*; it was more like he was a person of interest. This all happened a couple of years after Melissa went missing. It was in 1997. You were only five, so you wouldn't have known about it."

"I went to live with my grandparents when I was five."

"You've heard of the Jilliande Richardson case right?"

"Of course."

"She was killed in 1997. She was a pretty little girl with blonde hair and the police suspected her parents had something to do with her death. A lot of people thought her father killed her. So I think that got the cops out here to thinking that maybe there was foul play with Melissa, you know maybe your father was involved. It was all speculation and they had absolutely nothing on him. And according to the press, at the time the carjacking took place, he was in the middle of a root canal. Not only did they release him, but they apologized profusely, mainly because the neighborhood was up in arms. Your father was really loved here. I'm sure he still is. He's done dental work for almost every kid in the neighborhood, including me."

The slight tension at the base of my neck dissolves after Ted declares my father's innocent. Maybe my family's right. Maybe I need to chill on finding Melissa.

"Maddie!" I jump when Ruby sneaks up on me. "Maddie, what's wrong?" she asks so loudly a hush falls over the room.

My parents, Ruby's parents, and my grandmother run to my rescue, but there's nothing to save me from. "What's wrong?" they all ask in unison.

My father turns toward Ted and asks, "What did you do to her?" Before Ted can defend himself, my father asks me, "Is he bothering you?"

"No, no. I'm fine, Dad. I'm fine. Nothing's wrong."

"I'm sorry. It's my fault," Ruby admits. "I scared her."

"You didn't *scare me*. You caught me off guard," I say, wishing everyone would calm down. "No worries, Ruby. It's fine. Let's eat some cake," I suggest.

"But you haven't eaten breakfast or lunch," my mother laments.

"It's her birthday, Millicent. If she wants to eat cake, let her eat cake," my grandmother says.

"Let's at least sing happy birthday first," my father suggests.

I force a smile and walk toward the cake along with my family and the other guests. Ted sidles up next to me and takes my hand. I look down at the white business card I'm now holding and then at him.

"I gotta go, Maddie. I can tell you have a lot of questions about what happened. A buddy of mine works for Dancing Hills Police Department. Give him a call. He might be able to help you. I'm not the right person to talk to. I don't know the right things to say, or how to say them, and the last thing I want to do is ruin your birthday or your life for that matter. Call him. He's good people. I think he might be able to help you get closure. I put my number on the flip side."

I take in everything Ted's saying, grateful he has loose lips. He kisses me on the cheek, and before I can say thank you, he bolts.

My mother and Ruby approach and lead me to the table.

I stare at the flames on the two candles and shut my eyes. "Happy birthday to you. Happy birthday dear, Madeline, happy birthday to you," they all sing perfectly off-tune. "Make a wish."

Dear God, please let Melissa be alive.

♊

Sitting at the dining room table that's covered with half-eaten cake, used dishes, and silverware, I wait for my parents to join Ruby, my grandmother, and me. It's after eight and all our guests have gone home. My mother approaches with my father following.

"Maddie, why don't we talk in the living room? It's such a mess in here," my mother says.

"Who cares? Let's hear what the birthday girl has to say," my grandmother counters.

"No, mom's right. Let's go to the living room," I suggest.

"Last one there's a rotten egg," my father says, leaving us behind.

"Your father's a trip sometimes," Ruby says under her breath.

"I heard that, Ruby," my father says.

The living room fills with laughter. My parents sit on the loveseat, my grandmother relaxes on the avocado green recliner, and Ruby and I sit on the tan sofa.

"Look at my little girl, all grown up," my father says, his eyes shifting from my mother to me.

"Don't remind me," my mother says.

"Millicent, did you expect for her to stay a kid

forever?" my grandmother asks. She removes the birthday hat she's still wearing.

"No, I didn't, Alicia, but it's still not easy seeing your child leave home."

"Tell me about it," my grandmother says.

My mother rolls her eyes and purses her lips. My father places his hand on her leg and says, "Let it go."

"Maddie, what did you want to tell us?" Ruby asks.

I shift in my seat, glad to take the attention away from my mother and grandmother, who over the years tend to tolerate, more so than accept each other. "I had a dream about Melissa." My announcement is greeted with blank stares.

"Kiddo, you've dreamed about your sister before."

"This was different, Dad."

"In what way?" my mother asks.

"For crying out loud, let her tell us about the damn dream," my grandmother says.

Ruby coughs and passes her hands over her face.

"Melissa was a grown woman in this dream. In my other dreams she was three."

"I see," my mother says, averting her eyes.

"What did she look like?" my father asks, scooting to the edge of the loveseat.

"That's a stupid question, Alvin," my grandmother says.

"Alicia, why do you have to be so rude?" my mother asks. "How many drinks have you had?"

"Don't you worry about me and my drinking. You better be glad it's Maddie's birthday or —"

"Excuse me, but I really want to hear about the dream," Ruby says, casting a knowing look my way.

"Ruby's right. Mom, Millicent, please," my father says.

"I'm sorry, Maddie. You know I love you forever."

"I know you do, Grandma."

"I love you, too, sweetheart," my mother says.

I give my mother a smile and then say, "To answer your question, Dad, Melissa looked like mom and me. She had long, sun-kissed blonde hair, crystal blue eyes, and full lips."

"You know it's because of your mother's hair that we're together, Maddie. I fell in love with her hair in the seventh grade. One day I pulled her pigtails, and I got put in time out for twenty minutes."

"I couldn't stand that teacher of his. She was always picking on Alvin," my grandmother says.

"Anyway, she appeared to me as clear as I'm sitting here. I started to cry, because I was so happy to see her alive."

"Is that why you told me Melissa was alive right before you hid out in the shower?" Ruby asks.

"Right. I was trying to explain, but you cut me off," I say.

"Sorry," Ruby says.

I notice my mother's face redden. "Maddie, it was a dream. Why are you saying she's alive?"

"Because she *is* alive," I say.

"In the *dream*," my mother says.

"In the dream, out of the dream. Maddie says she's alive. What don't you understand about that?" my grandmother asks.

"Mom, are you ready to go home?" my father asks.

"When I'm ready, I'll go. I'm not a child."

"Then stop acting like one," my father says.

My grandmother rises.

"Where are you going?" he asks.

"None of your business," she says, heading to the kitchen.

"There's no more wine *or* champagne," he says.

My grandmother returns and flops down onto the recliner. "What else happened, Maddie?" she asks. Ruby tries to stifle a giggle, but it pops out. My grandmother turns toward Ruby and shoots daggers with her eyes. Ruby looks away.

"Melissa asked me why I was crying. I tried to tell her I was happy to see her, but the words were stuck in my throat. Then she moved toward me and my eyes got wide as saucers. And in that moment, I fantasized about going back to the beginning, when we were one egg, before fertilization, before the split. But she stopped and a horrified look crossed her face and she said, 'Help me. I need your help. Please, save me. I wasn't dead, Maddie!'"

I sit here waiting for them to respond, but the room is so quiet I can hear the refrigerator humming.

"Interesting," my father says.

"So what do you think it means?" Ruby asks.

"I think she's alive. I think she's reaching out to me, and I want to have her case reopened."

"What?" my mother asks.

"You heard her?" my grandmother says.

"Maddie, you really need to think this through," my father says.

"I have, Dad."

"Please, Maddie, let it go. Please tell me you're not going to do this," my mother says, tears pooling in her eyes.

"Are you okay, Mom?" Ruby asks my mother.

"No, I'm not okay and reopening Melissa's case is not okay."

I get a pang in my gut taking in my mother's reaction. I had no idea she would be so against me moving forward. But then again, I'm not her. It was hard for me losing a twin and I'm sure even more devastating for her losing a daughter. My mouth seems to have a mind of its own and I say, "Don't worry, Mom. I won't. I won't bother with it. And I'm sorry I got you upset. You're right, it was a dream."

"I appreciate that, Maddie," my mother says.

"Thank goodness," my father says, falling back onto the loveseat. "Maddie, we did everything we could to find Melissa. I had even hired a private detective because I didn't think the police were doing enough. On top of that, I was doing my own research. Trust me, kiddo, leaving well enough alone is the best thing to do."

"Mom and Dad are right. I think you should stay focused, Maddie. Let it go," Ruby says. She places her hand on mine and gives me an exaggerated smile.

"I need to get home," my grandmother says. "Thanks for sharing, Maddie."

"Be careful, Mom."

"You be careful, Alvin," my grandmother says, leaving.

I go to her and give her a hug goodbye and then return to the living room.

"I better head out, too," Ruby says. "I'll see you tomorrow. I'll drive."

"Okay, Ruby," I say.

"Bye, Mom and Dad." Ruby kisses my parents and leaves.

I sit on the sofa and my parents and I share a quiet moment.

"Great party," my father says, breaking the silence.

My mother and I exchange strained smiles, and now I

wish I hadn't made that promise.

Chapter 3

"Clay, now is not a good time. I'll call you later. Bye now."

Sitting across from Ruby in the patio area of a restaurant in Old Towne Pasadena, I watch her slip her Smartphone into her purse. Pasadena's a city in California known for hosting the annual Rose Bowl football game. I wonder to myself when Ruby's going to tell Clay he needs to really move on. She rolls her eyes and says, "What's wrong with him? Isn't it obvious I'm done?"

I start to tell her Clay can't read her mind and he obviously can't read *between* the lines and that she needs to be honest with him and tell him she's not going to change her mind about the engagement. But she gives me a look that unmistakably says, *You better say what I want to hear, Madeline Louise Patterson.* So I say, "I don't get it. I mean, you turned down the proposal. Most guys would be through."

She flashes me a 'thanks for cosigning' smile and then takes a forkful of her veggie spaghetti. After chewing and swallowing she asks, "Speaking of men, what did you think about Red Ted?"

Before answering Ruby, I look up at the overcast sky, wondering how long this June gloom is going to last. "I'm glad you brought him up," I say, wiping salad dressing off of my mouth.

"Can you believe how thirsty he was acting? He's probably married. I didn't see a ring, but you know a lot of married men don't wear rings. What were you guys talking about for so long?" Ruby asks.

"I saw a tan line."

"I knew it," she says.

"I'm not sure if he's married or not," I say. "Probably not. He gave me his number before he left, and I called him this morning. *He* and not a wife answered the phone."

"You called him? You didn't get enough of each other at the party? What were you talking about? You both looked caught up."

"I called to thank him again, because he gave me some important info," I say. Ruby takes a sip of her sugar-free lemonade, brows raised. I dig into my Cobb salad, waiting to jump knee deep into the subject I *really* want to talk about.

"What kind of info?"

"He was filling in some missing pieces about Melissa, the carjacking. I want to have her case reopened."

Her fork falling to her plate makes me jump. "Wow, Maddie. I thought we were past this. You promised us last night you would let it go. It's been almost two decades. You know how it almost destroyed your family. You told me yourself how long it took your mother to get past it. Why now when you're about to start your life as an adult? You have a great opportunity with the TV station. You're going to be a reporter. We have a fabulous furnished loft apartment downtown we're moving into tomorrow that accepts dogs, very big dogs. Why do you want to ruin all of that?"

"What makes you think I'm going to ruin things?"

"Because I know you, Maddie. Once you get fixated on something, you go overboard, and you have no idea what you're going to come up against. Think about your parents. Why bring it all up again? It's going to bring a lot of pain to a lot of people. You saw how your mother reacted yesterday. Maddie, you're the sister I never had, but always wanted, and if something ever happened to you, I would be devastated. So I understand how you feel, I get that you miss Melissa, but sweetie, you have to let it go. She's no longer with us."

I swallow hard, a little hurt that the most positive person I know believes my twin's dead, in spite of what I told her happened in the dream. "Please hear me out, Ruby."

"Go ahead, Maddie," she says, softening.

Right as I am about to argue my case, the waitress approaches.

"Ladies, can I get you anything else?" she asks.

"We're good. Thank you," Ruby says, still looking at me.

"Okay," she says, turning on her heel.

I take a moment and then say, "Ruby, there's a lot going on. I mean a lot. So much has happened since I had the dream. Strange coincidences I don't really think are coincidences."

"Okay."

"Last night, in bed, I spent a lot of time going over the dream. There were a couple of things I missed."

"Like what?" Ruby asks, leaning forward.

"Remember when I told you all Melissa asked for my help?"

"Yes."

"Well, I also told you all she said she wasn't dead. I mean, it wasn't like she was telling me she's alive. She said, 'Maddie, I wasn't dead.'"

Ruby scrunches her face and says, "I don't get it."

"Why would she say, 'I wasn't dead?' Shouldn't she have said, I'm not dead? It's like she's talking about a time in the past." I shake my head, torn between moving forward with my idea and letting it go. Why am I going down this rabbit trail? Ruby's right, I've worked hard in school for my degree. I want to do well at the station. I have my whole life in front of me. Now is not the time to lose focus. I cup my hands over my face, trying to figure it all out.

"Talk to me, Maddie."

I look up and say, "I know you're right, but I can't help myself. She's my twin. That's more than a sister. When I was a kid, there was nothing I could do, but I'm grown now. I can't let it go. I guess there's a part of me that feels guilty. Why was she taken and I wasn't?"

"You're probably really emotional about it because it's June — the same month Melissa went missing."

"Possibly," I say.

"Maddie, the chances that she's alive after all this time are…and even if she is still alive, what makes you think you can find her when the entire DHPD couldn't?"

"I know she's alive. It's a twin thing, and I know I can find her because she's helping me."

Ruby recoils and folds her arms across her small chest. "Okay, you're scaring me now. What do you mean she's 'helping you?'"

"Before I get into that, there's something else I need to tell you about the dream I didn't mention last night. I had forgotten about this."

"What?"

"She was floating on a ball—a colorful ball, with specific colors that stood out—purple, green, and orange." Ruby covers her face and closes her eyes. She tries to hide a snicker but it slips through the spaces between her fingers. "Are you laughing at me, Ruby Renee Flowers?"

"No, no," she says, sitting up straight.

"I know it sounds crazy, but I believe it means something."

"But how is she helping you?"

"We all know Melissa's favorite color was...is red."

"And?"

"I got the idea to wear all red yesterday. When have I ever done that on a birthday before?"

"Okay," she says, obviously still not convinced.

"What color is Ted's hair?" I ask.

"Red," she says nonchalantly.

"You don't see the connection?" I ask, my voice rising an octave.

Ruby gives me a blank stare.

"Melissa sent Ted to me. Why of all days would he show up like that out of the blue? Yes, he was doing some work for his father, but I don't think it was a coincidence. And then he gives me a contact at the police department." Sensing, Ruby about to add her unwanted two-cents, I say, "And the sermon today at your parents' church. First of all, when was the last time we've come out here to go to church with your parents in Pasadena? It's been forever, but for some reason we decide to go on a day your parents' pastor preaches about Jacob and Esau. Isaac and Rebekah get pregnant with a set of twin boys. The first boy to come out is *red* and very *hairy*. Now that's in the Bible. I'm not making it up. Melissa was born first and she loves red! And out of the two of us, she has the most hair. It's like Melissa's giving me confirmation that I'm on the right track."

Satisfied I've proven my case, I lean back in my chair. I take a swig of water and let the tension seep out of my limbs, waiting and hoping for Ruby to agree with me.

"Hmm," she says, nodding.

"What?" I ask.

"You might be onto something," she says.

I stop grinning and say, "Ruby, you believe me? Please tell me you're on my side."

"I've never not been on your side. I don't want you to get hurt. I don't want you to get your hopes up and…"

"What about Elizabeth Smart, Jaycee Dugard, the three young women in Cleveland? People thought they were dead, too," I add.

"Okay, okay," she says, placing her hand on mine. "I believe you. I think Melissa may be reaching out to you. Anything's possible. And if looking for Melissa makes you as happy as I just saw you get, then I truly believe you're doing the right thing, and I want to help you in whatever way I can."

I stare into Ruby's eyes that are filled with love and compassion and I lose it. Then she loses it. We forget about where we are, and who's looking, and who's not, and get up from our seats, and hold and hug each other like our lives depend on it.

"Don't worry, Maddie. We're going to find her," Ruby says between sobs.

I give her the biggest most appreciative smile I can muster. "Ruby, as your mother would say, 'from your mouth to God's ears.'"

♊

"Please God, please let it be true." I kick the covers off, get onto my knees, and look under my Cinderella pillow. "Hooray!" I shout, snatching the crisp five dollar bill I got in exchange for my front tooth.

"Maddie?"

Lost in my daydream, I gather my thoughts and turn my attention to my father's longtime dental hygienist/office manager. Hands in the pockets of her dental smock, she looks at me with a face coated in concern. "You okay?" she asks.

"I was thinking about the first tooth I lost and how the tooth fairy gave me five-dollars. All the other kids on the block got a dollar. And I think we both know who the fairy was," I say.

She laughs huskily and gives me a knowing nod. "Your father's a generous man. I guess that's one of the many reasons we all love him," she adds with a twinkle in her grey eyes.

"You're right." I rise and go to the wall near the reception desk that's covered in a gang of photos of children and adults. Admiring the smiling faces, I say, "It's nice when you can get paid to do what you love."

"Speaking of which, congratulations on landing your new gig. I'm really into that station. Get all my news from there and the Internet of course."

"Thanks, Emma. It's an entry level position. Basically, I'm a glorified intern."

"You gotta start somewhere. Show up on time, work hard, before you know it, you'll be runnin' the place."

We share a laugh, knowing she's actually talking about herself and the twenty years she's worked at Patterson Dental L.L.C.

"Tammy and Rachael are already at lunch, and I'm going to officially shut down for the next hour. I told him you were here. You can go on back."

"Great. Talk to you later," I say, heading toward my father's office. I walk down the corridor, looking at the numerous exam rooms, glad I'm not due for a cleaning. My father does great work, but once I started dating, I felt weird having him do my check-ups. Every time my ex-boyfriend, Richard and I would kiss, my father, wearing a facemask, would invade my head, and I'd make excuses to shut down our smooches. That's probably why Richard cheated on me and not because he's a *scum bag jerk*—Ruby's words.

Standing at my father's office door, I pause when I see him on the phone. He scratches his head and then motions for me to enter and sit. I've sat in this chair a dozen times over the years, but I still like looking at all the photos, awards, diplomas, and certificates that line the walls. My gaze zooms in on a picture of my parents in their twenties. They're snuggling and giving each other goo-goo eyes. Middle school sweethearts, they have one of the best relationships in town. Ruby's parents are close, too. Right next to my parents' photo is a picture of Grandma Patterson holding Melissa and me.

"Make sure you floss and use a good mouthwash. You'll be fine, Mrs. Brown...right...exactly. Okay, I have to go. Maddie's here...will do," he says, ending his call. He leans back in his ergonomic leather chair and says, "Mrs. Brown says hello."

"How is she?"

"Talkative as ever, but good. To what do I owe the honor of having KYON's star reporter in my office today?"

"Dad, I'm not actually a reporter yet."

"Yet, Y-E-T, you're eligible too. It's just a matter of time, kiddo."

"Thanks, Dad."

"No, thank you for being the wonderful daughter you are. How can I help you? By the way, I have something for you," he says, thrusting his hand into a briefcase that's on the credenza behind him.

Curious, I sit at attention. His checkbook in hand, he reaches for one of the many pens he has in the blue painted, macaroni-covered pencil holder I made him for Father's Day, when I was in the second grade. He begins filling in a check. "What's that?" I ask.

"You said you raised twenty-three hundred dollars at the party Saturday, I want to make it an even twenty-five."

"Wow, Dad. Thanks."

"My pleasure," he says, handing me the check.

I slip it into my purse and then ask, "Dad, have you ever been in trouble?"

"If you count pulling your mother's hair in the seventh grade, I have. I got told off pretty good and put in the corner by Mrs. McGruff," he says, shaking his head.

"You mentioned that the other night. I mean trouble with the police."

His face reddens and he tugs on his tie that's covered with miniature toothbrushes, each hand-painted a different color. "Trouble with the law? Why do you ask?"

I start to answer him, but I take a moment, realizing he didn't answer my question. "Ted mentioned at my party the police labeled you a person of interest two years after Melissa went missing."

Silent, he stares at me. He folds his thin arms over his

chest, pushing the tie upward, and purses his lips. "Maddie, after the party you had us all sit down and then you told us about the dream you had about Melissa. I, along with everyone else, gave you my undivided attention in spite of how difficult it was listening to a dream where Melissa is supposedly asking for help when no one in that room could help her. Maddie, you promised us you would let this go."

"I know, Dad, but—"

"But, nothing. I can't let you do this to your mother."

"Do what to her?"

"Dragging it all up again. We went through hell, Maddie. You were too young to know everything that happened. It nearly destroyed us. Honey, she's gone. It's been forever. We waited five years before we stopped looking. Maddie, we have a life now, a good life. Sweetie, you have so much going for yourself. Enjoy the life you have. I'm begging you to not dig this thing up again."

"Don't you miss her, Dad?"

"Of course. But I've learned to be grateful, kiddo. I could have lost you, your mother, *and* Melissa. But I was spared and I have you, and your mother, and my mother. We're a family, baby." Now standing, he walks to me and passes his hand over my twisted face. "Let it go, Maddie."

"But I feel guilty. Why her and not me?"

"No one can answer that question."

"There seems to be a lot of questions no one can answer," I say rising, moving away from him.

"What do you mean by that?"

"Why did the police suspect you? Why in this small town didn't anybody see what had happened? Why wasn't our SUV found? Why was she taken?"

"Stop doing this to yourself!" He pulls me onto his chest and caresses my back.

"I'm sorry, Dad. I'm sorry I bothered you at work. I didn't mean to upset you."

"It's okay. The police focused on me because of a little girl who went missing two years after Melissa. Her father was a major suspect, so I guess that got them to thinking about me again. That's why they questioned me. I wasn't arrested, I wasn't charged, because I'm innocent," he says, lifting my chin, looking into my eyes.

Staring into his tear-filled brown eyes, I swallow my guilt and shame. "I know you're innocent, Dad, but someone out there isn't, and I plan to find out who that someone is *and* find Melissa."

He moves out of our embrace and goes back to his desk. He collapses into his chair, looking defeated. "Okay, Maddie. I'm not sure who you get your stubbornness from, me or your mother. Before you went to church yesterday, you told your mother and me that you believe Melissa's speaking to you. I'm not going to scoff at that, but you're going to need more help than enigmatic messages in a dream. You'll have to get the case reopened. I'm not sure that's something DHPD can do with limited resources and manpower. You'd have to have some very substantial new evidence in order for that to happen."

"I know, Dad. But I do have a contact."

"What contact?"

I take the card Ted gave me out of my wallet and say, "Mitchell Faulkner."

"Who's Mitchell Faulkner?"

"A friend of Ted's. He's a detective. Ruby and I have a meeting with him tomorrow."

"Ruby's for this?"

"At first she wasn't but she believes me, Dad. I hope you'll stand by me, too."

My father takes a tissue out of the box on his desk and dabs at the perspiration sprouting from his forehead. "I see. Can you promise me something?"

"Of course."

"Be careful and please don't tell your mother. She's soft, Maddie. She won't be able to handle this," he says, reaching for more tissue.

"Okay, Dad. Will do. Are you okay? You're sweating."

"I was tinkering with the air and heat this morning and I may have screwed it up." His phone rings and he answers it, giving me the once-over. For a fleeting moment, I feel more like a double-crosser than his daughter. I wave and he gives me a smile that escapes his weary eyes.

"Bye, Dad."

Chapter 4

"Pepper! Pepper, where are you? Aunt Ruby and I have finished packing and we're ready to go." I look in my bathroom and closet for Pepper, but he's nowhere to be found. On my way downstairs, I almost have a head-on collision with my mother.

"Careful, Maddie. What's going on?"

"I can't find Pepper."

"He was out back a minute ago," she says, dabbing at her red-rimmed eyes.

"Mom, what's wrong? Have you been crying?" She clears her throat and turns away. I step in front of her. "You're crying."

"I'll be okay. It's...it's hard letting you go."

"Mom, I'm not leaving the country. I'm not even going *cross country*. I'll be less than an hour away. And you know Pepper's going to take care of me. And Ruby will be there. I'll be fine."

"But I'm going to miss you."

"You'll get used to it. Remember how upset you were when Ruby and I decided to stay on campus?"

"I do, but you came home every weekend. You still had your room here and a lot of your things here."

"I'm not taking my room."

"You might as well be. It's empty now. Your computer's gone. All your pictures and posters are gone. Your books are gone. Your closet's empty. Thanks for leaving your swimming medals."

I take her in my arms and hold her like I'm the mother and she's the child. I think about what my father said, about her being soft. He's right. She wouldn't be able to handle me looking for Melissa. And then what if I don't find her or what if we get confirmation that she's actually dead? God forbid.

"Come here, Mom." I lead her to my room. She sits on my bed that's covered in the blue duvet my grandmother bought me for Christmas. I sit next to her.

"See how empty it is in here," she says, pointing to the bare walls.

"Mom, I'm not my room. I'm here. I will always be here for you. We're a family."

She forces a smile and says, "I'm sorry for being such a big baby."

"It's okay," I say. My heart goes out to my mother, because unlike my father, she doesn't have a good relationship with her parents. In fact, she doesn't have a relationship with them at all. They've been estranged for as long as I can remember. Why? No one has ever enlightened me. It seems like I'm left in the dark about most things in this family. But that's about to change. "Mom, can I ask you a question?"

"Of course."

"What happened with you and Grandpa and Grandma Darcy? I can't ever remember them calling or coming over. It's almost like they don't exist."

She rises and walks to my dresser. Standing with her back to me she says, "As far as I'm concerned, *they don't* exist."

I go to her and wrap my arms around her waist, wanting to ask more questions, but afraid of upsetting her. She pulls away and faces me. "Maddie, we have to learn to let things go that aren't good for us in this life. We have to appreciate what we have now. We have each other. I know you miss Melissa, we all do, but we have to keep moving forward, sweetie. I appreciate you sharing the dream with us, but I'm glad you agreed to not try to have the case reopened. I don't want you worrying about Melissa, my parents, or anyone. I want you to enjoy your new place and do well at the TV station. You can have it all, Maddie. Soon, you'll be completely over Rich—"

"Mom, I am over Richard, completely. He cheated on me! He's a…a…scum bag jerk."

"I know, sweetheart, but there's still something there. I can tell by the way you snapped at me. When all feelings for him are gone, you'll be indifferent. And then your heart will be open for a new love—someone that will cherish and love you like your father has me over the years. He says he's always loved me. Grandma Patterson wanted him to marry a girl named Sylvia. She lived on their street when they lived in Long Beach. Her parents had money. She thought Sylvia was perfect. But your father thought I was perfect. He even once told me he would die for me if he had to. That's the kind of man you need, you should want, Maddie."

I take a moment to digest her wisdom. "You're right, Mom. I want you to be okay."

"Don't worry about me. Let's go find, Pepper."

"I found him," Ruby says, standing at my bedroom door.

"Where was he?" my mother and I ask in unison.

"Trying to get under the house again," Ruby says, brushing dirt and grass off of her jeans. The debris falls to the floor and she shrieks. "I'm sorry, Mom!"

"Don't worry about that, Ruby. I'll get it. It'll give me something to occupy myself with while I get accustomed to my empty nest."

"My parents are feeling the same way," Ruby says. "Maddie, we better go. I want to get moved in before it gets dark."

"Good idea," my mother says.

"Mom, you better have dad check out the cover over the crawlspace. Pepper nearly pulled it off. I'm not sure what he's after down there," Ruby says.

"I found him over there after the party Saturday. Scratching away," I say, my eyes locking with Ruby's.

"Hmm," my mother says. "You two better get going. I'll walk you outside."

We leave my room with our arms linked — my mother in the middle. I turn toward her, wanting to tell her I haven't let it go and that I still plan on finding Melissa, but I remember what my father said about her being soft and decide to keep quiet. It's better this way. I get giddy when I imagine how freaking surprised she's going to be when I show up at our front door one day, with her long lost daughter by my side.

♊

Sitting on the floor of our new apartment, surrounded by unopened boxes, we all stuff our faces. Ruby, Pepper, and me. Ruby and I scarf down Chinese food and Pepper drowns himself in a bowl of organic dog food, compliments of his Aunt Ruby.

Smacking loudly, Ruby says, "I don't know if this food's actually as good as it tastes or I'm just hungry. Moving sure works up an appetite."

I nearly choke on a forkful of orange chicken. I take a drink of my bottled water, glad to be able to breathe again.

"Careful, Maddie. Don't hurt yourself," Ruby says. Pepper seconds her motion with two loud barks.

"I'm okay. I think it's a combination of good food and big appetites. I'm full," I say, pushing my paper plate to the side and patting my stomach.

"Me, too. Now I want to go to sleep. Can we unpack tomorrow?" Ruby asks.

"Of course, after our meeting with Detective Faulkner."

"Crap, I forgot about that," Ruby says, struggling to get off of the floor.

"Are you okay?"

"I'm fine. Just stiff. I need to get back into my Pilates class. But anyway, I have bad news," she says, finally standing.

"What?"

"Like I mentioned, I totally forgot about our meeting at DHPD and accepted one of the available orientation slots on my new job tomorrow. Once you confirm, you can't back out, because they're juggling a lot of schedules."

I give Ruby a questioning look, wishing she would have told me about her schedule earlier.

"I know how important this meeting is to you, but I have a lot on my plate and it slipped my mind. I do plan to make it up to you."

"Make it up to me how?"

"Hold that thought," she says, going into her new room.

Pepper walks to me and licks the side of my face. He whimpers and sits at my feet. "Thanks, Pep, I know you have my back. We're going to find Melissa. Yes, we are —"

"BAM!"

"What's that?" I ask, standing, wondering what Ruby has in her clutches. Whatever it is, it must be heavy, because there's a long vein protruding from her forehead.

She sets the contraption down on the floor and it lands with a loud thud. "Hold up." Pepper and I exchange inquisitive glances waiting for Ruby to return. She enters with a towel and begins wiping the plastic oblong box, revealing what looks like a computer? "This, Miss Thing, is a computer case, aka, the hard drive."

"*Okay,*" I say, yawning. Pepper groans and slumps to the floor.

"Don't get too excited you, two," Ruby says with more than a hint of sarcasm.

"And what am I supposed to do with that?"

"You're not going to do anything with it and it's not just a *that.* It's the computer I found in the garage at your house when I was loading your box of text books into the U-Haul truck. It's a computer that I asked your mother if I could have, and she said yes to *it,* and any and all other broken down, haven't been looked at in years, items your father had out there, that he's been promising to have hauled off to the junk yard." She takes a few beats to catch her breath, seemingly waiting for me to respond.

"So why did you want the computer?"

"You're kidding me right?"

"No, I want to know."

"Maddie, your mother says your father bought this computer in the Stone Age. That means there's a boat load of info I can get my hands on. Word docs, Internet history, stuff that might help us find Melissa."

I stare at the computer case, wishing I could kick it and a genie would appear and grant me three wishes. The first one would be for Melissa to come home, the second one would be for Melissa to come home, and the third one would be for Melissa to come home. Then we all could take a collective sigh of relief, and I wouldn't have to go see a strange detective tomorrow and Ruby wouldn't have to hack into our old family computer. Who knows what's on there. What if my parents were into porn?

"You said the police suspected your father at one point. You and I both know he's innocent, but he may have unknowingly stumbled across some information that could help us. Remember after you told us about the dream how he said he had worked with a private investigator at one point and that he was doing his own research. Sometimes a person is too close to something, so they can't see the proverbial forest for the trees. We might be able to pick up where he left off. Who knows, but it's worth a shot."

Ruby's reasoning hits me like a sledgehammer. Pepper moves next to me and I lean on him for support. "Ruby, you're a freaking genius. Can you get started tonight?"

"I would love to, but I had planned to go by the electronics store tomorrow to get a couple of cables to help me get this bad boy up and running, and I'm really exhausted," she says.

I kill the frown pushing its way onto my forehead and

give her a faint smile. She barely could get off of the floor a few minutes ago, and I have to admit, she did most of the heavy lifting today. As much as I want her to power up that hard drive and get the bugs out, I say, "No worries. Do it tomorrow."

"Thanks, Maddie. Thanks for being so understanding," she says, padding toward her bedroom.

"No problem," I say to her back. Pepper, with his tail wagging, slinks over to the computer and sniffs. "Can you get the computer going for me, Pep?" I ask. He looks at me like I'm crazy and then makes his way over to his deep dish dog bed, snuggles with his stuffed turtle, and falls asleep.

I know I should get some rest, too, but I'm wired for sound. I grab my Smartphone, make myself comfortable on the tan sofa that came with our loft, and press the Google icon. I stare at the search box and then type D-E-T-E-C-T-I-V-E M-I-T-C-H-E-L-L   F-A-U-L-K-N-E-R, D-A-N-C-I-N-G H-I-L-L-S. The screen fills with different versions of his name: Mitch Faulkner, Mitchum Falkner, and so on. I click IMAGES and am bombarded with a collage of faces. I think about my brief conversation with Detective Faulkner and try to match his voice to one of the photos. I'm meeting him at the station, so it's not like I have to know what he looks like, but I want to get a feel for the kind of person he is, and sometimes you can tell from a photo. He didn't sound like he was older than forty, but voices can be deceiving. I think I'll have a better chance if he's in his twenties or thirties. Younger people tend to be more opened-minded.

I come to a squared-jawed, clean shaven man with dark wavy hair and bushy brows. Looking into his deep set brown eyes, I wonder what he was thinking when the photo was taken. My gaze drops. There's something about the way he holds his mouth. Great lips. He's wearing a navy blue tie with a light blue shirt and a navy jacket. He looks like he's in his late twenties to early thirties. He actually looks more like a cross between a rapper and a runway model than a cop. I click on the photo and he and the background come into full view. I read the caption out loud. "Detective Mitchell Faulkner — Dancing Hills Police Department Cold Case Unit." I set my feet on the coffee table and study his mug. "He looks nothing like he sounds." If he's as nice as he looks, I might make some progress tomorrow.

Pepper snoring, reminds me it's getting late. I start to power my phone down, but stop when it rings. RESTRICTED flashes across the screen, and I pause before answering, wondering who could be calling me after midnight. I can't stand restricted calls. If the number isn't in my contacts, it's most likely a pushy telemarketer. I glance at the time on my phone. I doubt anyone's trying to sell something at this hour. Against my better judgment I answer. "Hello," I say, ready to hang up.

"Is this Melissa Lorraine Patterson?"

A chill runs through my veins, and I get up from the sofa, wondering if the woman calling is playing a bad joke.

"Who is this?" I ask.

"I'm sorry to call so — "

"Who is this?"

I can hear the woman's gravelly voice, but I can't make out what she's saying, because Pepper is howling and Ruby is screaming at me.

"What's going on?" Ruby, asks. She goes to Pepper and gives him a hug. "Calm down, boy."

"I had no idea I was that loud. I'm sorry, guys. I'm trying to find out who's on the phone." Not wanting to lose the call, I put it on speaker and say, "Hello, hello, are you still there?"

"Yes, I am. I'm trying to reach Melissa."

"Melissa's not here. This is Madeline."

"Oh my goodness. I'm sorry. I meant to say Madeline. Madeline Patterson, not Melissa. I have it all written down here and got it screwed up. It's late," she says.

"Tell me about it," I say. "What do you know about my sister, Melissa, and how did you get my number, and who are you?"

"My name is Kaitlin and Ted Wright gave me your number. Again, I'm sorry for mixing up the names. I must have really spooked you."

"You think?" Ruby says.

My eyes follow Ruby as she joins me on the sofa. "You said Ted gave you my number?"

"Yes, Ted. We used to call him Red Ted in elementary school," she says, chuckling. "He told me he ran into you recently and that you're trying to find your twin sister." Ruby and I grab each other, bracing ourselves for a miracle. "Hello?" the voice rings out.

"I'm here. I'm still here," I say. "Do you know where my sister is?" I ask. I press my hand on my chest, trying to calm my racing heart.

"No, but—"

Completely deflated, Ruby and I release each other.

"But what?" I say, shaking my head.

"When Ted told me he ran into you, we started talking about all the stuff that went down back in the day and it made me remember something I had forgotten—something strange."

"What?" I ask, losing my patience.

Ruby jerks the phone away from me and says, "This is Ruby, Madeline's best friend and roommate. It's late and not to be rude, but you need to get to the point or we're going to have to end this call. This is a very sensitive issue and—"

I take the phone from Ruby, afraid she might run the woman off. "I got this, Ruby," I say. "Can we meet in person?" I ask.

"If you don't mind meeting in Hawaii?"

"Hawaii?" Ruby and I say at the same time.

"Look, the thing I remembered is that there was this dude that wanted to rent our house. We lived directly across from your house. You probably don't remember us. The Burhenns?"

"I never knew your family name, but I remember a family across the street. There was a large camping trailer in your driveway," I say. "My father always warned me to stay away from it."

"That's us!" she says. "Anyways, like I was saying, this man wanted to pay us to rent our house, but our house wasn't for rent. He wouldn't take no for an answer."

"When was this? Was it around the time of the carjacking?" I ask.

"That's the funny thing. It was about three weeks before the carjacking."

"Three weeks?" Ruby asks.

"Are you sure?" I ask.

"Damn straight I'm sure. He paid my dad two-thousand dollars and that was a lot of money back then for one month."

"So your folks rented the house to him?" I ask.

"It was eight of us. Money was tight."

"Did your folks tell the police?" Ruby asks.

"Unfortunately not," she says. "My dad took the money and we went on a camping trip. It was the first of June. By the time we came back, he had moved out. But I do know this; he was there during the carjacking."

"How do you know?" Ruby and I ask.

"Because it was summer time like it is now. It was June and it was a hot June. There wasn't that much June gloom that year." Ruby and I share an eye roll, wishing she would get to her point. She must sense we're annoyed because she unleashes a flurry of words that make me think at one point she's speaking in a different language.

"Excuse me…uh…excuse me," I say.

"Kaitlin. Like I said, earlier, my name is Kaitlin."

"Kaitlin, can you slow down and repeat what you just said?"

"I'm sorry. I'm so excited; you know that maybe this could help you. I was saying that the man rented our house in early June and we went on our camping trip. We had been gone about three weeks when the man sent my father a 911 page. You know cell phones weren't that popular yet. We were already at the camping grounds and my father was bitching about having to go and find a pay phone to call the guy at our house to see what was up. The air conditioning at our house wasn't working. So my father was trying to tell him how to fix it over the phone. Talk about frustrating. All this happened the day before the carjacking."

"Are you absolutely sure?" I ask.

"Yes, because the carjacking happened on my tenth birthday — June 28, 1995, and my father talked to the guy the day before my birthday. We didn't find this all out until we came back home a week later and found the neighborhood invaded by the media. The man had already moved out. When we were camping, we were isolated from anything that was going on in the outside world. My father liked it like that. But when we got back home, my parents started following the case right along with everyone else, but they never did think about the guy who had rented our house. I remember trying to bring it up one time, but in our house, kids were to be seen and not heard. I feel horrible now because what if that guy was the one who carjacked your mother and took your sister."

Ruby, shaking her head, says, "It doesn't make sense, Kaitlin. There were two carjackers."

"Maybe he wanted to stay in our house so he could spy on your family. And then when he saw your mother leaving that day, he followed her. Maybe he stole your sister so he could sell her to some rich guy overseas. Maybe the second guy was staying somewhere else."

I press down on my head that's starting to pound. This is too much. I wish Ted would have gotten my permission before he gave this woman my phone number. I hope he hasn't given it to anyone else. "Kaitlin, I really appreciate you sharing this information, and I'm going to mention it to the detective I'm meeting with tomorrow," I say.

Ruby grabs the phone out of my hand. "Kaitlin, do you remember the man's name? Do your parents have any information on him?"

"I'm already on it," she says. "My father has to pull some stuff out of storage, but he's sure he had the man fill out some paperwork. And, get this, he had a gun. I saw it."

"Where did he have the gun?" I ask.

"In his waistband."

"Was he a cop?" Ruby asks.

"I don't think so."

"Okay, Kaitlin. Can you give me your number? It came up restricted. I want to stay in touch," I say.

She rattles off her number and Ruby gives me thumbs up that she has it memorized. Exhausted, I take the phone from Ruby, thank Kaitlin, and disconnect the call.

"Wow, she's a piece of work," Ruby says.

"That was a lot of information. Whether we can use it or not, I'm not sure. It is kind of creepy that he wanted to rent a house directly across from ours and that he had a gun. Why couldn't I have been older? I missed so much. Maybe my father remembers the man."

"Kaitlin has a point though. What if he was stalking your mother?" Ruby asks.

"Wow. That's true. This whole conversation is freaking me out," I say, rising and stretching. "It's after one and I have to walk Pepper before my meeting."

"We better get some sleep," Ruby says.

"My body is tired, but my mind is on overdrive," I say.

"I'm going to bed, and Maddie, you should, too. Pepper, back to bed," she says.

I watch Ruby and Pepper head to bed, and I go to the picture window in our living room and gaze at the L.A. skyline, wondering if Melissa is out there somewhere. Could she be a homeless woman living in a cardboard box, minutes from our apartment? What if she's no longer in California or God forbid in some foreign country, like Kaitlin suggested? Hopefully, Detective Faulkner will be able to help me figure it all out. Note to self: send all Christmas money to the downtown mission.

Chapter 5

Standing under the awning of our apartment building, I exchange smiles with an elderly woman walking her dog. I keep a tight grip on Pepper's leash while he eyes the miniature white poodle dressed in a little pink outfit with matching booties. I remember when my parents surprised me with Pepper five years ago. He was a baby, so small and cute. I wanted to dress him up, too. I'll never forget approaching him with an adorable pullover sweater. He snatched it with his teeth and ripped it to pieces. That was the end of any ideas I had about dressing up Pepper.

I put the dog waste bag in my pocket along with a packet of wipes and say, "Come on, boy," gently yanking Pepper's leash. He runs forward, pulling me behind him. "Slow down, boy." I catch up with him and we fall into a nice comfortable pace. He walks with his head held high and his chest out, daring anyone to mess with me. It's early Tuesday and the neighborhood is bustling with people rushing off to work and children already on bicycles and skateboards, enjoying the beginning of summer. Pepper and I stop at the corner and wait for the light to turn green while the bumper-to-bumper traffic trudges at a snail's pace. I love the energy downtown, but it was a culture shock when the realtor, my father referred us to, initially brought us here. Dancing Hills has wide streets, manicured lawns, and two-story, three or more bedroom houses with long driveways, big backyards and two or more bathrooms. I look up at the skyscrapers and the rows and rows of condominiums that have become home to the white collar crowd—and get a twinge of middle class guilt—thinking about the homeless that have been pushed further eastward.

"What's wrong, Pep?" He pulls away from the corner, dragging me with him. I let him lead as he heads to a grassy area where he does his business. I give him his privacy and when he's done, I do the part I hate most. He gives me the apologetic look he always does, and I pat his head to let him know that I know he would clean up behind himself if he could. I dispose of the bag at the pet waste station and wipe my hands.

"Come on, boy, the light's green," I say, running back to the intersection. We cross and continue our brisk walk. It's still overcast but not too cool. A woman wearing a designer suit and sneakers winks at Pepper. She gives me the idea to dress up a bit for my meeting with Detective Faulkner.

"Maddie! Maddie!" I motion for Pepper to stop and we both turn to see who's approaching. Pepper pulls hard and I lose my grip on the leash. Before I have a chance to order him to stay, he pounces on my grandmother, nearly knocking her to the ground. "I missed you too, Pepper," she says, letting him lick her like she's a double scoop of vanilla ice cream.

"Down, Pep. Let Grandma breathe."

Pepper calms down and stands between my grandmother and me. He looks from me to her with his tail wildly wagging. I go around him and give my grandmother a hug. "What are you doing here?"

"I wanted to bring you a few things for your new place. Ruby let me in. I left everything at your apartment, which I might add is fabulous. Ruby told me to tell you good luck and that you had just left. She said she was running late to some kind of orientation. Poor girl, she looked wiped out. I don't think I've ever seen her look that tired before."

"That's my fault, Grandma. I kept all of us up last night."

"What's going on? And why did she wish you good luck?"

"It's a long story," I say.

"I have nothing but time," she says, pointing to the watch she's worn since I was a little girl.

"Unfortunately, I don't have a lot of time," I say, pulling my phone out of my pocket.

"Let's run over to that coffee shop," she says, pointing. "I could use a nice latte and it looks like you could, too. Spend some time with an old lady."

"You're not old, Grandma."

Pepper barks and we both laugh.

"He looks good, Maddie. I see you've been keeping up with his grooming."

"I try to. I might have to find a place nearby."

"Come on, my darling Maddie," she says, pulling Pepper and me across the street.

We sit outside on the patio with Pepper at our feet. A waiter comes by and we order our lattes and scones. Once we have our goodies, we sit in silence, sip, and eat.

"Have any more dreams?" my grandmother asks.

I almost choke, surprised at her question. "No, at least

not yet," I say. "Grandma, can I make a confession. I hope you don't get angry or upset with me."

"What is it?" she asks, gripping her cup.

"I know I said I was going to leave well enough alone when it comes to Melissa, but I can't. I have to find out if she's still alive and I think she is. That's why Ruby was wishing me good luck. I meet with a detective this afternoon about reopening Melissa's case." My grandmother sets her latte down and parts her lips to speak and I say, "Before you—" She cuts me off with loud applause. "Why are you clapping?"

"I'm glad you're moving forward, my darling. I'm glad someone in this family has the balls to find out what really happened to little Melissa."

After picking my jaw up from the gum-stained ground, I say, "What do you mean by that? Didn't the carjackers take off with her?"

"That's what your mother told the police," she says with a contorted face.

I press my hands together, not sure what to make of her comment. "Are you saying my mother lied?"

"No, goodness, no. That's not what I'm saying. It's just that your mother was a very nervous person back then. She's so much calmer than she used to be."

"Nervous in what way?"

"I think having twins may have been a bit too much for her. She and Alvin were in their early twenties, and he was trying to get his practice off the ground. It was a lot going on, and I got sick right after you and Melissa were born, so I couldn't help out in the beginning. And your grandfather was still working on the docks. He hadn't retired yet. Your mother was a little overwhelmed. Don't get me wrong, she's a great mother, she loved having you and Melissa, it was a bit much…that's all. So to be attacked by strangers and to have someone put a gun to her head, I'm surprised your mother got through that. I'm not sure if she really remembers what happened. She told the police several different versions of what took place. I'm sure she was in shock."

Sitting here listening to my grandmother, I grip the arm of the chair. I hear the words coming out of her mouth but they're not making sense. The woman she's describing is not the mother I've known all my life. She's describing someone who I don't recognize. Nervous? I've never known my mother to be nervous. Soft, sensitive, yes, but not nervous. Calmer now? Where have I heard that before? *She hasn't changed much at all. Well, I guess a little, I mean she seems much calmer.* Ted said the same thing. "Grandma, what happened to Grandpa and Grandma Darcy? Why doesn't my mother have a relationship with them? Do you ever talk to them?"

She starts to speak, but says nothing. I notice a hint of fear in her eyes. I scoot to the edge of the chair, anxious for her to give me the 411 on my mother's parents.

"Give me a minute," she says, removing a silver flask from her purse. She opens it and pours its contents into the cup containing what's left of her latte. She returns the flask to her purse. I watch her while she guzzles her drink, remembering the first time I saw her taking her "medicine" as she calls it.

"Are you okay, Grandma?"

"I'm fine now. Your mother's people, hmm. Not sure where to start. Strange pair, Jean and Jerome. I don't blame your mother for cutting them off. They were two of the coldest people I've ever met. They didn't even come to your parents' wedding. They were so aloof. Your mother left home at eighteen. Alvin said she couldn't stand to be around them. I'm not sure what happened there, but whatever it was, it wasn't good. That's probably why she was such a

Nervous Nellie. You know at one point your mother thought someone was following her."

"Really? When?"

"That was a long time ago."

"Was it around the time Melissa went missing?"

"Before then. As far back as high school. Darling, your mother was and still is a stunning woman. I'm sure she was being followed. What man wouldn't follow her? In her twenties, she used to stop traffic. And you're a Mini Her. Every last man that has walked past here, now has a case of whiplash," she says, laughing. "I've never seen anything like it. Your hair is in a bun, you're wearing worn sweat pants and a T-shirt, and you still turn heads, Maddie. Be careful. I know you're grown up now, but you're still a woman, a young woman." She looks around, her demeanor suddenly changing. "They've tried to clean this place up, but it's still a cesspool filled with predators, looking to get their grimy claws into someone like you. Pimps, prostitutes, drug addicts. My goodness, why here, Maddie? Couldn't you and Ruby have found something on the Westside? I'm sorry. I've said too much. I just worry about you."

I place my hand on my grandmother's, hoping to ease her anxiety. Raised in a small town in Iowa, her attitude doesn't surprise me. "We'll be okay. Don't worry, Grandma. It's not as bad as it seems and it's convenient and affordable." Changing the subject, I ask, "Do you remember the people who lived across the street from us? They lived there during the time Melissa was taken and a few years after that."

"The campers? They had that big ugly box of a thing in their driveway."

"That's them. Do you remember a man living there the summer Melissa went missing?"

"It was a bunch of them. I remember the father."

"No, it was another man. He rented their place."

"What did he look like?"

Her question stumps me. What did he look like? That was something Ruby and I never asked Kaitlin. "I'm not sure," I say, feeling like an idiot.

"Can't say I do, sweetie. I'm sorry. Why?"

"Never mind," I say, glancing at my phone on the table. "I need to go home and get ready for my appointment."

"I really appreciate you spending time with me, Maddie. You know I love you forever."

"I love you, too, Grandma."

II

White dude, early thirties, dirty blond hair, obese, sweaty. Sitting in the lobby of the Dancing Hills police station, I study the text Kaitlin sent me. Based on his age, the man who rented Kaitlin's house would be in his late forties, early fifties now. Hopefully, over the years he's taken better care of himself and hasn't croaked from a heart attack, or diabetes, or any other disease that could be attributed to a person being overweight. Last night I wasn't sure if The Renter had anything to do with what happened, but I've been having this nagging feeling that he's one of the many pieces to this puzzle I'm trying to put together. He has to be. Melissa led me to Red Ted, and Red Ted led me to Kaitlin, and Kaitlin has led me to The Renter. I turn my attention to the empty lobby, surprised how quiet and small the place is. It's nothing like the police stations you see on the CSI shows. Dancing Hills is a small town and although we do have to lock our doors now and then, it's still relatively much safer than cities like Los Angeles or New York.

"Miss Patterson?"

I look up and my eyes meet the inquisitive brown eyes of the man standing before me. He knits his dirty blonde brows and passes his hand over his dirty blonde hair. My gaze moves to the sweat stains spilling out from both his armpits and the perspiration beading on his forehead. He snatches a handkerchief from the back pocket of his wrinkled brown slacks and dabs at his face. I hear someone behind him, but can't see beyond his wide girth. I glance back at the description Kaitlin sent me of The Renter and shake my head. If this man was twenty years older, he could possibly be a dead ringer for The Renter.

"Yes, I'm Miss Patterson. You can call me Madeline. I told the desk officer that I'm here to see Detective Mitchell Faulkner."

He extends his wet hand and says, "I'm Detective Mitchell Faulkner, ma'am."

My eyes widen when I flash back to the Detective Faulkner I saw on Google Images. What the fu...this is definitely not the same man. "But—"

He pulls his hand back before I get a chance to shake it and says, "I get that reaction all the time, ma'am. You must have Googled me."

I nod.

"There used to be another Detective Mitchell Faulkner on the force, but he got discovered by this photographer when he was on vacation in Boston and now he's a fulltime model. He resigned a year ago, ma'am."

"That explains it," I say. *I wish he would stop calling me ma'am.*

"Why don't you bring her to the back office?" Mitchell and I exchange glances when the man I had heard earlier approaches. "I'm Detective Warren, Sam Warren. Mitch and I are partners...in crime." He follows up his witty remark with a husky laugh.

"Hello, I'm—"

"Madeline Louise Patterson, twin sister of Melissa Lorraine Patterson," he says.

"Right," I say, not sure if I should be impressed or thankful.

"This way," he says, turning on his heel.

Detective Faulkner shrugs and we follow Detective Warren. I can't help but notice the contrast—Detective Faulkner—dumpy and disheveled, and Detective Warren—dashing and debonair. I pick up my pace to keep up and stop when we come to a large door at the end of the hall. Detective Warren opens and holds the door and then motions for me to enter. He and Detective Faulkner follow me. They nod and make small talk with other officers passing through the corridor and when we come to a dead end, Detective Warren speaks.

"Right there to your left," he says.

"Sure," I say.

We enter the small office that's furnished with a table and a few chairs. I notice an accordion folder on the desk with M.L. PATTERSON written across the front in black. I remain standing, not sure if and where I should sit.

"Have a seat right there," Detective Warren says.

I do so, wondering to myself if the two detectives take turns being in charge or does Detective Warren always run the show.

"I'm going to turn on the air. It's sweltering in here," Detective Faulkner says, smoothing his hand over his wet shirt.

"While you're at it, can you bring us some water? Would you like some water?" Detective Warren asks.

"Water would be good," I say, shifting in the wooden chair.

Detective Faulkner leaves and Detective Warren sits on the edge of the desk with his legs spread. He gives me the once-over and I feel heat rising up my neck, filling my cheeks. He doesn't take his piercing green eyes off of me. I want to look away, but I find myself staring back at him. He smiles, revealing perfect white teeth and deep dimples. I return his smile.

"My sister and I used to do that when we were kids," he says.

"Do what?"

"See who could stare the longest without laughing," he says. "You win."

"I wasn't —"

"It should be getting cooler in a minute," Detective Faulkner says, entering with water. He hands each of us a bottle and sits in the chair near the desk.

"Ma'am, how do you know Red Ted?" Detective Faulkner asks.

"He used to help his sister, Sarah, babysit Melissa and me," I say.

"Lucky guy," Detective Warren says.

Detective Faulkner rolls his eyes and says, "Don't mind my partner, he's a work in progress, ma'am."

If he calls me ma'am one more time, I'm going to scream. "Detective Faulkner, I appreciate you being so respectful, but you don't have to keep calling me ma'am."

"I'm sorry, ma'am. As you can see, it's a habit, but I'll try not to call you ma...I mean...what you said."

Detective Warren, seemingly amused, shakes his head and takes a swig of his water. "Let's cut to the chase. You want to reopen your sister's case."

I get a burst of energy and sit at attention, hoping Detective Warren is ready to move forward. "Yes, that's right."

"We appreciate your situation, Miss Patterson, but there has to be a valid reason to reopen a case," Detective Faulkner says.

"What he's saying is, do you have any new evidence — substantial evidence?" Detective Warren asks.

"I guess that depends on what you mean by substantial," I say.

Detective Warren stands and paces. I look up at his over six-foot frame, hoping he tells me getting a visitation from Melissa in a dream is substantial.

"Substantial would be new witnesses, solid leads, such as someone knowing the whereabouts of Melissa. Substantial would mean someone confessing to the crime. The SUV being discovered, a body being found..." I grimace when I hear *body being found,* and Detective Warren blanches when he notices my reaction. "I'm sorry," he says. "But I think you get where I'm coming from."

"Yes, I understand."

"Do you have any new evidence?" Detective Faulkner asks with what appears to be hope in his eyes.

"I'm not sure if this counts, but my sister came to me in a dream and told me she wasn't dead." Before I even finish getting all the words out of my mouth, I feel like a doofess. Sitting here with these two no-nonsense detectives, I feel like I have totally wasted their time and mine. I wouldn't be surprised if they throw me in jail for wasting good taxpayer money.

They share curious looks and then meet for a sidebar while I strain to hear what they're saying. They break away from each other and put their focus back on the idiot.

"When did you have the dream?" Detective Faulkner asks.

"The morning of my birthday. This past Saturday."

"Happy belated birthday," Detective Warren says.

"Thank you," I say. "It's not just the dream. A woman Ted knows called me and said that around the same time my mother was carjacked and Melissa was taken, a strange man rented their house that's directly across from ours and he had a gun. We believe he was spying on my mother. He could have had something to do with it."

"What's the man's name?" Detective Warren asks.

"I don't know, but I'll have a name for you by tomorrow. I'm sure this all sounds crazy, but I've never had a dream where my sister's a woman and she's asking me for help. She's out there somewhere," I say, standing.

Detective Warren picks up the accordion folder on the desk. "You see this? There are hundreds more like it in hundreds of boxes down the hall. There's a paper trail on this case you wouldn't believe. Mitch and I were in elementary school when all this went down, so we're no experts, but we're familiar with the case and we want to help you out, but to be honest with you, you don't have enough for us to go to the Chief with. It would take weeks, months, maybe even years to sort through the files, to recall witnesses; you're talking about a lot of time and money the department doesn't have."

I stand here feeling like I just got sucker punched in the gut. My grandmother told me that if I wore my blue Donna Karan suit with matching shoes and wore my hair down, I would have Detective Faulkner eating out of my French manicured hands. But she was wrong. The room's silent and filled with tension.

"Miss Patterson, please don't be upset," Detective Faulkner says.

"It's okay," I say. "I understand. I'm not upset." I bolt out of there with my head held high, ignoring the men and women in uniform giving me questioning looks. I find my way to the parking lot and grit my teeth. "I don't need you," I say, getting into the BMW my father bought me for my twenty-first birthday. I start up the car and pull out of the parking lot. A familiar voice gives me pause. I slam on the brakes when Detective Warren jumps in front of my car.

Chapter 6

He motions for me to let my window down. "Don't ever do that again!" I say. "I could have knocked you off of your feet."

"You already did," he says, under his breath, pulling on his tie.

"What was that?" I ask.

"Why did you run out like that?"

"I didn't want to waste any more of your time."

"Take my card and call me when you find out the name of the guy who rented the house and if you come up with any more *substantial* leads. I want to help you. I remember the case, and I remember how afraid everyone was, and I remember seeing your folks on TV holding press conferences. I talked to one of the retired detectives who worked the case and he told me he felt like there were a lot of holes in your mom's story. Please don't take it the wrong way. It's not that she was lying, things just didn't add up.

But because of your folks' standing in the community, the Chief didn't want to push too hard and your mom was already going through it. Mitch and I are going to do some research on our own time. Don't worry; we're going to help you."

I'm grinning so hard my face hurts. "Detective Warren, that's the best thing I've heard in a long time. Thank you so much." I reach my hand out to shake his and we hold hands longer than we should. He finally let's mine go.

"Don't forget to call me. I'm heading to New York tonight, but I'll be back this weekend. My cell number is on my card, so you can leave messages."

"Are you from New York?" I ask, hoping the answer's no.

"No, my sister is graduating from NYU, and my whole family's going there to see her graduate. It's the sister I used to do the staring contests with," he says, laughing. "I hate flying, and I really hate taking the redeye, but it's the best I can do. By the way, you can call me, Sam."

"Okay. Have a safe trip, Sam." I start my car and drive away and then it hits me.

"*Redeye!*"

Ⅱ

"Roses are red, violets are red, and Madeline, I wasn't dead. He saved me. The man saved me. Now I need you to find me. I'm not crying anymore, so don't you cry anymore. Here, take the pillow so you won't cry."

Pillow? I thought it was a ball. "I'm coming, Melissa," I say. She reaches out to me, but I can't move. My feet feel like lead. I try to tell Melissa that I can't move, but my words won't come out.

Panic crosses her face. "Please save me, Maddie. Why won't you save me? Why won't you come?"

"I'm trying, I'm trying!"

I sit bolt upright in bed. My UCLA jersey is drenched with sweat and I'm shivering. I turn toward the door and my eyes lock with Ruby's and Pepper's eyes.

"You're trying to do what?" Ruby asks.

"Wow, I had another dream."

"From here it looks like you had a nightmare. You look sick and you're soaking wet," she says, approaching. Pepper leaps onto the bed.

"Down, boy. Not now, sweetie," I say. He groans and jumps to the floor. "What time is it?"

"A little after nine. You better get out of those wet clothes," she says. "Are you ill?" she asks, planting her hand on my forehead.

"No, definitely not. I don't have time to be sick."

"Well, change and come join Pepper and me in the living room. I have something to show you."

I swing my legs over the side of the bed, stand, and stretch. Walking to my bathroom, I pull the jersey off and step out of my sweats. I grab my terrycloth robe that's hanging on the back of the bathroom door, put it on, and return to my room that's filled with unopened boxes. It's Wednesday and we still haven't unpacked. Yesterday, after her orientation, Ruby ended up hanging out with a few of the software developers that start work with her next Tuesday. After I left DHPD, I stopped by my parents' house to spend a little time with my mother. Then I stopped by my father's practice. Big mistake, because I ended up stuck in rush hour traffic. I have no idea why they call it rush hour, because nothing is rushing. I was moving so slowly on the Santa Monica Freeway, I could have gotten out of my car and walked, and made it home faster.

I grab my Smartphone off of the dresser to see if Kaitlin has sent me any messages. I hope she gets the name of The Renter to me, because I want to get it to Detective Warren, I mean Sam, as soon as possible. My face breaks out in a smile when I think about him and then it morphs into a frown when I think about Melissa. The dream I had floods my mind.

"Please save me, Maddie. Why won't you save me? Why won't you come?"

"Ruby, you have to hear this," I say, heading to the living room like a child with a secret.

I hear a burst of laughter. *What the hell has her cracking up?* Ruby at my computer, buried in boxes and piles of printouts, pinches her nose and shoots me a knowing look.

"What's so funny?" I ask.

"Pepper let one rip and he's trying to act like he's innocent."

"Pepper, is that true?" I ask.

He slumps to the floor and puts his paw over his eyes. Ruby and I laugh.

"I'm glad you're feeling better, Maddie. You look a whole lot better than when you first got up," she says.

I watch her fingers fly across the computer keyboard and when I see her pause I say, "I need to tell you about the dream I had."

"Sure. Afterwards, I need to give you an update on what I've found so far," she says, giving me her undivided attention.

Standing, I shut my eyes for a moment, so I get it right. "Melissa asked me to save her again. But this time, she said some other stuff, too."

"Like what?"

"She told me to take the pillow she was holding."

"So now there's a pillow? What about the ball?" Ruby asks.

"The pillow *is* the ball. Somehow it changed form, but it's a pillow. And she told me to take it so I wouldn't cry. And then get this; she says that the man saved her."

Ruby, now standing asks, "What man?"

"I don't know, but she said the man saved her and then she begged me to come and get her and I couldn't move. It was so damn frustrating. And she said she wasn't dead, again. I forgot to mention, she's three again in this dream. She's not grown up."

Ruby sits at the computer, creates a word document, and says, "Let's recap the dreams and everything we've learned so far." Her fingers moving at the speed of light, she compiles a list:

1) In the first dream, Melissa's all grown up.

2) She asks you to save her and she says she 'wasn't dead.'

3) She's floating on a ball that we now know is actually a purple, green, and orange pillow, that's supposed to help you stop crying.

4) In the second dream, she's three.

5) She said a man saved her and she wants you to come and get her.

6) According to Red Ted and Grandma Patterson, your mother used to be really nervous.

7) Detective Warren, aka Sexy Sam, *your words*, says the retired detective felt your mother's story had holes in it and Grandma Patterson feels the same way, but neither of them feel your mother wasn't telling the truth, it was just her truth.

8) According to Kaitlin, the man who rented their house could have been spying on your mother and stalking her and may have been a part of the carjacking. Also, he was there three weeks before the carjacking and he had a gun. Grandma Patterson also said your mother felt she was being followed at times, as far back as high school.

9) Your mother doesn't have a relationship with her parents.

10) Two years after the carjacking, your father was a person of interest, but was never arrested, or charged, and had an alibi.

Ruby turns toward me, takes a sheet of paper off of the stack on the floor and hands it to me. "What's this?" I ask, scanning the paper.

"It's some search history I was able to recover from the computer. I haven't sorted it yet, so don't pay attention to the order."

"Construction in Dancing Hills, Body Car Repairs, Private Investigators, Statute of Limitations in California, Postpartum Depression, Pregnancy Week by Week, Twins, Cryptophasia:Twin Language, Colic, Plumbing for Idiots, Open Adoption vs. Closed Adoption, LLC Formation, Carpet Cleaners, Hair Salons, Metal Shops...Wow, Ruby, this list goes on forever."

"I know. I highlighted the things that stick out."

"Like private investigators, statute of limitations, those obvious things," I say,

"Right," she says.

I hand her the paper and flop down onto the sofa. "This is a lot. Where do we start?"

Ruby sits next to me and says, "We need to take it one step at a time, or we'll both get overwhelmed. I think you're right about The Renter. We find him, we solve this conundrum."

"Good," I say.

"Let's agree that he was spying on your mother. The question is, why?"

"He was a pervert," I say. "A Peeping Tom."

"Perverts and Peeping Toms don't rent houses to fulfill their twisted fantasies and they don't throw money around," Ruby says. "He was the 'P' word, but not those two. I believe he was *Paid*."

"Paid?"

"I think someone was paying him to watch your mother."

"But why?"

"That's a good question, Maddie. Have you heard from Kaitlin? We need to I.D. The Renter."

"Not yet. If I don't hear from her by noon, I'm going to call her again."

"Okay, let's look at what else we have." Ruby goes to the computer. Two copies of the list she made comes flying out of the printer and onto the floor. She grabs them and hands me one.

"Wait a minute," I say.

"What?" Ruby asks.

Pepper, who's been a silent observer, starts to bark. "Calm down, boy," I say. "Mommie's going to take you for your walk soon. Has he eaten?"

"Everything *and* the kitchen sink," Ruby says. "Why did you say, 'wait a minute?'" she asks.

"A thought just came to me," I say, going into our small kitchen for water. "What if my father was paying The Renter to watch my mother? What if The Renter is a private investigator? *That is* one of the searches on the list."

Ruby cups her chin in her hand and gives me a curious look. "But why would your father spy on your mother?"

"Maybe he was insecure or jealous. My grandmother said he was spending a lot of time trying to get his dental practice up and running, and my mother was probably home alone. My mother's a cougar now, but according to my grandmother, in her twenties, she was a real hottie. My mother told me the other day my father said he would be willing to die for her, he loves her so much. Doesn't it sound like he was somewhat obsessed?" I open the empty refrigerator, grab a bottle of water, and guzzle.

"You may be onto something, Maddie," Ruby says, patting her afro like she always does when she's trying to solve a complex problem. "But why would he go that far and how is the carjacking connected?"

"What if he set it up to freak my mother out so she would be more dependent on him? Maybe The Renter was working with the second guy."

"But what about Melissa being taken?"

"Maybe things got out of control...and...never mind. I'm tripping for real. I am way off base," I say.

"I agree, "Ruby says. "Your theory had all the makings of a bad made for TV movie."

"You're right," I say, leaning on the wall and sliding

down to the floor. Pepper walks over and licks me on the cheek. "What do you think, Pepper?" I ask, hoping by some miracle he'll start talking.

Ruby massages her long neck and moves her head from side to side. "Okay, we'll agree The Renter was paid to spy on your mother, but I don't believe your father hired him. I think he searched for private investigators to help him find Melissa when the police had given up. But there are some other things on the list that stand out, like statute of limitations and postpartum depression, and open versus closed adoption."

"You're right," I say. "Someone wanted to know how long it would take before they or someone else would be immune from criminal prosecution. It was probably my father, worried that too much time might pass before the carjackers would be found."

"There's no statute of limitations on murder," Ruby says.

"Please don't go there," I say, bristling.

She gives me an apologetic nod and then asks, "What do you think about postpartum depression and the adoption stuff?"

"My mother may have been suffering from postpartum. Maybe all that nervousness was her hormones being out of control. Now the adoption thing, I have no clue."

Ruby throws her hands up and says, "This is driving me crazy. I can't figure it out. And the pillow, what does it mean?" She flops down on the floor beside me. "We start our jobs next week. How are we going to get to the bottom of this once we start work?"

"You're right," I say. "Wait a minute. My grandmother said my mother mentioned being followed as far back as high school. Maybe my mother's parents know something about it. Maybe that has something to do with their strained relationship. I really need to talk to them."

"Will they talk to you?"

"It's worth a try. They live in Long Beach. Unfortunately, I don't have the address. I remember the street name is some sort of animal. Giraffe, Kangaroo?"

"What are their names?"

"Jean and Jerome Darcy."

"What the...wait a minute," Ruby says, scrambling to her feet.

"What's wrong?"

"Hold up." She goes to the computer and I follow her. "There's a folder on the drive labeled Darcy." She clicks on the directory and there are about a dozen word documents.

"Open the one that says L-Darcy," I say.

We stare at the screen wide-eyed when a letter appears.

Chapter 7

May 15, 1995

Mr. and Mrs. Darcy
53158 Zebra Lane
Long Beach, CA 90801

Hello, there. It's been a long time. The girls will be three next
month. I thought

"That's it?" Ruby asks.

"It looks like she was trying to reach out and changed her mind. But that's okay because that's the address."

"Cool," Ruby says, extending her hand for a high-five.

"You want to ride over there with me?" I ask.

"Of course," she says.

"Let me shower and get dressed," I say.

"I'll walk Pepper while you get ready."

"Thanks, Ruby."

"No problem. You know I like hanging out with Pep."

"I meant thanks for believing in me."

II

I squint when we approach my grandparents' block in Long Beach, a city in Los Angeles County. It doesn't seem like much of anything, but it's actually the 36th largest city in the United States and the seventh-largest in California. Despite its size, it wasn't immune to the infamous subprime lending scams that ravaged neighborhoods across the country. A few of the houses bear foreclosed signs and have overgrown lawns with tall reedy grass. In my peripheral vision I can see Ruby squirming in her seat. I wonder if she's as nervous as I am.

"There's the house right there," she says, holding the unfinished letter we printed out.

"Right, I remember it being on the corner and it still needs a paint job," I say, parking behind a black pickup truck.

"How old were you when you visited your grandparents?"

"I was eight, but I didn't actually visit. My mother left me in the car. She stood on the porch, my grandparents came outside, she had a few words with them, and that was it. They're like strangers to me. If I saw them on the street, I wouldn't know them. Outside of a couple of pictures I found in my father's office at home, I don't have much to go on."

"That's deep," Ruby says. "Hopefully, they're here. Too bad we don't have their phone number."

"It's just as well. I think we'll get more out of them with a surprise visit."

"You're right," Ruby says.

We get out of the car, and I lead the way to the green and brown house trimmed in red brick. Ruby slides her hands into her jean pockets and I wring mine. We step onto the porch, and I stand in front of the door that's behind a security iron gate and ring the doorbell.

"If my parents knew I was here, they would kill me," I say.

Ruby stretches her neck and peeks into the curtained window.

"You see anything?" I ask.

"Nope."

"Dang, they're not home."

"Oh, well," Ruby says.

We turn to leave and stop in our tracks at the sound of the door creaking open. "Can I help you?" a woman with a high-pitched voice asks. When we turn around she screams. "Millicent! What are you doing here?"

Ruby and I give each other surprised looks. "I'm sorry, I'm Madeline," I say.

Now standing on the porch, the woman covers her face with her meaty hands and giggles. "I'm sorry; you look like my sister, Millicent—just younger. I'm Caroline, the oldest."

"My mother's Millicent...Millicent Patterson. And this is my best friend, Ruby."

Ruby extends her hand and Caroline reciprocates. There's a couple of beats of uncomfortable silence and it hits me that she referred to my mother as her sister. I give her the once-over, taking in the overcoat and robe she's wearing, her greasy hair, puffy, pockmarked face, and wonder who in my mother's family she took after. "You said you and my mother are sisters. I never knew my mother had a sister."

She bats her eyes. "Why don't you two come in? It's okay," she says, motioning for us to enter the house. Ruby casts a 'let's be careful,' look my way and I nod. "I won't bite," the woman says, grinning, revealing tobacco-stained, jagged teeth.

When we enter, we're greeted by a wave of heat. She shuts the door and the sound of the lock makes the hairs on the back of my neck rise. For a fleeting moment I feel like James Caan in Misery and it takes everything in me not to grab Ruby by the hand and take off running. The sound of Ruby coughing takes me out of my head. "Ruby, are you okay?" I ask.

"You know I can't stand the smell of smoke," she says. "And I'm sorry, but it's burning up in here."

"Forgive me for that," Caroline says, putting out a cigarette in a full ashtray. "And I apologize that it's so hot, but I'm severely anemic. Can I get you girls anything?" she asks.

"No...thank you," Ruby and I say in unison.

"Please have a seat," she says, motioning to the small plastic-covered floral sofa that's flanked by a worn recliner and an end table literally on its last leg.

We tentatively sit and eyeball the room that's covered in boxes, books, clothes, dishes, and only God knows what other creepy-crawly things are lurking within the nooks and crevices of all this debris. Caroline, or whoever's responsible for this clutter, would be a perfect candidate for one of those hoarder shows on cable TV.

Caroline, flopping down onto the recliner, tugs on the faded green smock that's peeking up from under the coat and robe, and rocks. "What can I do for you, girls?"

I start to answer her, but something underneath the seat

cushion is poking me. I move about and then stand.

"What's wrong?" Caroline asks.

"Something's poking me," I say.

"I'm sorry," she says, removing the cushion. "Well I'll be. I've been looking for this." She holds up a huge hardcover thesaurus, and says, "Your mother and I used to wear this thing out when we did our school papers. Here, you have it." She thrusts the book my way.

"No, that's okay," I say.

"Please, your mother used it more than I did. I have to get rid of all this stuff anyways. You'll be doing me a favor."

"Oh, okay," I say, taking the book. I set it on the arm of the sofa. Caroline replaces the seat cushion and we both sit. "We actually came here looking for my mother's parents...your parents," I say. "And excuse me for asking, but are you my mother's half-sister?"

"No, I'm her adopted sister."

"That's what I was thinking," Ruby says. I glare at her, surprised she would say something like that out loud. "I'm sorry. I didn't mean—"

"No worries. Everyone knows Millicent is the pretty one and I'm the ugly one." She pauses as if she's waiting for us to debate her, but we take her at her word. I notice a hint of a scowl, but she covers it up with a forced smile.

"Wow, I feel so clueless," I say.

"What do you mean?" Caroline asks.

"I didn't know my grandparents had an adopted child, that my mother had an adopted sister."

"Yep, your mother and I are adopted. She was adopted a couple of years after I was. She was seven and I was nine when she came here."

I tilt my head, not sure I had heard her correctly. "Excuse me, what did you say?"

"I said your mother was adopted two years after I was."

"My mother's adopted?"

"She didn't tell you?"

"No, I had no idea. Where are the Darcys?"

"Florida. They moved there a little over a year ago. Right after Jerome had a massive stroke. He can't walk or talk. He got just what was comin' to him."

I sit here bug-eyed with an open mouth. *Why didn't my mother tell me she was adopted? Does my father know? Does my grandmother know? This is crazy.*

"You okay?" Ruby asks.

"I'm trying to be," I say.

Ruby removes her phone from her purse and takes notes.

"I'm sorry this is all such a shock to you. It's kind of a shock to me, too. I didn't know I had a pretty niece like you. Millicent swore she would never have kids. She said she didn't want her kids to go through what she had gone through. Poor thing. Her real mother was something else. I don't know it for a fact, just what I heard through the grapevine."

"And what did you hear?" Ruby asks, jutting her chin out.

Almost salivating, Caroline leans forward and says, "Judy...that's her name, Judy Gardner, was a drug addict and a prostitute. She had left Millicent to fend for herself when she was barely out of diapers. She was in and out of foster homes until she got adopted."

Sitting here, I let Caroline's words hang in the air, so I can look at them from a distance, so I can decide whether I want to believe them or not. Her words are like a foreign or made up language. They don't make sense to me. My mother, the middle class, stay-at-home-mom who made me chicken soup when I was sick, who baked cookies for my Girl Scout troop, who kissed my boo-boos until they didn't hurt anymore. How could she have come out of the womb of a drug addict, prostitute? *That totally did not come out right.* I know that everyone in life doesn't get a fair shake and that things happen. Look what happened to our family, but on the surface, my mother shows no signs of her screwed up background, if indeed Caroline is telling the truth.

Ruby reads my mind. "How do we know you're telling the truth?"

"I have no reason to lie," she says, pulling her jacket closed.

"Do you know where Judy is?" I ask.

"Sure don't."

"Do you know if it was a closed adoption?" Ruby asks.

"It was open, because Millie, that's what we used to call her, knew her mother. Like I said, she was seven when she came here. The Darcys wanted it to be closed, because they didn't want Judy having any contact with Millie. But Judy was determined to get her back. She really didn't want to give up Millie. I overheard conversations with the social worker and my mother. Judy was forced to give her up. She used to show up unannounced. She would drive the Darcys crazy. I remember when we were in middle school; someone was calling here a lot and hanging up. Our dad got so pissed because he thought it was some boy calling and he wasn't having it. At first I thought it was this boy in her class that was always pulling her hair, but when I thought about it some more, I realized it was Judy. I think she was obsessed with getting Millie back. Millie even thought Judy was stalking her, but it could have been anybody. Millie had boys chasing her from elementary through high school. She had stalkers before the word was even popular. At one point I heard Judy had gotten clean and sober. That was after

Millie moved out. You know she hasn't been back since. Maybe once or twice, but I was long gone by then."

"Caroline, you don't seem too broken up about Mr. Darcy having a debilitating stroke. You even said he got what he deserved. What do you mean by that?" Ruby asks.

Caroline grips the arms of the recliner and her face reddens. Rising, shaking her head, she gets teary-eyed. "Yeah, I said it and I meant every word. That fucking bastard raped Millie and me. He took turns with us while that bitch wife of his watched. She watched it all. How sick can anybody be? Who does that? I used to try to get Millie to run away with me, but she was afraid to be back on the streets like she was with Judy. I couldn't even convince her to go to the police or report him to anybody and she begged me not to. I couldn't blame her. Over the years, with the economy failing, things have gone south, but there was a time we lived good. We went to private school; we had the best clothes, and toys, and ate well. We had all the material things we could want, but it came with a price and in my opinion, that price was way too high."

Ruby scoots next to me and places her hand on my juddering leg. I sit here stone-faced, numb. I think about every time I rolled my eyes at my mother behind her back, the times I called her bitch under my breath. I grimace when I think about all the grief I caused her when I was going through my terrible teens. I even had the unmitigated gall to tell her I hated her. If I had known then what I know now, I would have awakened her with kisses and breakfast in bed every morning. I would have cleaned up my room and done my chores. I would have not only shown her, but told her how much I love her on a daily basis.

"Are you okay?" Ruby and Caroline ask.

Now more than ever I want to find Melissa. After everything my mother has gone through, she deserves to get her daughter back. I look from Ruby to Caroline. "I'm fine," I say with steely resolve.

"Caroline, are you sure you don't know where Judy is?" Ruby asks.

Her face crumples and she shakes her head. "I wish I did. I think she spent some time up north. When Millie first got here she talked about the city with the hills and the golden bridge. She said when she was little she used to be afraid when Judy would drive up hills or over the bridge."

"We need to go," I say, rising.

"Give me a minute," Ruby says. "Caroline, do you mind if I use your restroom?"

"No, of course not. It's down the hallway, the last door on the right."

"Thanks," Ruby says, leaving the room.

"Don't forget the book," Caroline says to me.

"Right," I say, picking it up.

"I hope I didn't upset you too much," Caroline says. "I don't know why Millie didn't tell you about her life, but I can't blame her. It's not a good look," she says, scratching her head. "I need to wash my hair," she says, yawning. "You have pretty hair like your mother. You know she was the pretty one and I was the ugly one," she says again.

I nod and shift my weight from one foot to the other, wishing Ruby would hurry back. I can't believe she's using the restroom here. She's the only person I know who will hold it until she gets home.

"Thanks," Ruby says, returning.

"No problem," Caroline says, walking us to the door.

Ruby rushes ahead of us, holding her jean jacket closed. I follow her with Caroline on my heels. I want to keep moving and never look back, but she digs her fingernails into my shoulder. I spin around, facing her, wondering why she would do that. I start to ask, but an evil grin creeps over her face. She quickly covers it with a fake smile.

"Again, I'm sorry about all of this. It was nice meeting you. You're pretty—like your mother. Your friend is pretty, too. Pretty girls are so interesting. You know, I was the ugly one," she says, narrowing her eyes.

"Maddie, let's go," Ruby says, bolting to the car.

"Right," I say. "I'm behind you."

We get in my BMW, I toss the thesaurus onto the back seat, and drive away. I turn toward Ruby who's now holding a plastic bag filled with papers and mail. "Where did that come from?"

"I picked it up on my way to the 'restroom,'" she says, making little quote marks with her fingers. "I noticed a bunch of boxes in the hallway and gabbed whatever looked interesting. Who knows, there might be something in here that could help us solve this mother of a puzzle."

"I was wondering why you asked to use the restroom."

"That woman's a trip," Ruby says. "Jealous as hell. She couldn't wait to tell you all she had heard through the 'grapevine' about your real grandmother. She relished every moment of it. I'm sorry you had to hear all of that. I was so tempted to leave."

"It's okay, Ruby," I say, stopping at the traffic light. "I needed to hear it all. I wonder if she's telling the truth."

"It does explain why your mother cut the Darcys off. And it does give us another name for your mother's stalker list."

"You think my grandmother hired The Renter?"

"She could have."

"What if she was so obsessed with getting my mother back, years later she settles for the next best thing, a granddaughter. What if she hired The Renter and someone else to carjack my mother and take Melissa? She could have been after both of us. My mother says she had already taken me out of my car seat and I was standing by her side —"

"What's going on?" Ruby asks.

"I was thinking about one of the very few memories I have of the day of the carjacking. I remember Melissa and me in our red and blue jackets with the fake fur lining. My mother was wearing her coat, too. But it was a hot June that year, according to Kaitlin. We wouldn't have been wearing our jackets. Why do I see us in our jackets that day?"

"That's something to think about," Ruby says. "And I agree with you. I think Judy hired The Renter. You need to meet with Sam and bring him up to date. He should be able to verify the adoption for us and if Judy was involved in the life, she most likely has a record that Sam should be able to access. Hopefully, there'll be an address on file somewhere."

"I also need to ask him about Jerome Darcy being brought up on charges. I don't think there's a statute of limitations on child molestation in California," I say.

"There is and there isn't. Clay and I got into this discussion once when he was working on a child molestation case at Harvard. He was assigned California. There's a ten-year statute of limitations, but the crime can still be prosecuted within one year whenever the victim tells the police even if ten years has past."

"That doesn't make sense," I say.

"I know. It's confusing."

"It would take a miracle for my mother to tell the police."

"Girl, you got that right."

"I love your spirit, Rubik's Cube. What would I do without you?"

She laughs hysterically. "You haven't called me that in a

long time. Anyway, the question is, what would I do without you? When no one would talk to me at Dancing Hills Elementary, you did. You never judged me and you inspire me. Losing your twin at a young age and now finding out all this horrible stuff about what happened to your mother and you're still not giving up."

"My father said he doesn't know why I'm so stubborn. Now I know. My mother went through hell and back, but she never gave up. She made a life for herself, for my dad, for Melissa and me." The MESSAGE icon on my phone gets my attention. "I have a text, check it out, please." The light turns green and I continue driving onto the freeway.

Ruby grabs my phone and says, "It's from Kaitlin."

"Please, God let her have the name of The Renter," I say, gripping the steering wheel.

Chapter 8

J.F. That's what was on the faded piece of paper my father found in storage. Sorry, wish we could have found more.

Sitting at the breakfast nook, in our small kitchen, I study the text Kaitlin sent. Who the hell has initials J.F.? Ruby and I have been racking our brains since yesterday. I click over to the message I received from Sam.

Hey U. Graduation 2day. Now returning 2morrow. Got yr message about yr mom being adopted. Let's meet asap. I have some ideas. J.F.?

Where there's a text from Sam, there's a smile. It's something about him that makes me feel better. Maybe it's those lively green eyes of his or his thick dark hair he runs his fingers through when he's being bossy. Maybe it's that blinding smile and all that swagger. *Hmm.*

"Breakfast must have been really good," Ruby says, entering, clutching a sheet of paper.

I give the barely eaten eggs and toast on my plate an eye

roll and say, "It was okay. I'm not used to eating breakfast. Actually, I was catching up on my recent text messages."

"I should have known. That explains the orgasmic look on your face when I walked in. Have you and Sam decided on a *date*? I mean meeting."

"Ruby Renee Flowers, you are not right," I say, popping her with a nearby dishtowel.

"Ouch," she says, laughing and sitting at the table. She looks around the kitchen, sizing it up. "We should paint it green and white in here."

"I was thinking blue and white."

"Why am I not surprised? How are you doing with your boxes?" she asks.

"I'm almost done unpacking. I still need to go through those things my grandmother gave me. I really love it here, but I wish the kitchen was bigger."

"It could have been if you didn't need three closets for your clothes and shoes," Ruby says.

"You're on a roll," I say. "My grandmother hates the neighborhood but loves our place. It is great. The hardwood floors, the skylight in the living room, the spacious bedrooms..."

"Yes, it is all that," Ruby says, patting her afro.

"What's that?" I ask, my eyes zooming in on the paper in her hand.

"It's the search list. I wanted to revisit it. Construction in Dancing Hills, Body Car Repairs, Private Investigators, Statute of Limitations in California, Postpartum Depression, Pregnancy Week by Week, Twins, Cryptophasia:Twin Language, Colic, Plumbing for Idiots, Open Adoption vs. Closed Adoption, LLC Formation, Carpet Cleaners, Hair Salons, Metal Shops, and more."

"Adoption!" we say at the same time.

"Either my mother or father was looking up adoption. You know what, I remember my mother using the computer more than my father. She may have been trying to find out how much access her mother had to her," I say, scrunching my face. "I think...I'm not sure."

"Have you decided whether and when you're going to tell your mother about our meeting with Caroline?"

"I'm still thinking about it. I don't know how'll she'll take it, and I had told her I wasn't going to try to find Melissa. It's hard. I don't want to hurt her. And what if my father doesn't know she's adopted and about the rape. I know my grandmother doesn't know. She would have told me. I feel so bad for my mother. And then what if none of it's true?"

"I still get pissed off when I think about that asshole Jerome putting his hands on your mother. I know we don't have proof, but I have a feeling Caroline was telling the truth. You can tell she's really messed up, and Jerome and Jean are probably the reason why."

"I hope my mother got some counseling or help."

"Maybe she did. Remember how your grandmother said your mother was really nervous in her twenties and now she's calm."

"But is she calm because of therapy or is she medicated? I did notice a bottle of Valium in her medicine cabinet. That was a long time ago though."

"Let's try to be positive," Ruby says. "You know what else on the list is interesting?"

"What?" I ask.

"The construction stuff and the body car repair thing."

"Why?" I ask.

"You told me Sam said finding the SUV your mother

was driving that day would be substantial new evidence."

"Yeah, he did. It's really strange that the police never found it. So do you think there's a connection with the construction and the body car repairs?"

"I don't know. Usually when someone steals a car, the first place they go to is a chop shop," Ruby says.

"That's where they take cars apart and sell the parts?" I ask.

"Exactly."

"That's probably what happened to our car."

"Maybe your father was trying to see if anyone around town had been trying to get rid of an SUV. I don't know. I feel like I'm grasping for straws," Ruby says, dropping her head onto the table.

"Don't be so hard on yourself, Ruby. You're doing good. I feel as lost as you do. I was thinking about the construction site Ted mentioned—his father's construction site. I don't remember it that well, but I do remember always seeing those big yellow trucks. What if the carjackers stashed Melissa in a hideaway and then got rid of the car. You know, left it at the construction site so that it would be buried in cement. Maybe my father thought the same thing and was looking up construction sites to visit."

Ruby gives me a blank stare, and I drop my head onto the table, too. She giggles and I join her and then we break out in uproarious laughter.

"Girl, who do we think we are?" Ruby asks. "Olivia Pope from ABC's Scandal, we are not."

"Let's not quit our day jobs," I say.

We quiet down and sit in silence and then I see a spark in Ruby's eyes, the one that means she's gotten her second mental wind.

"What are you thinking?"

"Let's regroup. Let's make sure we're on the same page."

"Okay," I say.

"We both agree that your maternal grandmother, Judy Gardner, hired The Renter because of her longtime obsession with getting your mother back. By the way, off the chain analysis, Miss Patterson."

"Thank you," I say.

Ruby continues. "We believe the drug use, coupled with her life on the streets, and your mother being taken from her, probably pushed her over the edge mentally. And as a result, she had The Renter and another unknown assailant carjack your mother so she could get you and Melissa, but she ends up only getting Melissa. In her mind, it would be her second chance to raise your mother."

"If our theory is true, then Judy has Melissa," I say. "Now we have to find Judy or J.F., or both. And Sam is going to help us find Judy."

"It looks like we might be getting closer," Ruby says, giving me a high-five.

"There's only one catch," I say.

"What?" Ruby asks.

"This is all speculation and hearsay. We don't have any proof," I say.

"Right," Ruby says.

"What about that plastic bag you took when we met with Caroline?"

"I've already gone through it. It was junk mail."

"Are you sure?" I ask.

"Yep."

"Do you still have it?"

"It's in my room. I was going to throw it out."

"Can you get it?"

"I told—"

"I know, Ruby, but sometimes a fresh pair of eyes can see what tired ones can't."

"You're right," Ruby says. "I'll be right back."

I stand and pace, waiting for Ruby to return, wondering if, and hoping the smoking gun is in that plastic bag. Even a firecracker would do at this point. The sound of Pepper's nails on the hardwood floor give me a sense of hope. He enters the kitchen and jumps on me, showering me with hugs and kisses. "Good morning to you, too, Pepper. I love you, too, boy." I pat his head and he moves away from me when he spots his bowl brimming with the organic food he's become addicted to. Chomping on his breakfast, he now ignores me.

"Pepper is going to town," Ruby says, returning.

She sets the bag on the table and I go through it. "You're right. It's junk."

"Now what?" Ruby asks.

"Let's take a break."

"I'm all for that. I need to call Clay anyway."

"What's going on with you two? I notice a lot of calls lately."

"He's lobbying for my love, for my hand in marriage."

"Is it working?"

"I guess time will tell," she says, leaving me in the kitchen.

I go to the living room and grab my phone, checking for messages. I notice the thesaurus Caroline forced on me sitting on the coffee table. I put my phone down and began rifling through the book. "What's another word for stumped?" I go to the S's and pause when a folded piece of paper falls onto the floor. I pick it up. It's actually an envelope. I unfold it and peer at the cursive writing on the front. *Millicent Darcy, c/o Jerome and Jean Darcy.* "What the hell? Ruby! Come here. Quick."

"What's going on?"

I show her the envelope. "It's a letter to my mother."

"Where did it come from?"

"It was in the thesaurus."

"Shut the hell up. Do you think Caroline knew it was in there? Maybe that's why she wanted you to have the book."

"But she didn't know we were coming there," I say. "You saw how jacked up that house was, who knows where anything is in that place."

"That's true. Who's it from?"

"It doesn't say."

"Open it?" Ruby says, going toward the kitchen.

"Where are you going?" I ask.

"To get some gloves. You've already touched the outside, but we should at least not touch the actual letter. Sam might be able to get some prints."

"I don't know if there is a letter."

"Open it and find out, but wait for me," Ruby says.

She returns with two pairs of gloves and we put them on. Holding onto the envelope like it's the last lifejacket on a sinking ship, I set it on the table. Ruby sits next to me and we share inquisitive looks.

"Are you going to open it?" Ruby asks.

I nod and open the envelope. I remove the letter.

♊

May 1, 1989

Dear Millicent,

I'm sorry I won't be able to celebrate your 17th Birthday with you. I miss you so much, my sweet Honey Bunny. I've tried to see you and call you, but I'm blocked at every turn. Don't worry, I have something in store for Jean and Jerome, and I don't care if they read this. God don't like ugly and what they are doing is pure evil. I have eyes and ears on every corner, and what is done in the dark will soon come to the light. I know that evil man is doing things to you a decent man wouldn't do to a dog and I blame myself. If I had been a better mother, you wouldn't have been taken from me. I shouldn't have had you out on the street like that and your no good daddy wouldn't help. He's locked up now. Don't know when he's gettin' out. Anyway, I never wanted to give you up. That social worker played mind games on me, got me all confused. I didn't know I was permanently signing my baby away. I vowed to get you back, to be the mother you never had, and that I should have been. Baby, I tried to get you back. I came by your school looking for you, I spied, I had people spying. I was going to snatch you, take you back, but I was too high to get the job done. I'm in rehab now and am doing a twelve step program. You would be so proud of me, Baby.

I love you so much, Millicent, it hurts. It hurts, Baby, and sometimes I want to stop the pain. I want to use, so I don't have to feel this hell. It's hell not being able to hold you, to talk to you, to see you. Ten years, ten fucking years, the system has taken you from me. Forgive me for my bad language, Baby. I'm working on that. But sometimes I get so angry at myself, at the system. The streets is no good. Don't ever get on the streets like I did. You're a pretty girl and there a lot of wolves out there. Be careful, my Honey Bunny. God help me to accept the things I cannot change, the courage to change the things I can, and the wisdom to know the difference.

I have to go. Stay sweet. And one day soon we'll be together. I swear to that.

Love your mother that will always love you,

Judy Gardner

Sitting in the sand at Venice Beach with Pepper by my side, I try to imagine my mother's mother writing this letter. I can feel her determination seeping from the paper. I've read this letter a hundred times since Ruby and I first laid eyes on it yesterday. It took everything in me not to drive to Dancing Hills to show my mother, and to let her know I know about what happened, and that I want to be there for her. But after thinking things over, I decided I would be still and wait. I don't want to hurt her any more than she's already been hurt, and before I talk to her, I want to run things by my father. I'm not sure how much he knows, but now I suspect he may know it all. I'm not sure if my mother has ever seen or even read the letter, even though it was in a book Caroline claims she used on a regular basis.

Sam's back in town today, and I can't wait to fill him in on everything and for him to start searching for Judy. Deep down I know she has Melissa, but why wouldn't she come forward knowing how much it hurt my mother to lose Melissa? It doesn't make sense. Every time Ruby and I think we've solved this mystery, a million other questions rear their ugly heads. In a few days I'll be starting at KYON, but I'm not sure how focused I'll be with everything going on. I'm not sure how I'm going to react when I see my mother again. I hope I don't lose it.

I put the copy of the letter in my purse, lean back, and take in the expansive blue sky. I can see the sun's rays trying to push through the clouds. I love coming out here when I'm feeling stressed. The smell of the salty sea relaxes me and clears my head. I think about the few times my father took us to Venice Beach. It's more than forty miles west of Dancing Hills. My mother said my father didn't really like coming out here because of all the guys flexing their muscles. He's always been on the scrawny side. But what he lacks in brawn, he more than makes up for with business acumen. He's turned his practice into a gold mine with his charisma and skills.

Pepper looks at me and I pass my hand over his back. He's such a loyal friend. I love him. I couldn't imagine him being taken from me. How did my mother endure Melissa being taken? A text from Ruby makes me laugh out loud.

You're not fooling anybody, Madeline Louise Patterson. Tell Sam I said hello and that I look forward to meeting him.

"Pepper, your crazy aunt thinks we're out here with Sam. Speaking of which," I say, clicking over to a message from him.

Madeline, I'd luv2cu...that is 2go over the case. Call me when u can. Sam.

I gaze at his message and then click over to his number in my contacts. Looking around, I smile at the families and couples enjoying the beach, wondering if Sam is into water sports. I wonder could he hold his own on a pair of jet skis or riding a wave.

His ringtone comes on and then he answers. "Hey, you," he says.

"So you like Pitbull?" I ask.

"Huh?"

"Your ringtone is 'Timber.'"

"Right," he says.

"I like him, too," I say, twisting my hair.

"Good. Did you get my text?"

"That's why I'm calling," I say.

"You make me nervous."

Furrowing my brows, I say, "Make you nervous. You're

a big bad cop with a badge and a gun. How in the world could little ole' me make you nervous?"

"You just do," he says, sounding a little breathless. "Where are you?"

"Venice Beach."

"Oh...Muscle Beach. You like the water?"

"I love the water."

"Can you swim?"

"Not to toot my own horn, but I was captain of my swim team in high school *and* a Junior Lifeguard. I love the water and the sun."

"I can tell by your hair — sun-kissed. Boy I wish I was the sun."

"Excuse me," I say.

"I said my trip was a lot of fun."

"Right...you'll have to tell me more when I see you again."

"I'll tell you about my trip, but I also want to share some ideas with you I have about the case."

"That sounds good. When do you want to meet?"

"I'm at LAX. I can meet you in thirty minutes...that's if you're available. There's a coffee shop on Sepulveda and La Tijera — Carmen's Coffee."

"I have my dog with me."

"They like dogs there. Bring her. I'd love to meet her."

"She is a he," I say.

"Then bring *him*," he says.

I glance over at Pepper, wondering if he's okay hanging out. He wore himself out chasing his Frisbee and the seagulls when we first got here. "Okay, sounds like a plan. I'll see you there."

"Great," he says, hanging up.

"What do you think, Pep? Are you up for some coffee?"
He barks three times and I say, "Will do."

Chapter 9

Pepper leaps out of the car. When he was a puppy, I had to make sure he waited for me. When mastiffs are little, if you let them jump or play too hard, you could cause permanent damage to their ligaments. I close the passenger door and motion for him to stay. "Carmen's Coffee," I say, looking up at the sign painted on the glass window. "You want some caffeine, Pepper?" He barks, but not in response to me. I pull on his leash when he tries to make a sudden move toward a terrier walking by. Pepper's a peaceful dog, so I know he just wants to play. "Come on, boy, let's go get our buzz on," I say, pulling him toward the entrance to the café.

When we step inside, I notice a man at the counter with his back to us. Broad shoulders, nice ass, slightly bowed legs. It has to be Sam. Pepper barks and the man spins around, all smiles and winks.

"Hey you, what's your name?" he asks, approaching Pepper. Pepper jumps on him and gives him a big lick. "That a boy. You're strong and tall. What's Madeline been feeding you?" he asks.

"It's not Madeline who's been feeding him, it's his Aunt Ruby," I say, impressed with how he's handling my baby boy. "He likes you," I say, reining Pepper in. "Come on, boy. Let the nice man breathe." Pepper relaxes and stands between us, looking from Sam to me.

"He's a great dog, but then again I shouldn't be surprised," he says.

"His name's Pepper and you can call me Maddie."

"I like both names," he says. "Why Pepper? How'd you come up with that? It's unusual."

"When I first got him, I started having sneezing fits. I thought I was going to have to give him up. But we discovered it was the powder his groomers were using on him. That's where the name comes from."

"Are you ready to order?" the lady at the counter asks.

"Sure," he says, turning toward her. "Maddie, Pepper, it's on me."

I join him at the counter with Pepper by my side. "I'll have a latte and a scone," I say. "And Pepper..."

"We have dog bones," the clerk says.

"We'll take one," I say.

Sam laughs and says, "I'll have a latte, too."

He pays for everything and we find a nice table near the window. He pulls my chair and I sit. Pepper slumps to the floor with his bone in his mouth. Sam and I share more laugher. I wish I had met Sam at this coffee shop and not at DHPD. I wish I didn't have a missing sister or a mother who grew up in hell. I wish everything was normal. But Ruby says normal is a setting on a washing machine and not what are lives are supposed to be.

"What are you thinking about?" he asks, sitting across from me.

"I was wondering how your trip was," I lie.

"It was great. My sister graduated with honors. She wants to be a doctor."

"She must be really smart."

"She is. Made my folks really proud."

"Did you get a chance to do any sightseeing?"

"Not really, but we did get around to checking out some nice restaurants. And I saw a show on Broadway."

"What show?"

"I knew you were going to ask that. I think I fell asleep half way through. It was something about boots. My sister wanted to see it."

"Kinky Boots?"

"Right. That's it. Do you like theatre?"

"I do, but I'm not too fond of musicals."

"I guess we have that in common," he says. "My sister was telling me Alan Alda is going to be in a show called 'Love Letters.' My dad's a big fan. I'm thinking about taking him for his birthday."

"That sounds like a great idea. Speaking of letters." I reach into my purse and hand him a plastic bag. Inside is the envelope containing the letter. Then I give him a copy to read. "I found it in a book my mother's adopted sister gave me."

Sam takes a sip of his coffee and his green eyes move from left to right. I study his face, but it's stoic, like I'd expect. I'm sure as a cop he's probably seen so much blood and gore, that nothing shakes him. He finishes the copy and hands it to me. He pockets the original.

"I'm sorry, Maddie. I'm sorry for your mother and your grandmother. So your mother never told you she was adopted?"

"No, I had no idea. I thought she was estranged from her parents. I didn't know they weren't her biological parents and that they had assaulted her. I'm not sure if she ever received the letter. A part of me wants to show it to her in case she's never seen it. I think it would make her feel better knowing her mother never meant to give her up or for her to have gotten hurt." I look into Sam's eyes for permission. I want him to tell me he thinks it's the right thing to do, but his face turns slightly crimson and my stomach sinks.

"I think you've made the right decision to wait. You don't know how this information may help us in our investigation and you mentioned that your mother doesn't want you trying to reopen the case. She may not react well to you knowing about her past, Maddie. At least not now."

"You're right. I guess I'm a little anxious about how to behave around her. I'm having dinner at the house with my parents this weekend. I don't want to say the wrong thing and then explode. I don't know if I'll be able to control myself."

"I believe you have a tremendous amount of restraint. Personally, I doubt I'd be able to keep something like this to myself, but I think it's imperative you do. I'm going to have someone check into the adoption records for information and the whereabouts of your grandmother."

"Detective Faulkner?" I ask.

"No, actually he had to take some unexpected time off. I have someone else helping me."

"I hope he's okay."

"He's alright. He says he's dealing with a family matter. I talked to him yesterday. That's nice of you to be concerned."

I give him a warm smile.

"Anyway, don't worry. I also think you and your roommate may be onto something about your grandmother hiring The Renter. Now whether he was a part of the actual carjacking, I'm not sure. But based on that letter, your grandmother was watching your mother or had people watching her for a very long time."

"Do you think she has Melissa?"

"Honestly, I'm not sure, but I think she definitely knows something. When do you start your job at KYON?"

"Monday. Why?"

"Do you have a good relationship with your boss?"

"She was great in the interview, but I don't know her that well. Why?"

"I think you should pitch your story. Melissa going missing was big news back in the day. If you give the station an exclusive, they'd be all over it. I've worked with a lot of reporters and they always like to get scoops."

"Why would they be interested if the case isn't going to be reopened?"

"You have a degree in journalism, Maddie. What's journalism 101, something about a biting dog?"

"Dog bites man is not news, but a man biting a dog is news," I say. "Wait a minute. How did you know I have a journalism degree?"

"I'm a cop. I do my research."

"What else do you know about me?"

"I know you're smart, beautiful, determined, and you're unlike any woman I've ever met."

I feel my face flush. I take a sip of my coffee and avert my eyes. "Okay, back to man bites dog. They'd be interested, because it's not every day that a twin goes missing, and years later, the other twin tries to find her."

"Bingo," he says.

"Do you think they'd run the story?"

"I do and it would give the case some much needed exposure. You'd be surprised how after decades pass, people come out of hiding. Witnesses who were afraid to talk suddenly have diarrhea of the mouth."

I grimace. It's not only a cliché, but the image it conjures up, is beyond gross.

"Sorry, poor choice of words."

"But what if my mother hears about it?"

"You could blame the station."

"But I work there. She'll think I had something to do with it."

"Maddie, sooner or later your mother is going to figure it out. You can't keep something like this a secret. You *can* keep what you know about her past to yourself, but if you want to find Melissa, you're going to have to go all out. With that in mind, we need to put together a flier, with you at age three and you now. We need to put that flier everywhere. The caption would be something like, HAVE YOU SEEN MELISSA LORRAINE PATTERSON? SHE'S AN IDENTICAL TWIN. SHE WAS KIDNAPPED DURING A CARJACKING AT THE AGE OF THREE, NINETEEN YEARS AGO. SHE'S NOW TWENTY-TWO. We'd put the fliers everywhere — Long Beach, Pasadena, Compton, Beverly Hills, San Dimas, and especially up north. If Melissa's alive, someone has seen her. You also need to start a Facebook page. Call it Missing Melissa or whatever you come up with. You can put pictures there, make comments. Invite the world to like the page. You'd be surprised what kind of leads we could get. You have to basically create a campaign. You could garner so much public support and sympathy that the Chief would have to reopen the case."

"Thank you, Sam. I don't know what to say. You've put a lot of thought into this."

"Maddie, as I mentioned before, I have a sister and I love her. I couldn't imagine losing her. That's what drives me, that and you, lady. How could I not want to help?" He glances at his watch and says, "I gotta get going. I'm working on two other cases. Let's talk soon. Let me know how you're doing with the Facebook page and work. I'll give you an update on your grandmother as soon as I hear something. He reaches into his pocket and hands me a card. My uncle owns a printing company. He'll do the fliers for free."

"But—"

"Just say thank you."

"Thank you."

"You're welcome. Let me walk you and Pepper to your car and then I have to take off."

"Okay," I say, rising.

He motions for Pepper and me to walk ahead of him. We do so and he follows. He gets ahead of us and opens the door. We all leave. I thank him again and he heads toward his car. I stand here waiting for him to change into his superhero costume. But when he gets in his black Corvette, he's still wearing jeans and a short sleeve, yellow polo shirt. I pass my hand over my yellow sundress and think about Ruby's parents and how they wear twin outfits.

I open the car door for Pepper and he gets in. I join him, still thinking about Sam, but mainly thinking about taking my search to the next level and how it's going to impact my family.

♊

Pulling up to my parents' tan and green, two-story brick home, I park in front and peer across the street at Kaitlin's old house. I can't help but think about The Renter peeking through the blinds, sweat dripping from his face, his heart racing, while he watches my mother's every move. His accomplice was probably waiting in the cut, waiting for my mother to leave the house. They probably knew her routine by then. But how did they know we had a doctor's appointment?

I glance at the clock on my dashboard. Dinner is about to start. My grandmother's Lexus isn't out front so she hasn't arrived. I look in my rearview mirror at Pepper with his tongue wagging and get out of the car. I open the passenger door for him and he leaps out, runs around the side of the house, and to the backyard. Before I can call him, my phone rings. I take it out of my purse, wondering what Ruby wants.

"Rubik's Cube, what's going on? You miss us already? We've been gone for less than an hour."

"Look who has jokes," she says. "I was calling to wish you luck, and to tell you to stay calm, and that everything is going to be okay."

"Thanks, I appreciate the pep talk."

"Okay, call me if you need me. I'm on my way to the hardware store to get some green and white paint," she says.

"Ruby!"

"Just kidding. Bye now."

Shaking my head and grinning, I wave at the couple two houses over, watching their children playing in the yard. A group of boys on skateboards race up and down the middle of the street. The sun smiles down on all of us. July will be here before we know it—barbecues and fireworks on the horizon. I remember being a kid in the neighborhood, post the carjacking. We had a lot of fun chasing one another and the ice cream truck.

Entering the house, I step into the foyer, and sniff. My mother's cooking pot roast, potatoes, and asparagus. The sweet aroma wafting in the air pulls me toward the stainless steel kitchen. On my way there, I stop in the living room, surprised to see my swimming medals on the mantle. I see my mother has been redecorating. Speaking of which, where is she and my father? As I approach the kitchen, the sound of muffled voices coming from the garage gives me pause. I walk to the door that separates it from the house. The door's slightly ajar. I'm surprised to hear my father's voice, laced with attitude and exasperation.

"*Millie*, how many times have I asked you not to bother my things?"

"Don't call me that. You know I don't like that name," my mother says. "And I didn't know it was important. We have a new computer. Why did we need the old one? It was just taking up space."

"That's not the point."

"Then what is the point, Alvin?"

"You gave it to Ruby."

"And?"

"She's a computer whiz. What if she goes snooping around on there? God knows what she might find."

"Why would she care about what's on our computer?"

"Because she and Maddie are trying to—"

"To what?" my mother asks with panic in her voice.

"To...to."

Think fast, Dad.

"They're trying to do some social networking project."

"Oh, okay. Well, I'm sorry. You're right. I wasn't thinking."

"That's okay, Millicent. Don't worry about it."

"Are you sure?"

"Yes. Maddie's going to be here soon. Whatever you do, don't let anyone else in here, and don't let anyone take anything without checking with me first."

"I understand."

I move away from the garage and rush to the front of the house. I open the door as if I'm just arriving. "Mom, Dad, I'm home," I say, hoping they're now in the kitchen and within the sound of my voice.

"We're in the kitchen," my mother says.

"Okay, coming," I say, wiping my sweaty hands on my jeans. Entering, I give them an exaggerated smile and hug them. "Smells good," I say, opening the oven door, giving the broiling roast the once-over.

"How's my favorite reporter doing?" my father asks, sitting on a stool adjacent to the marble island.

"I'm great," I say, feigning cheerfulness.

My mother goes to the oven and checks on the roast. "Are you hungry?"

"I'm starving. Where's Grandma Patterson."

"I'm right here," she says, standing in the doorway.

"Mother, you're like a Ninja," my father says, going to her. She ruffles his hair just as he's about to hug her and he rears back.

"Ma, don't. It took me thirty minutes to get it just right today," he says, whining, pressing his hair in place.

"Poor baby. Look at him, he's so spoiled. Millicent, you spoil him, I spoil him, and Maddie spoils him. Just spoiled rotten!" she says, tilting a bit.

I go to her and give her a hug. She reeks of alcohol. Wow, and she's driving. She used to live in Long Beach when my grandfather was alive, but now she only lives a few minutes from here, but still. "Grandma, let me fix you some coffee," I say.

"Okay, Maddie. You know I love you forever," she says, flopping down on a chair at the breakfast nook.

My mother and father exchange glances. Then they look at me and I give them the, "I think Grandma's had too much medicine," look.

"Ma, I want you to drink some coffee!" my father yells as though she's deaf rather than drunk.

"Maddie's fix...fix...fixing me coffee," she says, slurring her words.

"I can't believe this," my mother says, storming out of the kitchen.

My father runs after her. "Millicent, wait."

I get coffee into my grandmother and take her to the living room sofa where she lies down, mumbling and rolling her eyes. "Your parents are a piece of work, Maddie. Always conspiring, whispering, secrets here and secrets there. I can't figure them out."

"Are you okay, Ma?" my father asks, approaching.

I notice my mother lurking in the background, her face firecracker red. "All I wanted to do was have a nice dinner with Maddie. Why can't you stop drinking for at least a day? Why can't you stay sober, Alicia?"

My grandmother sits up and her eyes widen. "Maybe I drink to calm my nerves. Don't think because you take Valium that you're any better than me, Millicent. And why am I nervous? Because the only granddaughter I have left is living on skid row with a bunch of pimps, prostitutes, and drug addicts. What if she's taken like Melissa was? Why would you let her move there? What mother does that?" She rises and extends her short arms to keep balance. "It's because of you, Melissa is missing. Who knows what you did to her," she says with rage in her voice and eyes.

My mother stumbles backward with her mouth open so wide you can almost see her tonsils. She shuts her mouth, takes a moment, and says, "How dare you, Alicia. How dare you say those things?"

"Ma, it's time for you to leave," my father says, grabbing her by the arm. "I'll call you a cab."

"Let go of me, Alvin," she says, breaking free of his grip. "You're always on me about my drinking. But what about yours? At least I'm not falling out in my own vomit, spending days in a drunken stupor, putting holes in the wall. Do you remember those days, Alvin? Your drunken antics. You almost lost your practice and your license. Millicent, starving herself to death. Do you remember how your father and I came and rescued Maddie from this mad house? Now because I had one too many, I'm the bad guy. I don't think so," she says, leaving. My father, mother, and I run after her.

"Ma, don't you get in that car. Don't you drive drunk," my father says, blocking the front door.

I stand here like a stranger, watching a movie featuring actors I've never heard of, performing scenes I've never knew existed. Who are these people? My grandmother and father have a tug of war at the front door, while my mother looks on in dismay. Pepper, clamorously barking on the other side of the door, snaps them back to some semblance of sanity, and they compose themselves, averting each other's accusing glares. My father opens the door and my mother and I scream.

Chapter 10

Pepper, with blood on his nose and paws, jumps on my father and sends him reeling back onto his butt. He then limps over to me, rubs against my leg, and slumps to the floor with his eyes closed. My mother screams again.

"Is he dead? Oh God, please don't let him be dead," she says.

"Don't say that, Mom."

"He's breathing, Millicent," my father says.

"I can't tell," my mother says.

"He's not dead," my grandmother chimes in.

A trail of blood can be seen on the pathway leading to the front door. My father stumbles to his feet and grabs Pepper, trying to see where and how he's been injured. My legs go out from underneath me and I fall to the floor. My mother and grandmother come to my aid and help me stand. I hate the sight of blood. Why does it have to be red?

Why couldn't it be pink or yellow or green or even blue —
happy colors?

"What happened to him, Dad?" I ask in a shrill voice.

"I don't know, kiddo. I'm trying to find out."

Pepper yelps when my father touches his paws. "He's
been scratching on something. The blood makes it look
worse than it actually is. Millicent, get the first aid kit."

"Of course," she says, shutting the front door, then
sprinting to the guest bathroom down the hall.

"We need to take him to the vet," my grandmother says.

"She's right, Dad," I say. "What if he gets an infection?"

My mother returns with the kit and my father gets busy
doctoring on Pepper. My mother, grandmother, and I look
on with concern, hoping my dad can make him all better,
forgetting about the caustic words and accusations, that
moments ago were being fired like rocket-propelled
grenades in a war-torn third world country.

"Okay, Pepper. You're going to be okay, boy," my father
says, patting him on the head. Pepper, with his paws
wrapped in white gauze, looks at us with eyes bereft of their
usual liveliness. "He needs to stay down for a few days. No
running around."

"I still want to take him to the vet, Dad."

"They'll be open Monday and you work Monday," my
father reminds me.

"I'll take him," my mother says.

My grandmother rolls her eyes and pats Pepper on his
head. "What are you scratching for?"

"It's something under the house he's after," I say,
heading to the backyard.

"Leave it!" my father says. "I'll take care of it. Your
mother told me about the crawlspace. I'll clean up the blood,

too," he says. "I think the neighbor's cat had kittens underneath the house. Weren't they looking for their cat?" my father asks my mother.

"You're right, Alvin. You really need to get *down there* and see what's going on," she says, pointedly.

Still curious about Pepper's obsession with the crawlspace, I ignore my father and head to the backyard, but am stopped short when my grandmother begins twitching her nose.

"What's that smell?" she asks.

"Oh my God," my mother says. We all gasp at the sight of smoke coming from the kitchen, wafting into the foyer. "The roast is burning." My mother goes to the kitchen with all of us following, sans Pepper. Coughing, she opens the oven door, fanning away the smoke with her hand. We stare at the black piece of meat that's not fit for even Pepper to eat. "There goes dinner," she says, slamming the oven door closed. She turns it off and looks at my father.

"Let's order pizza," he says. "You wanna ride with me, Maddie? Like we used to."

"Okay," I say, needing to get some fresh air and some answers. "Let me check on Pepper first."

"Sure," he says.

I return to the foyer and kneel down next to Pepper. "It's going to be okay, boy. I love you."

He gives me a whimper and closes his eyes. I stare at him to make sure he's breathing, and then I meet my father outside so we can get dinner and I can get to the bottom of the Patterson family drama.

♊

My father and I sit in his white Range Rover in stony silence while we wait for our pizza. We're so close to the mountains, I feel like I can reach out and touch them. He clears his throat and says, "A long time ago Dancing Hills was voted one of the safest cities in the United States. You know how it got its name?"

I look at him, waiting for him to give me the answer, hoping he's going to give me all the answers.

"The hills are really the mountains. This area was populated with Native Americans, hundreds of years ago, and according to legend, there was a great Tribal Chief who had a beautiful daughter. She was not only beautiful, but talented and smart. Like you Maddie. She wasn't an award-winning swimmer, but she could dance magnificently. Her dancing was so unusual and beautiful that it would make people cry with joy. Her movements could restore crops and bring rain. The people of the land believed that their ancestors had blessed her with this dance that enabled her to perform miracles. Then one day the Chief became gravely ill. There was no doctor or medicine man that could heal him. The people of the land were distraught and the Chief's family, especially his daughter, was devastated.

On his death bed, the Chief had one request—for his daughter to dance for him. There was a big party and ceremony and the Chief's daughter was made up and dressed in beautiful, colorful ceremonial garb. The evening of the celebration she danced and danced and danced. She danced so hard the mountains began to shake and rumble. Then soon after, the mountains crumbled and fell and destroyed the town with all the people in it. They say that when there's a full moon you can see the mountains shimmering if you look at them at a certain angle. And that, kiddo, is where the name Dancing Hills comes from."

"That's such a sad story," I say. "I was waiting for you

to tell me she danced and her father's health was restored and they all lived happily ever after."

"When I first heard the story, I thought the same thing. It's amazing how her actions, her movements, instead of saving her father, not only destroyed him, but the entire town." My father looks at me, through me, and a chill goes through my bones.

"You know I used to dream about you being drunk and mom being sick, really thin. And then there were times I thought I had actually seen you drunk. It's so confusing when you're little; so many things are going on in the adult world you don't know about."

"Maddie, losing Melissa took a toll on all of us. Your grandmother's right. I drowned my sorrows in bottles of alcohol and your mother stop eating. The guilt was unbearable. It took us a few years to get it together. That's why I didn't want you to start your investigation."

"I'm sorry you and mom had to go through all of that."

"And I'm sorry it got so ugly today with your grandmother, but I had to stop her. And I'm sorry about the horrendous things she said to your mother, and I'm sure she'll be, when she sobers up. Your mother would never hurt you or Melissa."

"I know she wouldn't, Dad, because she's been hurt so much in her own life."

"What makes you say that?" he asks, pressing his hair.

"I went to see Caroline."

He swallows hard and says, "Caroline Darcy?"

"Yes. She told me everything. You know, don't you?"

"Know what?"

"About mom. About her being adopted and about her being...raped."

He shuts his eyes and drops his head onto the steering

wheel. The horn goes off, and startled, I jump.

He lifts his head and says, "Maddie, please. This is why I didn't want you trying to reopen Melissa's case. I knew this investigation of yours was going to uncover some things that need to stay buried. Yes, I know about your mother being adopted and about the Darcys and what they did to her, and I know about Judy and the life she led and how it impacted your mother."

"Why didn't you guys ever tell me?"

"Maddie, wait until you have kids, then you'll understand. No parent wants to burden their children with their sins and the sins of their parents. What good would it have done?"

I sit here listening to him, wanting to be mad, but feeling more sympathy for my parents than anger. "Did mom get counseling?"

"She said she did. I met your mother in middle school and by the time we made it to high school she had moved away. Then years later she had a toothache and ended up at my dental office. We rekindled our middle school romance and the rest is history. We never told your grandmother about Millicent's background because she wouldn't have understood, and we felt she would have tried to stop us from getting married."

"Dad, I think I know who took Melissa."

He turns toward me, red in the face, his lips parted, and with a timorous tone asks, "Who?"

"I believe my grandmother has Melissa."

He blinks rapidly as though something's caught in his eye. Then he says, "No way. My mother may drink a little too much now and then, but she would never harm Melissa."

"Not Grandma Patterson, Grandma Gardner. Judy

Gardner. Mom's real mother."

"What makes you think Judy has Melissa?"

"She was obsessed with getting mom back and we think—"

"We?"

"Ruby and I think that with her drug use and being on the streets, and everything that she went through, she's not all there mentally. We think she took Melissa, thinking it would give her the opportunity to raise mom vicariously." I gape at my father's contorted face, wondering and hoping he's believing me and that he'll join forces with Team Maddie.

"That's a stretch, kiddo."

"There's more, Dad."

Now sweating boulders, he rolls the window up, turns the engine on, and runs the air conditioning. "What?"

"A woman that used to live across the street from us said that the same month mom was carjacked and Melissa was taken, a man rented their house and he had a gun. We believe Judy hired that man to spy on mom and that he was working with someone else and the two of them carjacked mom and took Melissa. Melissa also came to me in another dream and this time she told me that a man saved her."

"What man saved her?" he asks.

"I don't know. We're still trying to figure it out."

My father shakes his head and leans back in his seat. He passes his hand over his face and roars with laughter. I feel like I'm in grade school all over again, vulnerable, needing and wanting his approval.

"I'm sorry, Maddie. I didn't mean to laugh…it's…it's so farfetched."

I turn away from him and get out of the car. I walk to the pizza parlor and go inside; surprised my father could be so cruel about something so sensitive. It seems like ever since I had the dream and I started searching for Melissa, my family has been possessed by a mean spirit. My grandmother's accusing my mother of hurting Melissa, my father and grandmother are dissing each other, and now my father's having a good laugh at my emotional expense.

"Miss, did you order two large pizzas, with the works?" a young girl asks.

"Is it under Patterson?" I ask.

"Yes," she says, pointing to two large boxes. "It's ready."

"Thanks. I'll be right back," I say.

When I step outside, my father is standing next to the driver's side door of his SUV. He bends his head looking into the side mirror, fussing with his hair. I can't believe that at this moment his hair is more important to him than what I've told him about Melissa. He looks up with a smile that's nowhere near his eyes.

"The pizza's ready," I say, going back to the car.

I get in the passenger seat and look straight ahead. He comes to me and I let the window down. "I'm sorry. I really am. I didn't mean to laugh. It was out of nervousness. The whole idea of you pursuing this search makes me nervous, it frightens me. I don't want it to destroy you like it almost did your mother and me."

"Dad, it's not going to destroy me. It's going to free me. At least I can say I tried. I have people helping me."

"Melissa?" he asks.

"Melissa, Sam, Ruby, Ted, Kaitlin, a lot of people and hopefully my boss. I'm going to pitch my story to the station and Ruby's working on my Facebook page. I'm having fliers made and we're going to be passing them out. I'm determined, Dad, and nothing is going to stop me."

Squinting, he leans forward and kisses me on the cheek. "I'm going to get the pizza."

I watch him go into the pizza parlor, wondering if I really know my father as well as I think I do.

♊

"I can't believe he laughed. That doesn't sound like your father at all," Ruby says, loading the dishwasher.

"He said it was nervous laughter," I say, wiping the table. "But there was this tone to it, a condescending tone. I don't know, maybe he was nervous. My whole time over there was weird—my grandmother accusing my mother of doing something to Melissa."

Ruby shuts the dishwasher door. She looks at me and then averts her eyes. I wait for her to react to my grandmother accusing my mother. I wait for her to plant her hands on her hips and to roll her eyes and shake her head, but she looks away. I take her silence to mean she's too disgusted to even comment on my grandmother's wack behavior. "What did your mother do?" she asks.

"My mother was too mortified to do anything because my grandmother was reminding my mother and father what screwed up parents they were after Melissa was taken, and how she saved me from 'the mad house.'"

Shaking my head in disbelief, I follow Ruby into the living room. We get comfortable on the sofa.

"So what happened when you and your father got back to the house?"

"The first thing I did was check on Pepper. I miss him so much already. After I saw that he was okay, my father, mother, and grandmother apologized. Then they ate the pizza and I sat there, with no appetite, trying to figure them out. After thirty minutes, I couldn't take it any longer and I came home."

"Are you going to be okay without your baby?" Ruby asks.

"I think so. He needs to be around a familiar environment right now, and my father put a large metal contraption over the crawlspace. I don't think Pepper will be trying to get into it anymore."

"What do you think he was after?"

"My parents said the neighbor's cat gave birth to kittens down there."

"Are they still down there?" she asks with raised brows and a hint of sarcasm in her voice.

"I didn't have a chance to check or ask because my mother almost burned the kitchen down." Ruby gives me a curious look and we fall over cackling. "That was the other surprise of the day. She burned the roast. I guess you could call it collateral damage. That's why we ended up ordering pizza."

"Girl, you weren't exaggerating when you said there was a lot of drama."

"I forgot to tell you, but when I first got to the house, I overhead my parents in the garage arguing about the computer my mother gave you."

"What did they say?" Ruby asks, sitting at attention.

"My father didn't like that she had given it to you because he knows how good you are with computers."

"But why would he care if I got access?"

"Probably the same reason I wouldn't want anyone hacking into my phone. I don't have nude photos or anything like that, but still…"

"I feel you. And you're sure your mother doesn't know what we're up to?"

"Yes and my father hasn't told her either."

"You know if KYON does your story, she's going to find out."

"True. Maybe I'll tell her before that happens. That way she won't be blindsided."

"Right," she says, with a questioning air.

"Are you okay?" I ask.

"Yeah. Why?"

"You seem a little strange," I say.

Before she can respond, my cell phone rings, and I pick it up from the coffee table. Ruby stretches her long neck, trying to see who's calling. "It's Sam," I say.

"Answer it," Ruby says. "Put it on speaker."

"Sam, how are you?"

"I wasn't expecting to call you so soon, but you've been on my mind — "

I take the phone off of speaker, sensing this call may be more personal than business. "Sam, can I call you back?"

"Sure. No problem," he says.

I hang up and turn toward Ruby who's staring at me. "Why didn't you talk to him?"

"I saw him the other day."

"But what if it was about the case?" she asks.

"I doubt it. He's been saying stuff. Making comments."

"What kind of comments?"

"Flirty comments. Telling me I'm smart and beautiful."

"But you are."

"I don't — "

"You don't what?"

"I don't want to get hurt again. Sam's handsome, brilliant, charismatic. He has everything *any* woman would want and that's the problem. I don't want to be one of many."

"Has he disrespected you, hurt you?"

"No. He's really sweet. But he's probably sweet to every female who ends up at DHPD needing someone to protect and *serve* them. I can't afford to mix business with pleasure. It's too complicated. I need to stay focused on finding Melissa."

"Maddie, do you like Sam?"

"Yes, but I have to protect myself."

"You could end up protecting yourself from a great guy."

"What if I get involved with him and our relationship sours? Don't you think that's going to have a negative effect on how he works on the case?"

"You are way over thinking this. Relax. Let things progress naturally. If you feel he's coming on too strong, tell him."

"You're right. I will. I'm going to call him back."

"You do that," she says, giving me thumbs up.

I go to my room and get Sam on the phone, ready to set him straight.

"Hey you. Thanks for calling me back."

"What's going on?"

"I wanted to say hello, and I wanted to wish you luck on your first day at KYON."

"Thanks, Sam," I say, feeling a little guilty. "I really appreciate that. You have a good day at work tomorrow as well."

"I'm working as we speak. When you're a cop with two

jobs, you work 24-7-365."

"Two jobs?" I ask.

"I work for DHPD and MLP."

"Hmm, I see."

"Maddie!"

"Sam, I have to go. Ruby's calling."

"Maddie, come quick. Hurry!"

"Bye, Sam."

"Bye."

"I'm coming. I'll be right there," I say, racing to the living room.

Chapter 11

I skid to a stop at the entrance to the living room. Ruby, holding a pillow, stares at me. It's not just any pillow, it's a purple, green, and orange throw pillow, and it's the pillow in my dreams. Creeping toward her, I ask, "Where did you get that?"

"It was in the box your grandmother left. I was moving it, tripped, and this fell out. There's a matching spread."

I pick up the box and dump the contents. The spread falls to the floor. Images of my grandparents' bedroom bombard my head. I press on my temples and walk in a circle.

"What is it?" Ruby asks.

"I remember this. This was my grandparents' old spread and pillow set. Where's the other pillow?"

"There was only one."

"Why didn't I figure this out before? It's the pillow Melissa was holding. She said it would help me not cry?"

"Why would Melissa have it, if it was your grand — ?"

"Shhh, let me think."

Ruby watches me while I pace, casting my eyes upward, hoping to jar my own memory. "No…no…wait a minute." I grab the spread and lay it on the sofa. "What size is that?"

"It looks like it fits a twin sized bed," Ruby says.

"It does. It fits my bed and Melissa's bed. When we turned three, we had our own beds. To celebrate us moving from our cribs to real beds, my grandmother bought us the bedspread and pillow set. They were on our beds, not my grandparents'. Why couldn't I remember that when I saw the pillow in the dream?"

"Because you were three. Who remembers things at three?" Ruby asks. "Unless something really good happens or something really terrible happens, most people can't remember that far back."

"Then I should be able to remember someone putting a gun to my mother's head and taking off with Melissa in our SUV. That's traumatic. Why can't I remember that, Ruby? Why?"

Ruby clasps her hands and leans against the wall. She pats her afro and says, "Maybe you can't remember because…because…maybe it didn't happen."

We stand here frozen, in a standoff, boring holes through each other. Please let her be thinking out loud. Please don't let what she said be based on some solo theory she's worked out, some hypothesis that concludes that my mother is a pathological liar, or worse…I don't even want to imagine that. Ruby walks to me, takes my hand, and leads me to the sofa. I sit and look up at her, waiting for an explanation.

She sits next to me and I ask, "What do you mean when you say I can't remember because maybe it didn't happen? Do you know what you're suggesting?" She stares into space. "Talk to me, Ruby?"

"Forget what I said." She jumps up from the sofa and walks toward her room.

I run after her. "Don't walk away. Talk to me."

"I can't, Maddie. I can't talk to you."

"Why?"

"Because you don't want to hear what I have to say?"

"How do you know that unless you tell me what you have to say?"

"I don't want you to hate me. I don't want to lose your friendship."

"Why would I hate you, Ruby? Why would I break off our friendship?"

"Because I'm having doubts about mom's story, and I'm not the only one."

I press down on my red face and take a step back. Looking at Ruby, I wonder to myself when she had come to this conclusion. Has she been leading me on this whole time, pretending to believe Judy took Melissa when she really believes my mother is the culprit? "Why are you telling me this now? When did you decide my mother is a liar?"

"Don't say it like that," she says, reaching out to me. She grabs my hand and I jerk it away. "I said I have *doubts*. I didn't say I'm one hundred percent sure she's not telling the truth."

"How am I supposed to say it, Ruby? How? You leave me no choice."

"This is why I didn't want to say anything."

"Ruby, all this week we've been brainstorming and coming up with various scenarios. Never once did it come up that my mother did something to Melissa. So is it wrong for me to be a little thrown for a loop?"

"I know this, Madeline. But for the past couple of days that I've had time by myself, I've done more research. I've read news articles, blogs, opinion pieces, hundreds of stories about the carjacking and every time I sit back and meditate on all the information, I keep coming back to the same conclusion—there never was a carjacking. No one saw your mother being held at gunpoint a mile from the Medical Center. That's a busy area, Madeline. How could there be no witnesses in broad daylight?"

"My grandmother said that when my mother called the police she was with me at a phone booth. She didn't have a car. Where was the car if she wasn't carjacked?"

"I don't know," Ruby says.

"And where was Melissa?"

"I don't know," Ruby says.

"Why would my mother lie?" I ask, clenching my fists.

"Calm down, Maddie."

"Don't tell me to calm down. You're making a life-changing accusation about my mother. What proof do you have there wasn't a carjacking?"

"What proof do you have *there was?*" she counters.

"The SUV is gone. Melissa is gone."

"What if your mother got rid of the SUV, what if those searches for car repair shops were to find somebody or someplace to stash the SUV? What if those searches for construction sites were to find a place to dump the SUV or—"

"Please don't say it. And don't you think I would have remembered her getting rid of the SUV?"

"No, I don't. You don't remember the carjacking. What if the search for statute of limitations was your mother trying to find out how long it would be before she would be in the clear?"

"Why would my mother hurt Melissa? That's wack. And if she did, then that means my father is guilty, too."

"Maybe she lost it. Maybe she was under a lot of pressure. Postpartum stress was on the search list. It wouldn't be the first time a mother hurt her child and made up a fictitious story to cover her own ass: Susan Smith, Andrea Yates…Maddie, you need to check under the house. I don't believe it's the kittens Pepper's after."

My stomach flips and my palms sweat. I press my hand to my side because it keeps wanting to slap Ruby in her regal face, it wants to shut her up. Before I do something I'm going to regret the rest of my life, I grab my purse and leave.

II

Sitting in Carmen's Coffee shop, I stare at the whipped cream on top of my latte. I can't believe I have the Sunday night blues. I should be 'exultant' as my mother would say. I should be thrilled to be starting my new position tomorrow. But I'm bummed. This has been the worst day ever. Starting with the melee at my parents' house and now Ruby has gone off the deep end. I don't even have Pepper to cheer me up.

The door to the café swings open and my face lights up when Sam walks in. I wave to him and he approaches, his expression conveying warmth and concern. "I got here as fast as I could. What's going on?"

"I feel so foolish now, calling you. It's not like it was a real emergency," I say, taking a sip of my latte.

Sam takes a napkin off of the table and dabs at my face. "You got a little cream on your nose," he says.

"Thanks."

"So what's up?"

"It's my roommate, my BFF."

"Ruby?"

"Yes."

"What's wrong with her?"

"She thinks my mother's lying about the carjacking. She thinks my mother did something to Melissa. I can't believe her. She used to be the most positive person I've ever known. All week we've been working together to solve this mystery and she comes to the conclusion that my mother's lying."

"She told you that?"

"Well, not exactly. She said she wasn't one hundred percent sure my mother was involved, but she definitely has doubts."

I wait for Sam to tell me Ruby has lost her mind and that she's wrong and that he believes my mother's telling the truth, but he sits there, with a far-off look plastered on his face, like he's debating in his head whose side to take.

"Sam, what do you think? Do you have doubts about my mother's story? You mentioned that retired detective did. But I need to know how you feel."

He passes his hand over his face and finally looks at me. "Does it really matter what I think, Maddie?"

"Yes it does. So what do you think?"

"I think you first and foremost should give Ruby the benefit of the doubt. You said she's your childhood friend and she's been there for you. She has doubts. It's human to doubt. You should appreciate that she trusts your friendship enough to tell you how she truly feels. True friends tell us what we *need* to hear, not what we *want* to hear."

I remain silent and absorb what Sam's saying, even though he has conveniently avoided answering my question.

He's right, I wasn't fair to Ruby. She has a right to her opinion, no matter how much it hurts to know she thinks my mother may have had something to do with Melissa's disappearance. Now I wonder how genuine our friendship is. Over the years, we both have been guilty of telling each other what we think the other one wants to hear.

Sam leans forward and asks, "What do you think about what I said?"

"You're right. I do need to give her the benefit of the doubt. But you didn't answer my question. Do you think my mother fabricated the carjacking and did something to Melissa? And if she did, then that would mean my father was involved. There's no way she could have faked the carjacking by herself. She would have had to have gotten rid of the SUV while at the same time taking care of me. And I'm sure at the age of three, I had to have been crying, maybe even throwing a tantrum."

Sam shifts in his seat and I notice perspiration beading on his upper lip. "Maddie, I can't make a judgment call like that without talking to your mother or interviewing her. I wasn't a part of the original investigation, so I have limited information. I did read the statement she gave the police, and there are some inconsistencies. And your parents refused to take lie detector tests."

"I'm sorry," I say, jumping up, running for napkins. Sam moves away from the table, eyeballing what's left of my latte as it drips onto the floor. I return and place napkins over the spill, trying to steady my hands. "I'm such a klutz at times," I say. We get everything cleaned up and move to another table. I grip the arms of the chair when I sit, wondering why my parents refused to take lie detector tests if they're innocent.

"Are you okay," Sam asks, sitting across from me.

I nod. "What kind of inconsistencies?"

"When your mother called 911, she said a man had carjacked her. She said he was Hispanic and that he had a gun. When she made her statement at the station, she said there were two men, one black and one white."

"Couldn't she have been nervous, in shock?"

"Of course, but the operator had asked her how many people attacked her and she asked your mother to specify their ethnicity. That's on tape."

"I see," I say.

"Also, there were some issues with her timeline."

"What issues?"

"In your mother's statement, she said you and Melissa had a 9:00 a.m. doctor's appointment. But she didn't call 911 until 9:45 a.m. The medical center where the doctor's office is located is thirty minutes from your parents' house. She said she left home at 8:30 a.m. That would have put her at the location of the carjacking at approximately 8:55 a.m. being that the carjacking took place a mile from the medical center. Carjackings are quick. Say it was all over around 9:00 a.m. Where was she and what was she doing from 9:00 a.m. to 9:45 a.m.?"

"What did she say she was doing?" I ask.

"After the timeline discrepancy was brought to her attention, she changed her statement and said she didn't leave the house right at 8:30. She said she was running late to the appointment and that after the carjacking she was in shock, in a daze, wandering around, looking for a phone booth."

"That sounds like my mother. She was really nervous back then. And look at her background. Being raped, never going to the police. Look how she had to live on the streets with her mother. Maybe she started having flash backs. Maybe she thought she deserved what had happened and that she wasn't worthy of help." A wave of pity washes over his face and I look away, feeling lost, feeling like I'm drowning in a sea of weak excuses.

"That sounds plausible, but Melissa was in that car. There's no way any mother wouldn't have been overcome with an instinct to save her child. She would have been overpowered with adrenaline that would have propelled her to reach out for help the moment it happened. She would have flagged someone down, she would have screamed."

"Maybe at that time my mother wasn't just any mother. Maybe she was mentally challenged. I believe she was suffering from postpartum."

"There's still a big question mark, Maddie."

"I don't get it. If there was such a big 'question mark,' why wasn't my mother arrested?"

"Because there was no evidence to prove her story wasn't true. Melissa and the car were gone."

"Did the police search our house?"

"Yes, but nothing was found. Maddie, this all happened before the tech boom. There were no Smartphones. Cell phones were just becoming popular. There was no Facebook, Twitter, or Instagram. People weren't committing crimes and posting them on YouTube so that they could go viral. People didn't even lock their doors in Dancing Hills. Your mother was and is a beautiful, articulate woman. She and your father were and still are pillars of the community. The people of Dancing Hills were not ready to believe someone like your mother could do the unthinkable. They couldn't imagine the woman they shared a pew with in church, who they stood in line with at the grocery store and the bank, who greeted them and their child when they came to get their teeth cleaned, could be a monster. Because if someone like your mother could commit such a heinous act, what did that say about them? So instead of breaking her down, they built her up, supported her while she grieved. Sure there were those who suspected her, but they kept their opinions behind closed doors only to be discussed among themselves. What are you thinking?"

"I don't know what to think. I wish I never would have gone down this road. My father tried to warn me. And now after hearing all of this, I can't turn back."

"Are you strong enough to deal with what you might uncover?"

"I have to be strong for Melissa."

"You should move forward with what we talked about and let things unfold naturally. I believe you're going to find the answers you're looking for. And Maddie, your mother is innocent until proven guilty. Don't let what we discussed here make you give up on her. Keep searching for the truth."

"I hope you're right. I need to go home and apologize to Ruby, and I need to get ready for work."

"I'll walk you to your car," he says.

♊

I pull into the parking lot behind our apartment building. I wish I would have gotten here before dark. I think about what my grandmother said and look around at all the cars, hoping there's no one lurking in the dark, waiting to attack. My phone rings and I jump so high I nearly hit my head on the roof of the car. It's my mother. I pause before answering. Could she have hurt Melissa? Am I deluding myself? Am I behaving like the people of Dancing Hills, looking the other way because I can't imagine or deal with the implications of my mother hurting Melissa? And why Melissa and not me?

"Hi, Mom."

"What took you so long to answer the phone?"

"I'm just getting home."

"It's late, Maddie. Where's Ruby?"

"Upstairs," I say, glancing over at her jeep parked two spaces over.

"You need to get upstairs, too. I got your message. Pepper's right here and he misses you, too. Pepper, Maddie's on the phone."

"Hi, Pep. How you doin,' boy?" He barks vociferously.

"I'm going to send him to bed, Maddie and you need to go, too."

"Mom, can I ask you a question before you go?"

"Sure. What is it?"

I take a deep breath, like I'm about to swan dive into an empty Olympic sized pool, hoping I don't break my neck, or worse, die.

"Maddie, what is it?"

Chapter 12

"Mom, did you kill Melissa?"

Ruby falls off of the sofa, and rolls on the floor, with her hands over her face. "No, you didn't ask her that!"

"Hell to the no I didn't ask her that. But I wanted to. God knows I wanted to. I asked her about our matching red and blue jackets with the fake fur around the collar. I asked her why we were wearing those coats in the summer. She said Melissa was obsessed with her coat and that was the only way she could get us out of the house to the doctor. And of course, Melissa was taken wearing her coat."

"Where's yours?" Ruby, asks getting up from the floor.

"My mother has it packed away somewhere. So can I see the Facebook page now?"

Ruby goes to the computer and I run up to her and give her a big hug. "Thanks for forgiving me, and I'm sorry again for acting like such a spoiled bitch."

"I totally understand. Again, like I said, I have doubts.

Everything Sam told you about your mother saying there was one guy, and then two, and then not being able to account for forty-five minutes after the carjacking, is what I've been reading about online. It's crazy."

"Ruby, I've decided I'm not going to focus on any of that. The best way to prove my mother is innocent is to find The Renter and Judy. And I think once we get this campaign going, it's going to lead us right to them. I think we should create a website, too."

"Great idea," Ruby says. She continues onto the computer and clicks on the Facebook icon. A smile breaks out on my face when the cover photo appears featuring a picture of me at three and a picture of me now. She took Sam's suggestion and named the page Missing Melissa. She scrolls down and there are photos and comments everywhere. She even filled in the timeline.

"You already have a thousand LIKES," she says. "By tomorrow there'll probably be a thousand more."

"This is incredible. How were you able to get me so many LIKES?"

"I reached out to all the friends on your personal page. I also sent a ton of friend requests out and when they responded I asked them to LIKE the page."

"This is beyond great," I say, reading all the comments:

Good luck finding your sister.

You're beautiful. I hope you find your twin. God bless you both.

I'm a twin.

Keep the faith.

I remember when your sister went missing. Such a sad story. Glad to see you haven't given up the fight.

My eyes sting and I get choked up reading the posts. For the first time in a long while I feel like I'm doing the right thing, in spite of what I've heard about my mother. The truth is going to prevail.

"Thank you so much, Ruby."

"When are the fliers going to be ready?" Ruby asks.

"Tuesday and I plan to start passing them out this weekend."

"I'll help."

"Thanks," I say, gazing at the Facebook page, hoping I'll get a post from Melissa. "Wouldn't that be amazing if somehow Melissa found out about the page and reached out to me?"

"It's not impossible. There are over five-hundred million people on Facebook," Ruby says. "Now we have to get you on Twitter and Instagram."

"It's getting late, I better go to bed, Ruby. I have a big day tomorrow."

"I need to start going to bed at a decent hour so I can get my body back on an early schedule. If I don't, I might end up oversleeping Tuesday. I want to tweak the page a bit and then I'll shut down," Ruby says.

"Okay, I say," heading off to my room. I go to my closet, thinking about what I'm going to wear on my first day at KYON. I want to look nice, but I don't want to overdo it. I really want to make an impression, so that I get on my supervisor's good side. I'm hoping she'll be interested in running a segment on Melissa and me.

II

Tina pushes her wire-rimmed glasses up the bridge of her pinched nose while she waits for me to put my purse and briefcase away in the cabinet adjacent to my cubicle. She pulls her dingy bra strap that keeps falling, onto her bony shoulder, and emits an exaggerated sigh. Then she tucks her tie dyed tee-shirt into her jeans, shifts her weight from one foot to the other, and shakes her head.

"Not to rush you, but things move pretty quickly around here. And I should have told you to dress down. I love your designer skirt suit and red bottom shoes, but you might have a little difficulty getting around today. Things move at breakneck speed and unfortunately, the only women here who get to look cute are the anchors and field reporters." She pushes her auburn hair off of her gaunt face and grins.

I smile, trying to play it off, but I feel like a fool. I spent an hour last night vacillating over whether or not to dress up or dress down. I should have listened to my gut and not Ruby. "Thanks for the heads-up. I'll make do. I'm really excited to be here."

"We're excited to have you here. Come on; let's go to the newsroom."

I follow Tina, who's the head news desk coordinator, down a meandering hallway. A photo of a dog on a cubicle we pass makes me think about Pepper.

"This way," Tina says, turning into a large room filled with people at desks with phones stuck to their ears, peering into computer screens, looking at overhead monitors, holding numerous conversations.

The room is abuzz and I can feel the excitement and electricity in the air. This is where it all happens, where the stories are gathered, written, edited, and assembled for news broadcast. I imagine the day the call came in about Melissa and the carjacking. This is probably laid back compared to that day.

"Madeline? Madeline?"

"I'm sorry, Tina. I was taking everything in." *Focus Maddie. Focus.*

"I was telling you that in five minutes the editorial meeting starts."

"What's the editorial meeting?"

"It's basically where reporters pitch their stories. It's where decisions are made about what stories are going to be covered for a particular day."

I listen to Tina intently, wishing I was already an established reporter so I can be a part of the meeting, but I'm going to have to settle for second best, and that means I'm going to have to network, schmooze, get to know the reporters here. I survey the room and see a few familiar faces, but most of the people look like they work behind the scenes: news director, news writers, editors, camera operators, technicians, engineers. I wonder where the popular anchor team is. I doubt they're here this early. Jim Hernandez and Julie Sumpter are loved by millions and have top ratings.

Tina and I observe a group of people walking toward a huge glass conference room. She waves at a tall bespectacled man wearing an obvious toupee. "That's Curt Walker. He's one of our top producers," she says, gaping at him with stars in her hazel eyes. "The meeting's about to start. While it gets underway, there are a couple of people I want you to meet."

We approach a short man with a handlebar moustache chomping on a powdered donut. He finishes it off and then wipes his hands with the sanitizer on his desk. I suppress a giggle when he brushes traces of the donut from his moustache with the tips of his fingers. He greets us with a warm smile. "Tina Lynch, my favorite news coordinator. What can I do for you?"

"Nothing at this very moment. I want to introduce you to our new junior reporter, Madeline Patterson. She's a

Bruin, too and she's from Dancing Hills. Madeline, this is George Berry and he works in assignments as a researcher. If you want to know something, like a victim's address, or someone's name, or occupation, basically if you want to know anything, George is your go-to person."

"It's nice to meet you, Madeline," he says, shaking my hand.

"The pleasure's all mine," I say, thinking about the box of donuts I'm going to bring to work tomorrow. He's definitely someone I want to get to know.

"You graduate from UCLA this year?" he asks.

"Yes."

"I'm in the class of too long ago to tell you," he says, laughing. "I'm probably one of the oldest people here," he says, folding his hairy arms over his pot belly. "I know where the bodies are buried," he says, curling over, cracking himself up.

"George is a real hoot," Tina says.

He straightens up, makes a clicking sound with his teeth and says, "Hey, Patterson? Patterson? Would that be Patterson as in the Pattersons whose daughter was kidnapped twenty years ago?"

"It was nineteen years ago this month, and yes, I'm the other twin. My sister is Melissa Patterson."

Tina's eyes widen and her mouth falls open. "Wow. Are you serious?"

"I always wanted to know what happened to the other twin," George says.

"Well, now you know," I say, mustering a smile when deep down I'm cringing, irritated that Melissa's been relegated to news trivia.

"That was some story," George continues. "Ratings went

through the roof. Everybody wanted to know what had happened to the little blonde girl with pretty blue eyes."

Tina casts a compassionate look my way. "I need to get Madeline started on her assignments, George," she says.

"Sure, sure," he says. "It's such an irony you're here at KYON. That was a pretty little girl. What am I saying?" He slaps his forehead. "You're the little girl all grown up. I mean, you're the sister of the girl."

"Right," I say.

"So how are your folks?"

"They're fine," I lie. "We still live in Dancing Hills."

"I call it Mayberry R.F.D. You know there's an interesting story about how the town got its name."

"Thanks, George. We'll talk to you later," Tina says, grabbing my arm. Under her breath she says, "Sorry about that. I hope he didn't upset you. George tends to be a talker."

"No, it's okay really."

"I'll introduce you to some other people later today."

We come to my cubicle and I sit. "Give me a minute, Madeline. I need to get the paperwork we're going to go over."

"Sure. I'll be here when you get back." She gives me a curious look and leaves. I fall back in my chair and relax while I can. There's nothing that can give you a tension-induced headache faster than starting a new position and meeting new people. I rub my temples and stop when I hear my phone ringing. I thought I had turned the ringer down. I go into the cabinet and grab it before Tina returns. I see the miss call and notice a text message.

Call me as soon as you can. Grandma. 911.

"Grandma, what's wrong? Is Pepper okay? What's going on?" I say, pacing.

"Calm down, Maddie."

"Grandma, you used 911. Only use that for emergencies."

"I'm sorry. Pepper's okay. He's acting stubborn. We can't get him in the car. We think he's acting out because he's been away from you for more than twelve hours."

"What about dad?"

"He already left for work."

"Grandma, I can't leave work, and I'm all the way in L.A. He really needs to get to that doctor's appointment."

"Can you talk to him, Maddie?"

I can't believe this. I look over my shoulder and around the office to make sure no one is within earshot, especially Tina. "Put him on the phone."

"Pepper, Mommie's on the phone. Come and talk to Maddie."

I tap my foot while I wait for Pepper to come to the phone. I hear him barking in the background and a smile takes over my face. The barking grows louder and I say, "Hey, boy. Mommie loves you. Now get in Grandma's car and let her take you to see Dr. Virgil. Then she's going to bring you home and we'll all be one big happy family again." I wait to hear him bark and I say, "That's a good boy."

"Maddie, that worked. He's already going to the car!"

"I'm glad. Call me after the appointment. If I don't pick up, leave a message." Satisfied with myself, I hang up the phone, beaming.

"How old is your son?"

"You frightened me," I say, turning toward Tina whose arms are filled with files. "That's not my son. Well, in a way he is. He's my dog, Pepper."

"Oh, okay. You two must be really close." She sets the folders on my desk.

"Yeah, we are. He hurt himself yesterday and we need to get him checked out."

"I see," she says, motioning for me to sit. And then she follows suit. "I'm not sure if they mentioned this in your orientation, but personal calls are frowned on. I mean, emergencies are an exception. Anyway, it gets really busy around here, so you won't have time for personal calls."

"I understand and you don't have to worry about me being on any personal calls. I'm here to work hard, to learn everything I need to learn."

"That's good," she says, passing her hand over the files.

"Am I going to be filing those?" I ask.

"No," she says.

Thank goodness.

"Our summer intern put these together and they're not correct. These are information packets our reporters use. This top one is correct. Use it as a template and correct the others."

"Okay," I say.

"I know it sounds tedious, but we need these done now. Things are going to get interesting, Madeline. You're going to get a chance to write some scripts and go into the field. You'll be paired up with one of our mid-level reporters. I'm also going to show you how to use the news computer system. You'll also be assisting the producers with researching and preparing news packets for the anchors and scanning wires. Trust me; you'll have a lot of interesting things to do."

With wide eyes and a growling stomach, I take in all Tina's saying, wondering when I'm actually going to get a chance to go on the air.

"I know what you're thinking," she says.

"Excuse me?" I ask.

"Every new journalist wants to know when they're going to be able to say those famous last words on the air. This is so and so reporting live from xyz."

I nod.

"You'll get your chance, Madeline."

"Thanks. I better get to work," I say. *Hmm, I had planned to take a peek at my Facebook page, but I guess that'll have to wait. I'm not trying to mess up on my first day at work.*

Ⅱ

"I'm home. Anybody here?" I ask, pushing the door open with my foot. I sit the two grocery bags in the foyer and put my purse and briefcase on the wall-mounted table. Before I have a chance to step into the living room, Pepper greets me with hugs and licks. "I missed you, too, Pep. Mommie missed you. How are you feeling?" I ask, gingerly pushing him off of me. I kneel down and examine his paws that are freshly wrapped in gauze. He pants and wags his tail. "Where's Aunt Ruby?" I ask, taking the bags into the kitchen.

"I'm back here. I'm on the phone with Clay. I'll be right out. Pepper's doing good. Your grandmother said Dr. Virgil prescribed some antibiotics. She had the prescription filled and I gave him one already."

"Thanks, finish your call," I say, kicking my shoes off. While putting the food away, I notice a large bouquet of red roses in a vase on one of the end tables. I walk to them and give them a sniff. My eyes shift to a white card lying next to the vase. I can't help myself.

Ruby, I can't eat, sleep, or study because you stay on my mind and in my heart. This distance is killing me. I love you. I hope you enjoy the roses.

Wow, he's serious. I replace the card and can't help but think about Sam. I wonder if he's the kind of guy that would send a girl flowers. I finish putting the food away then power up the computer, wondering how many LIKES I have. Pepper sits next to me. "Hey, Pep. Wanna be my Facebook friend? Maybe I'll start an account for you," I say, petting his massive head. The screen lights up and I click on the Facebook icon. Every time I see the cover photo featuring me at three and now, I get a little misty-eyed. "OMG!"

"What's going on?" Ruby asks.

"You have to see this."

"Here I come."

Pepper, excited, barks.

"What are you two so jazzed about," she asks, looking over my shoulder.

I point to the screen.

"Five thousand LIKES!" Ruby screams.

"When did that happen?" I ask.

"When I checked this morning you had twenty-five-hundred."

"This is freaking amazing," I say.

"Check out the comments," Ruby says.

You are the most beautiful woman I've ever seen. God was missing two Angels and he decided to bring one home.

Our church is praying for you and your family. God will answer your prayer.

Bruins make great lovers, but blondes have more fun.

Don't give up. I'm spreading the word in Arizona about your missing sister.

My sister was abducted ten years ago. Even with the help of the FBI, they never found her. We believe she's somewhere in Europe, in the sex slave industry. This world is evil.

Ruby and I share curious looks. "They're so many comments," I say. "It's a miracle they're so clean."

"They haven't all been. I've had to delete some people."

"Thanks. Oh, Ruby, I'm sorry. Were you still talking to Clay?"

"I told him I'll call him back and guess what?"

"What?"

"He's coming out here next week. Wants to see me."

"How do you feel about that?"

"I don't know yet," she says, patting her afro.

"Those roses are beautiful," I say.

"They are aren't they," Ruby says.

"Clay's a good guy. You really should give him a chance."

"He's been working on me. Calling me, leaving sweet messages. Texting me inspirational thoughts. Girl, he's been talking to my father, too. My dad's all excited because he thinks there's hope. You know he was too through when I turned Clay down after Clay had asked him for my hand in marriage."

"I remember that. I hope you don't miss out on a good thing. Harvard *is* coed. And Clay *is* a good catch." Ruby gives me *the look.*

"Do you know something I don't?" Ruby asks.

"No, not at all," I say.

"I know Clay's a great guy, but I don't want to get married at twenty-two. It's too young."

"Because you get engaged, doesn't mean you have to get married right away."

"That's true," Ruby says.

"Do you love, Clay?" Her face brightens and her eyes light up and I know the answer is yes, but I still wait to hear it from her.

"I think about him all the time. I get butterflies when I see his name flash across my phone. I get all juicy when he talks to me at night while he's in bed. His voice has that tired deep sound. It's something about it that turns me on. And those big brown eyes and his athletic body. But more than that, he's brilliant and we talk about everything from global warming to international politics. He's almost perfect, Maddie. Do I love him? Hell yeah. I do love him," she says, looking past me as though she's realizing it for the first time.

"I know it's a cliché, Ruby, but love conquers all, even long distance."

"You're right, Maddie." She takes a moment and then asks, "How was work?"

"Busy and I was way overdressed."

"Sorry," she says.

"No worries. I got to work on some copy today, and I met some interesting people. Tina's really cool. I mean, she's by the book, but nice. Are you ready for tomorrow?"

"Yep. Got all my clothes laid out, too. What do you want to eat for dinner?" she asks going to the kitchen.

"I bought a few things. I was thinking about making veggie tacos," I say, joining her.

"That sounds good," Ruby says, pressing on her washboard stomach.

"What's that noise?" I ask.

"You have a message in your inbox," she says returning to the computer. "What the hell!"

"What?" I ask.

"You have fifty messages."

I return to the computer. "Missing Melissa is so popular. I didn't get this response when I set up my personal account."

"It's the picture and the topic. It's capturing people's hearts and their imaginations," Ruby says.

I click on messages hoping there's something about Melissa.

*Plz checkout my new video. **www.lovesexandwonders.com***

Thanks for the ad. Best of luck in your search!

I'll suck yours if you suck mine.

"Asshole," Ruby says. "Report him."

"I will. Let me read some more," I say.

Hello, Honey Bunny.

"Honey Bunny!" Ruby and I say at the same time.

"Judy? Could it be Judy?" I ask. "My grandmother. She called my mother Honey Bunny."

"I know, but no way," Ruby says. "Click it so we can read the whole message."

What if it's her? What if she's found the page and is reaching out? What if it isn't her? There's only one way to find out.

Chapter 13

Dear Honey Bunny,

You're so funny. You're so cute. I wanna touch you I wanna f_ _ _k you. I wanna.

"Damn! These freaks are driving me crazy!" Ruby screams.

"Don't worry. I just reported it as spam and I deleted it," I say, going to the next message. "Here's one that looks decent," I say, scrolling down. I click on the picture of the Heart.

"I hope this message finds you doing well. Please don't delete me. This ain't a hoax. I know you must be getting hundreds of emails because you are such a beautiful young woman. I can tell you're beautiful inside and out. Actually I know you are because we have a lot in common."

I stop reading and give Ruby a questioning look.

"Keep reading," she says.

"You don't know me, but I know you. I don't know how to say this, because I don't want to come off as crazy. Let me just say it. I'm your grandmother. My name is Judy Gardner and I would love to meet you. I think I have the answer to your question. Meet me at Oliver's on 3rd and Figueroa Street in Downtown Los Angeles tomorrow at 7:00 p.m. I'll be wearing all red. I can't wait to see you.

Love you always, your grandmother Judy Gardner.

P.S. You look like your mother, Millicent."

I step back from the computer with my hands over my mouth. Ruby jumps up and sits on the sofa, rocking. I run to the window and open it for fresh air.

"No freaking way," I say, turning back toward Ruby. "That has to be a hoax. Did you send it?" I ask.

"No. Hell no." Ruby returns to the computer and clicks on the Heart.

"What are you doing?" I ask.

"Checking out her page."

I join her. "There's nothing here but hearts everywhere," I say. "Click on 'About.'"

"It's blank," Ruby says.

"Do you think it's real?" I ask.

"At first I didn't, but who on Facebook knows your grandmother's name is Judy Gardner? Two weeks ago, you thought your maternal grandmother was Jean Darcy."

"I'm going to reply to the email," I say, sitting at the computer.

Thank you for your message, I'd love to meet you. Can you give me your phone number? Where do you live? Do you know where Melissa is?

"Do you think she's going to respond?" I ask.

"She isn't online right now. Let's keep checking back to see," Ruby says.

"Okay," I say, squinting, pacing.

"What's going on with you, Maddie?"

"I'm thinking about meeting her tomorrow."

"Hold up, Madeline Louise Patterson. You're not going to meet anybody. Do you know how dangerous that is? You don't know who the other person is on the other side of that computer and even if it is your grandmother, you don't know what she's been up to. Remember, if our theory is right, she had two men put a gun to your mother's head and had Melissa kidnapped."

"You're right. We need to at least let her respond. But what if it is her? That's why we set this page up in the first place. Sam was right. We can't assume it's not her, Ruby."

"And we can't assume it is. You should touch base with Sam on this. We could have him intervene and get a location on this person through Facebook."

"Are you serious?"

"It's usually done if someone is harassing or threatening another person."

"That's not the case here."

"I know, but please wait until we get more informa—"

"What's wrong?" I ask.

"I hear my phone. I was supposed to call Clay back. Let me finish this call."

"Okay, I'll start dinner," I say. I watch Ruby return to her room. When I hear her door close, I copy the message, paste it onto a word doc, and hit print. Then I slip it into my purse. My heart's racing and my hands are sweaty. I sit at the breakfast nook for a few minutes to calm my nerves. I know in my soul The Heart person is Judy. A heart is red. A heart is about love. It makes sense. She knows too much. It's her and she has Melissa, and Ruby doesn't know it, but I'm going to meet my grandmother tomorrow, and if I'm lucky, she may even bring Melissa.

II

Standing in front of the bathroom mirror at KYON, I do a three-hundred-and-sixty-degree turn. I don't look too shabby in my skinny jeans and blue pullover sweater. I stare at my flats and grimace. I miss my heels and dressing up. I have to admit, it's much easier running around the newsroom in no heels versus four inch ones. The editorial meeting starts in fifteen minutes and I get to be a spectator. Tina says it's her way of thanking me for all my hard work yesterday. She also mentioned Curt Walker, that top producer, took notice of me. I hope it was because of my work ethic, and not my *good looks*, George's words.

"Good morning."

Embarrassed, I get out of the mirror and feign washing my hands. I hate being caught primping. "Good morning..."

"Maria, Maria Rojo. You're the new junior reporter. I heard about you," she says, giving me the once-over.

"You have?"

"You're the twin sister of the little girl who was kidnapped."

"Right. I'm Madeline Patterson. Word travels fast," I say.

"According to George, that was a big story here at KYON. He was the one who told me about you. I was thirteen at the time, living in Guadalajara."

"How long have you been in the U.S.?"

"I came here to go to school fourteen years ago, and I became a citizen. I went to Northwestern and I've worked in a lot of small television markets. That's the best way to make it in this business. Start in the smaller markets, learn the business, and then transition into the big leagues. It's great you're getting a start here, but it's rare for someone to get on the air in a market this big straight out of college. But then again, you are breathtakingly beautiful and let's face it; looks do count in this town."

I stand here trying to hold my own, wondering if I've just been insulted. "I plan to pay my dues, Maria. I'm not looking for any handouts, and I definitely have no intention of using my looks to make it to the top. I worked very hard in school and I graduated with honors. I may appear to be just another pretty face, but as you and I both know, looks can be deceiving."

"I like that. You got fight, spunk. You'll do well here. It was good talking to you, but I have to *pee* before the meeting starts. I have to sell the news director on my Amnesty Bill piece."

"Good talking to you, too," I say, leaving. The restroom door shuts behind me and I lean on it, gathering my thoughts. I just had words with Maria Rojo, one of KYON's top reporters—at least in my mind. I didn't recognize her at first. I've seen her report on sex crimes, hit and run stories, fraud. She's really good. I get it together, go to my desk, grab my notepad, and head to the editorial meeting. I notice Tina already seated and she beckons for me. I go in and sit next to her, while scanning the faces of the managers, reporters, and producers who are in the room. As soon as I sit, Maria runs in and sits next to Curt. They whisper and point to me. I squirm in my seat and look the other way.

The meeting starts and the news director opens the floor for pitches. Several reporters present their story ideas and I take copious notes, while at the same time thinking about meeting my grandmother, Judy Gardner, tonight. She never responded to my reply, but no news is good news. Thinking of news, I notice Maria and Curt talking again. She runs her fingers through her long black hair, shuts and opens her doe-shaped eyes, and then she jumps in with her pitch.

"As you all know, Amnesty is a hot-button issue right now and I'd like — "

"Pardon me for interrupting, Maria, but I want to throw something else your way, something you actually brought to my attention."

The room grows quiet. Maria, red in the face, turns her attention to Curt. "Go ahead," she says. Noticeably pissed, she returns to her seat and Curt takes center stage.

He straightens his toupee and clears his throat. "In case you didn't know, almost two decades ago, in a quaint town called Dancing Hills, a young mother was accosted by two thugs at gunpoint and they stole her SUV. No one wants their car stolen — but in the back seat of that car was something far more precious. There was a three-year-old girl in that car — a precious baby with hair as golden as a field of daffodils and crystal blue eyes — pure innocence. No one knows what happened to the car or the child. In spite of the DHPD's very hard work, the countless volunteers, the searches, to this day, it remains a mystery. Whatever became of that child? We can imagine, we can wonder. What could have life been like for her. She never got a chance to go to kindergarten. To have graham crackers and milk, hear a good story, and take a nap with the rest of her classmates. She never got to feel the excitement of taking driving lessons and getting her license. She never got to attend a school dance, or the prom. She never got to wear her cap and gown and receive her diploma, making her parents proud. Remember how excited you were to register to vote and then actually exercise that right? That little girl was denied those experiences. That little girl's name is Melissa Lorraine Patterson." He momentarily ends his soliloquy and walks toward me. The sound of mumbling and whispering fills the room and then Curt takes my hand. "Is it okay?"

I look at him, not knowing what to say, feeling like I'm a freak on display, but if it means KYON is going to give exposure to my story, then I'll be the freak of the day, the week, the month, the year. I nod and say, "Yes."

"Ladies and gentlemen, this is Madeline Louise Patterson, the identical twin of Melissa Lorraine Patterson, the little girl who went missing. Madeline is a junior reporter here at the station. She recently graduated from UCLA with honors. She's an award winning swimmer. She's a philanthropist." Curt's gaze moves toward the door and I notice George grinning broadly. He gives Curt a big thumbs up. "If it's okay with Madeline, I want KYON to do a feature story about her and her sister. I want to revisit what happened back then, and I want to show how her life has been impacted and how she feels today. Does she feel enough was done? Madeline was there that day, and if her mother hadn't already gotten her out of her car seat, she wouldn't be here with us right now. Who knows how witnessing that horrific incident has impacted her? She's a walking miracle. Not only will this feature give us great ratings, but perhaps by bringing attention to this story, someone will be compelled to come forward with some answers."

I look out at the faces of everyone in the room, many of them twisted, sympathetic. I hear sniffles and turn to see Tina dabbing at tears streaming down her face. She approaches and throws her arms around me. I feel like the luckiest girl in the world. Not only is KYON embracing my story, but tonight, if my luck holds up, I might get to meet my grandmother and maybe even Melissa. That would be so freaking awesome. KYON would have a blockbuster of a story. I peer into Tina's face and mouth "Thank you." I look over at Maria who's obviously fighting back tears and give her a knowing nod.

II

"I'll be getting off work in a couple of hours, and I have to pick up the fliers, Ruby."

"It's my turn to cook," she says. "What do you want to eat?"

"Don't worry about me. I know I said I'm getting off in a couple of hours, but I could actually end up working overtime, you know with the station covering my story. It's been assigned to Maria."

"Maria Rojo?" Ruby asks. "I love her."

"Yeah. So she may need to meet with me and you know after I get the fliers, it's going to be late. So don't wait up for me tonight."

"Are you sure?" she asks.

"Yes. How's work going?"

"Busy. I better get off of the phone. Before I go, what did Sam say about the email you got from Judy?"

"It's been so crazy here; I haven't had a chance to talk to him yet."

"I can call him if you want," Ruby says.

"No, I'll talk to him. I better go."

"By the way, you're up to ten thousand followers on Twitter," she says.

"That's beyond freaking amazing," I say.

"You sure you don't want me to call Sam?"

"No! I mean no, it's okay. I have to go. I'll talk to you later," I say, hanging up the phone.

I sit at my desk feeling like a fake and a fraud. I hate lying to Ruby, but she's totally against me meeting Judy tonight, but I have to go. Everything is falling into place and I can't stop now. And I definitely don't want her talking to Sam. He would probably arrest me before he let me meet with Judy.

After work, I'll swing by the printers for the fliers and that'll give me just enough time to make it to 3rd and Figueroa by seven. Shoot, I may not even need the fliers now. Maybe seeing all the messages and reading my journey on the Internet, Judy's conscience has gotten to her and she wants to come forward. Melissa couldn't have known she was abducted all these years. I'm sure Judy raised her as her own daughter and probably with a different name. So if she's coming forward, then she would have to have confessed to Melissa. She would have to have told Melissa the truth. But how would Melissa feel knowing her mother is actually her grandmother and that her grandmother had her kidnapped? This is way deeper than Ruby and I thought it was.

I glance at the time on my phone and jump up. Crap, I have to get this copy to Tina. I slip my phone into my purse and make a mad dash for the newsroom.

"I'm sorry, George. I almost knocked you down."

"It's okay. I didn't see you coming and thanks for those donuts. That was so sweet of you. No pun intended," he says. "By the way, I heard Maria's been assigned to your story."

"She has and why do I have this funny suspicion you had something to do with my story being picked up?"

"Moi? Well, of course I got the dirt on you. You have a pretty impressive background, young lady. And I love the

Facebook page. I LIKED you today."

"You saw my Missing Melissa page?"

"I ran across it doing my research. I think it's great and I hope you find your sister. You're a brave young woman."

"Thanks, George," I say, noticing Tina across the room, stretching her neck, looking my way. "I have to go."

♊

Standing in Perfect Printing, I wait behind a tall man who unfortunately has a complicated order. I should have been careful about telling Ruby I may have to work overtime, because I self-prophesized and actually did end up meeting with Maria. She's such a good reporter. She asked all the right questions. But our meeting put me behind, and I may not make it to Oliver's on time. Perspiration building up on my neck, I lift my hair with one hand and fan myself with the other. The customer finally finishes with his order and leaves. I take in the cool breeze that sweeps through the door when he exits. It's still light out, which is a good thing.

The man behind the counter motions for me to come forward. He has to be Sam's uncle. I emailed my order, so we've never met. With green eyes and dimples, he looks like an older version of Sam. He pushes his greying hair off of his face and says, "You must be Madeline."

"And you must be Walter, Sam's uncle."

"Yes, we spoke on the phone. My goodness, he wasn't exaggerating when he spoke of your beauty. The pictures don't do you justice. It's no wonder Sammie can't stop talking about you."

"Thank you," I say. "Are the fliers ready?"

"Yes, they're right here." He sets an enormous box on the counter and his cheerfulness dissipates. "Such a sad thing to happen. I pray you find your sister. My nephew's good at what he does. You listen to him. Do what he tells you. You'll find her."

"You're such a kind man, Walter. Sam told me you were going to do this for free, but I have to pay you," I say, fishing around in my purse for my wallet.

"It's more than my pleasure. Don't you dare try to pay me. You take these fliers and find your sister. You see over there." He points to the window and I notice one of the fliers posted.

"I don't know what to say."

"You've said enough. Now go. Get to work."

"I will." *Now I know where Sam gets his bossy ways.*

"Let me help you," he says, lifting the box of fliers.

"I got a parking space right out front. I'll be okay."

"No, this is too big for you. Let me carry it," he persists.

"Okay, thank you," I say.

We go to my car, I open the trunk, and he places the box inside. I shut it, thank him again, and wave goodbye. He returns to the store, grinning and pointing to the poster in the window. I return his smile, get in the car, and make haste to the restaurant.

Chapter 14

Pulling into the parking lot of Oliver's, I notice Ruby's call coming in. This is the third time she's called me and I've let it go to voicemail. I can't talk to her right now, because I'm too close, and I don't think I can keep my lie up. Most times she can tell when I'm fibbing or leaving something unsaid.

I get out of the car, glancing around, trying to see if I can spot Judy. She's probably already inside. It's exactly seven o'clock. If she doesn't have Melissa, or God forbid, doesn't know where Melissa is, I plan to put fliers on the windshield of every last car in this parking lot.

I take a deep breath, smooth my sweaty hands over my jeans, and walk to the entrance. I've never heard of this place, but from the packed parking lot, it looks like it's pretty popular. I open the door and an attractive hostess greets me with a cheerful smile. I nod at the tall, freckled faced brunette and scan the room, looking for a woman in all red. The cacophony of clinking glasses, plates, silverware, and the dinner crowd's laughter and lively conversation fill the air.

"Welcome to Oliver's she says. Do you have a reservation?"

"I'm meeting someone," I say, eyes still roaming.

"You can hang out over there if you want." She points to a waiting area.

"Thanks. I think I will," I say, taking a seat.

I pull out my phone. It's a little after seven. I hope I didn't miss her. Then again, what if she's backed out? Got cold feet. Damn! That never crossed my mind. I log onto the Internet and check my messages. There's nothing from The Heart. I get a sinking feeling in my stomach. Please don't let her stand me up. Great. Now I have to pee.

"Where is your restroom?" I ask, approaching the hostess.

"It's right past the bar," she says.

"Thanks." Stretching my neck, I take one last look at the patrons and then make my way to the ladies' room. I press the door open and stop when I see a young woman about to enter one of the stalls. She's my height with hair like mine. Her back's to me and she's wearing a red dress and red shoes. The hairs on the back of my neck rise. Time seems to stop and I feel like I'm moving in slow motion. I part my lips to call out, but it seems like it takes an eternity for the words to flow. "Me…lis…sa. Melissa. Melissa is that you?"

She stops, jerks her head in my direction, and her long blonde locks fly through the air, partially covering her face. She widens her blue eyes and puckers her full lips. "I'm sorry, but you have the wrong person. My name is Cathy. I don't know anyone named Melissa."

Embarrassed, I duck into the stall next to hers, do my business, wash my hands, and get out of there before I have to face her again. I take a moment to get it together and head back to the entrance. I go around the other side to get a full view of the dining area and I spot Judy. She must have been there the entire time. She's in the corner in the back wearing oversized shades, an oversized red hat, and a red suit. She's alone. Okay. Melissa could be in the car or at home.

This is the moment I've been waiting for, and I don't want to screw it up. She's so close, but yet so far. Every step takes everything out of me. I squeeze pass the tables that are too close together, saying, "Excuse me," "I'm sorry," pushing myself forward, making my feet move, so I can get to the woman who I believe can make my life okay again. Now a few feet away, I can see her looking at me. She smiles slightly. As I near her, I notice something off about her. I hesitate for a moment. She seems familiar. She smiles, saying nothing. I pull the chair and sit across from her, forcing myself not to lose it.

Numb, and not able to speak, I wait for her to do so. I want to yank her glasses off and look into her eyes. I finally force out words. "Judy Gardner? Where's Melissa?"

"Excuse me, what are you doing?"

I look up at the young woman who I saw in the restroom.

"What is your problem and why are you in my seat?"

Confused, I get up, my gaze shifting from the young woman to the older woman. I notice a folding blind cane. "I'm sorry. I thought she was someone else."

"Cathy, what's going on?" the woman asks, moving her head from side to side.

"Nothing to worry about, Nana. This crazy girl was bothering me in the ladies' room, and if she doesn't leave us alone, I'm going to have the manager of the restaurant have her thrown out," she says, shooting daggers at me with her blue eyes.

"Forgive me. I'm sorry," I say, leaving in a hurry.

"Did you find who you were looking for?" the hostess asks.

"Ignoring her and blinking back tears, I exit, feeling like a fool. I look over my shoulder for a second and then turn to go to the parking lot and run into my father. *My father? What the hell.* "Dad what are you doing here? Did Ruby send you?"

"I sent you the email, Maddie."

"You sent it?"

"Yes, I made it all up. Grandma Gardner, wearing red, the whole thing."

"Why would you do that? That's really crappy. You set me up."

"I did it for your own good. I wanted you to see that what you're doing is dangerous. I was hoping and praying I wouldn't find you here."

"And I was hoping and praying Grandma Gardner was going to be here," I say, bursting into tears of disappointment and anger.

"I'm sorry," he says, reaching out to me.

"Don't touch me," I say, moving away from him. "I'm really pissed at you. That was wrong. You had no right to do that."

"Come here, kiddo. Don't cry. I did it for your own good," he says, pulling me onto his chest. "Don't be upset."

"Let me go," I say, jerking away from him.

"Let her go!"

My father and I turn and gasp at the sight of Sam standing before us with his jacket pushed to the side, revealing his revolver.

"I said let her go."

"Sam, this is my father."

"I'm her father."

Sam, shaking his head, pulls his jacket closed and says, "I'll be damned."

♊

My father emerges from my bathroom with a smirk on his face. Sam leans against the wall, shaking his head. Ruby and I, sitting on the sofa, share knowing looks.

"Mr. Patterson, what you did was not only stupid but very dangerous. People could have been hurt." Then he turns toward me and says, "And Maddie, you're no better. What possessed you to meet with someone you met on the Internet? I know you're smarter than that. You better be lucky that you have someone like Ruby in your life, who knows you well enough to tell when you're lying and who cares about you so much she's willing to do something about it."

I sit here feeling like I did when Ruby and I were in the fifth grade and got caught smoking in our garage. Her parents grounded her for a month. That's why the mention of cigarettes or the smell makes her crazy. Both my parents took turns preaching to me about the dangers of cigarette-smoking and then my grandparents gave me an even longer speech. I wished they would have spanked me and saved me from the harangues. Just like I wish Sam would just lock my father and me up for stupidity. Now I realize what a mistake it was. Not only was it a devastating let down, but Sam's right. *What if my father and I had ended up in a tussling match like he and my grandmother? Sam could have thought he was attacking me. My father could have been shot or even killed. I could have been caught in the crossfire.*

"You're right, Sam. What I did was stupid. I'm sorry, Ruby, for lying to you."

"And I was an idiot," my father says. "I called myself teaching you a lesson, Maddie. I knew you were all over the Internet and that thousands of people were making contact with you. And in my mind, you're putting yourself at risk. I know how badly you want to find Melissa and that makes you vulnerable to the nutcases out there. So I wanted to prove to you that you never know who's on the other side of that computer. It's not safe and I'm praying that after this, you'll let it go; you'll end this search, and get back to living your life. Please, if you can't do it for me, do it for your mother. Do you know how devastated she would be if she knew all this was going on?"

"Mr. Patterson, you're right about Maddie not meeting with strangers, but handled correctly, her Internet presence can help us find Melissa, not to mention the fliers and the piece KYON is going to do."

"With all due respect, Detective Warren, I appreciate what you're doing for my daughter, but you know better than all of us that the chances of anything coming out of this are a million to one."

"No, I don't know that. I know that anything's possible, and I think you owe it to Maddie, to help her, and not hinder her, in her pursuit to find the truth."

My father grits his teeth and then presses on his head, obviously stressed. Ruby gives me an 'I hope they don't go to blows' look. "What do you mean by find 'the truth?' You want to know the truth? My wife was carjacked by a couple of punks who took our SUV with Melissa in it, and the DHPD failed to catch the guys who did it. That's the truth. It's been nineteen years and we're no closer to finding Melissa now, than we were then."

"Mr. Patterson, the detectives at DHPD did everything

they could with the little evidence they had. I believe there are some people out there that saw something, that know something, and with new attention brought to the case, there's a chance something will be discovered."

"This is ridiculous," my father says, throwing his hands into the air. "Maddie, I'm sorry for everything. I need to check on your mother. Please let me know when the KYON feature is going to air so that I can keep your mother away from the television. You may not care about how this will impact her, but I do," he says, storming out of my apartment. He slams the door on the way out and Pepper lets out a loud bark.

"Your father has quite a temper," Sam says, sitting.

"I'm sorry about that. He doesn't want to upset my mother after all she's been through."

"Well, one good thing has come out of all of this," Ruby says.

"What's that?" Sam and I ask at the same time.

"I finally got to meet Sexy Sam."

I narrow my eyes at Ruby and try to change the subject. "So, where do we go from here?" I ask.

"No, not so fast," Sam says. "What's this Sexy Sam all about?" he asks, laughing, bringing a beacon of light into the dreary atmosphere.

"That's Maddie's nickname for you," Ruby says, cracking up. "I'm going to get dinner on. Can I interest you in joining us for dinner, Sexy Sam?"

"Based on the sour look on Maddie's face, I'm not sure she wants either one of us here right now, Ruby."

Rolling my eyes, I join Ruby in the kitchen and pen her against the wall. In a stage whisper I say, "Are you crazy? What's with telling him I call him Sexy Sam? And why did you invite him to dinner?"

She pulls out of my grasp and says, "We need to lighten things up a bit. According to Sam, that was a real heavy scene downtown, and I'm still trying to get my nerves to calm down. I can't believe you lied to me. Anything could have happened."

Back on the defensive, I drop my head and surrender. "Okay, okay."

"No worries, ladies. I can always put a TV dinner in the microwave," Sam says from the living room.

"No way," Ruby says.

"Maddie, can I stay for dinner?" Sam asks sheepishly. He enters the kitchen and says, "Pretty please."

II

Sitting next to Sam in the dark, I study his strong angular jawline that's illuminated by the full moon, wondering how this night is going to end. He stares out of the window in our living room at the L.A. skyline.

"Thanks again for coming to my rescue," I say. "Even though I didn't need to be rescued. I hate that you had to meet my father that way."

"Yeah, I do, too," he says.

I notice a slight smirk.

"What's wrong?" I ask.

"I was thinking about your father and what he did. That was really over the top. Him sending that email. Either he's madly in love with his little girl or..."

"Or what?"

"Nothing," he says, averting his eyes.

"No, that's a something kind of look?"

He chuckles. "What's a 'something kind of look?'"

"It's a look that says you don't want to tell me what you're thinking. What are you thinking, Sam?"

"I have an uneasy feeling in my gut about what your father did. It's almost like he was trying to throw you off the track, frighten you, keep you from searching, looking. Maybe...maybe your father has something to hide."

My stomach sinks and I get the feeling I did the day Ted told me my father was a person of interest. "Do you really think that? My father was cleared. He was at work when the carjacking took place."

"True. But what if he's protecting someone?"

"Someone like my mother?" I ask, rising, turning on the light.

Sam stands and thrusts his hands into his pockets. "I've said too much. I really shouldn't be discussing this with you."

"I thought we were working as a team, Sam?"

"We are."

"Then you can't keep your thoughts about the case from me."

"It's awkward. It's your parents we're talking about. I know that's a sore spot for you."

"No, I don't want to think the worst about my parents, but I have to be open, and I have to let you be free to make judgments. I don't want to do the same thing I did with Ruby. You have a right to your opinion. So what are you going to do about my father?" I ask.

"I'm not sure right now. I have to think about it."

"Do you really think he was trying to sabotage me?"

"Like I said, I have to give it some thought. I do want to revisit his statement to the police. Don't worry, I'll keep you in the loop. Right now I'd like to continue our conversation, unless you're ready for me to leave."

"No, it's okay," I say, sitting on the sofa. He glances at the light switch and I nod, letting him know it's okay to dim the lights. He does so and then sits next to me. "I wish it would have been your grandmother at the restaurant and that you could have gotten what you were after. I'm expecting to get some news on her last whereabouts this week. She gets around—Nevada, Texas, and of course California. She has quite a resume. She's done a few sprints in jail, no hard time and it looks like she's cleaned up her act lately. Not even a parking ticket in the last five years. Actually, no trace of her in the last five years, but I have someone digging. We'll find something."

"Was there any mention of a child? Would her record reflect that?"

"Just your mother and her being put up for adoption in the late seventies."

"I need to find The Renter."

"You will," he says.

"By the way, your uncle is a really sweet man. I met him today when I picked up the fliers."

"Yeah, he's good people. He's my mom's brother."

"Are you close to your mother?"

"Yep. She's my heart, her and my sister. She's a high school teacher and my father's retired now."

"Sounds like you have a good family."

"We have issues like every other family, but when it's all said and done, we try to stick together. You know, when Ruby called me and told me she suspected you were going to the restaurant, I got the jitters. That reaction surprised me, and then when I got there and saw you in distress, I had this...this...feeling to hurt somebody. I guess what I'm saying is…I don't know what I'm saying."

"I think I understand."

"Do you?" he asks, fidgeting with his keys. Obviously trying to change the subject he says, "Ruby's a good cook. So what's her story?"

"What do you mean?"

"Like you, she's a looker, educated, funny. I'm surprised no guy has swept her off of her feet."

"There's one right now trying to do just that. He proposed to her last year and she turned him down. She says she doesn't want to be in a long-distance relationship. I used to think she didn't want to be in a relationship period, but lately she seems to be warming up to the idea."

"What about you? Do you want to be in a relationship?"

I try to keep from smiling, but I lose the battle.

"What's funny?" he asks.

"Nothing. You make me smile," I say.

"Like you make me nervous?" he says.

"You don't seem nervous to me?" I say.

"Woman, I'm shaking in my boots. My hands are all sweaty. I'm tongue-tied."

We share a moment and then I turn away from him and say, "It's getting late and I have to be at work early tomorrow. Maria's interviewing me for the feature story she's doing on Melissa"

"Good luck with that," he says.

"Thanks," I say, getting up from the sofa.

He does the same and then says, "Maddie, I was wondering, you know, uh."

"What?"

"There's a play at the Ahmanson Theatre that I thought

you might like."

"What's playing?"

"A play called 'The Last Confession.' It's a mystery about a Pope who's killed."

"Sounds a little creepy."

"You're right. Not quite a date play."

"So you're officially asking me out on a date?"

"Yep."

I think about the conversation Ruby and I had and decide to let things flow. "I have an idea. Why don't we go see 22 Jump Street? It's a funny cop movie."

"I'm familiar with it. Did you see 21 Jump Street?" he asks, with dancing dimples.

"I did. It had me cracking up."

"Well, great. Then it's a date. I'll touch base with you tomorrow on logistics."

"Cool," I say.

We creep to the door, trying not to wake Pepper who's snuggled in his bed with his turtle. Sam glances over at him and says, "He's got it made."

We laugh as I let him out. He goes to the elevator and motions for me to shut and lock the door. I do so and walk to the window, so I can see him get into his car. I watch him, hoping and praying his suspicions about my father are wrong.

Chapter 15

Sitting in the studio, waiting for Maria to return, I go through all of my social networking sites, responding to posts, deleting spam, and replying to email. Overall, the response has been good, but unfortunately, nothing concrete has come in. I can't wait for Maria to get to part two of the interview. Between makeup, hair, and lighting, I feel like I've been sitting all day. I miss the hustle and bustle of the newsroom.

"Sorry it took so long, but I received an unexpected tip, and I had to check its veracity," Maria says, entering.

We turn our attention to the cameraman, the sound operator, and the glam squad while they do what they do best. Maria tilts her head back when her face is dabbed with powder. I stand still while my hair is lightly brushed.

"Your hair is so perfect, it barely needs touching up," the hairstylist says.

"Thank you."

Maria gives me what appears to be a snide look, but then she grins.

The sound operator adjusts the lavalier microphone that's on the lapel of my blue blazer. It feels good to be dressed up for a change. Once everything is perfect, Maria and I take seats across from each other.

"Feeling okay?" she asks.

"I'm great."

"I had a chance to view some of the earlier footage and it looks fabulous. You're a natural. I gave Bill, our cameraman, a heads-up about the B-roll we're going to need. I want to get some shots of you at your parents' house, with your dog—"

"That sounds great, but my parents' house is off-limits."

Maria widens her eyes and shares curious looks with the cameraman. "I wish I had known that because I've written my story with your house and family as the backdrop. It's really needed to add feeling and texture to the piece, especially being that your family was living in that house when Melissa was abducted."

I shift in my seat, now wondering if this is all a mistake. I need the exposure, but Maria's in charge, and I'm not sure if I'll have any say so in how the piece is edited. What if she puts my family and me on blast? Okay, I am really tripping, as Ruby would say. *Calm down, Madeline.*

"I'm sorry, Maria, but filming at my house is not negotia—"

She puts her diminutive hand up to silence me and says, "Think about it. That's all I'm asking. Sleep on it."

"But—"

Ignoring me, she takes a pen and pad from a nearby table, returns to her seat, and motions for the cameraman to begin rolling tape. The makeup artist runs to me and dabs at my forehead that's now dripping with sweat. I compose myself and wait for her first question.

"Madeline, nineteen years ago your mother and father experienced every parents' worst nightmare—their child was abducted and as we discussed, that lost took a huge toll on them. But what people fail to realize is that you have gone through a great deal yourself. Albeit, you were three, but as a twin, there was a strong emotional bond. What has it been like for you all this time?"

I take a moment, trying to choke back tears. "It hasn't been easy, Maria. I still have vivid memories of us as toddlers. We had our own language, and we loved for our father to push us in our swings. Her favorite color is red and mine is blue. Over the years, I've always had this feeling that some part of me is missing."

"Is it safe to assume that what happened impacted you mentally?"

"It impacted me mentally, emotionally, and spiritually."

"It's my understanding you're currently under psychiatric care for hallucinations you've been having about Melissa—visions where she talks to you and serves as a guru or guide."

"Excuse me?"

"Didn't she direct you to meet a perfect stranger at a downtown restaurant? And you ended up being attacked."

"Who told you that? That is not true. That's a lie. How dare you twist my experience and turn it into something freakish and weird. And I am not under a doctor's care."

Maria, with a smirk on her face, motions to the cameraman to keep rolling tape. I take my jacket off and throw it over the camera. "This interview is over," I say, storming out.

Standing at my cubicle, the reality of what I did sweeps

through me like a wild-fire. I spent twelve years being an upstanding student in elementary, middle, and high school. I worked my ass off in college. I impressed my professors. I graduated with honors and in one fell swoop I may have blown any and all chances of having a career as a journalist. I could be blacklisted, unemployable. What was I thinking? I pace and stop in my tracks when Tina approaches, jaw clenched, fists balled.

"What the hell happened?" she asks, getting in my personal space. She glowers at me. I flinch, watching the scowl grow deeper on her face. "Maria said you cursed her and the cameraman out and abruptly left the interview."

I remain silent, strategizing my next move. Now I get it. Maria wants to get rid of me. This entire interview was a setup, and I fell right into her trap. I have to give it to her, she's smart. She went on the Internet, read about me, and totally distorted and out right lied about my dreams and what happened at the restaurant. Now she's accusing me of cursing her out. One of my journalism professors who's been in the news business for over thirty years told me about the "Triple S-Effect" — Sabotage, Set up, and Stab your colleagues in the back to maintain your position and or move up to a higher one. I didn't see it coming, but now that I know what's up, I need to counter attack. I need this job. I deserve this job, and I don't plan on anyone getting rid of me.

"Tina, I'm not sure what happened back there. It's all a blur. I had no idea doing the interview would stir up such deep emotions in me, and I reacted without thinking. I owe Maria and the cameraman apologies. I hope I haven't jeopardized my position here with this incident. I would like to continue with the interview as soon as possible. I didn't have a chance to mention this, but several competitive stations have been calling me for exclusives. A few have even offered monetary compensation. However, I wouldn't think of accepting money for my story. As you know, there's a lot of buzz about Melissa and me because of my popularity on social media. I understand if you have no choice, but to let me go, if my services are no longer wanted or needed at KYON."

Before Tina has a chance to respond, Curt appears. "Your services *are* wanted *and* needed here and we wouldn't dare let you go outside of the family. I didn't mean to eavesdrop, but I just left the studio and Maria filled me in. She's still open to conducting the interview and she wants to apologize for overstepping her bounds. None of the offensive footage will be used."

"Thank you, Curt."

"What are you waiting on?" Tina asks. "Get to hair and makeup so we can make this happen."

"Will do," I say.

Ⅱ

"Mr. Toupee has a crush on you," Ruby says, stretching on the living room floor.

"No, Mr. Toupee knows a good story when he sees one. That's why he's an Emmy- winning producer."

"Well, I'm glad things worked out with you and Maria."

"She still wants to get some footage of me at my parents' house, but that's not happening. I'll have to cross that bridge when I come to it."

"By the way, who are these stations that approached you about your story?"

"I made it up. I didn't want to lose my job. I figured mentioning the competition would give me some leverage."

"You're becoming quite the liar, Maddie. You lied to me, your mother, your job…"

"Yikes. Please don't make me feel guiltier than I already do. Contrary to popular opinion, my hair isn't perfect and nor am I."

"No worries, Maddie."

"My LIKES are starting to slow down. Not as many this week."

"You haven't been online that much and neither have I," Ruby says.

"How can we with demanding jobs? I can't wait until Saturday to pass out fliers and Sam is having them sent to the surrounding states. He has some kind of law enforcement database connection," I say.

"That's great. Have you thought about what we talked about?"

"We talk about a lot of stuff."

"I'm talking about giving Sam a chance."

"I've thought about it," I say. "Have you thought about giving Clay a chance?"

"I've thought about it," Ruby says.

We exchange knowing looks and burst into girlish giggles. "We're crazy," I say. "And I need to get ready."

"Ready for what?" Ruby asks.

"My date with Sam."

Her eyes widen and she says, "You're kidding right."

"No, he's taking me to see 22 Jump Street."

"Get the hell outta town," Ruby says.

♊

Walking past the Staples Center, Sam holds my hand. I look down and he releases it and thrusts his hand into his pocket. I glance over my shoulder at the Regal Cinema marquee, thinking about how funny the movie was and what a great time I'm having so far. I want to tell Sam I don't mind him holding my hand, but I'm not really sure if I do or if I don't. One part of me wants to fall head over heels for Sam, but the other part is scared shitless.

"So you liked it?" he asks.

"Couldn't you tell," I say. "It was funnier than the first one and that's rare."

"Right. Most sequels suck," he says. "By the way, I love the way you laugh."

"Are you sure I didn't embarrass you?" I ask.

"No way." He motions to a nearby Chinese restaurant and we head in.

"How many?" the hostess asks.

"Just two," Sam says.

She leads us to a booth near the rear and we sit. Handing us menus, she says, "Someone will be with you shortly."

"Thank you," we both say.

Sam, facing the door, watches her leave then turning toward me he says, "Thanks for hanging out with me tonight."

"Thanks for asking," I say.

"The barbeque spare ribs are really good. I usually get those with a side order of vegetables and rice," he says.

"I'm not that hungry. The popcorn really filled me up."

"Why don't I order and you can share mine."

"I'll try a little," I say.

Sam orders when the waiter comes by. Afterwards, we

give him our menus, and I take in the quaint restaurant that has more plants then patrons. I turn back toward Sam and am greeted with an inviting smile. He leans back in his seat, seemingly satisfied.

"So what made you want to become a cop?" I ask.

"My grandfather was a lawman. I think he indoctrinated me. He wanted my father to join the force, but my father was in love with numbers. He almost became a mathematician but ended up in accounting. He's a retired CPA."

"Ruby's father is a CPA," I say. "So your grandfather pushed you to become a police officer?"

"I wouldn't say he pushed me. I admired him — the way he carried himself. I remembered how particular he was with his uniform and how shiny his shoes were. He loved being a cop, getting the bad guys."

"Are you still close to him?" I ask.

"He was killed in the line of duty fifteen years ago. He had answered a domestic abuse call and this woman's crazy boyfriend ambushed him."

Sam gets a little misty-eyed. I place my hand on his. "I'm so sorry."

"It's okay. He was my hero. Great guy. Every day I do my job, I think about him. I do it for both of us. Check this out." He reaches inside the inner pocket of the green blazer he's wearing and sets a gold pocket watch on the table. "My Gramps gave me this."

"Is it okay if I look at?"

"Please do."

"It's heavy," I say. "January 5, 1985 – SGW."

"The watch belonged to his father. He had my birthdate and initials engraved."

"This is really special, Sam. So you're twenty-nine and a

Capricorn. What's the "G" stand for."

"Gregory. That's my grandfather's first name."

"You must feel honored," I say, handing him the watch.

"I do," he says, putting it away. "What about you? Why journalism? You look more like a fashion model or a movie star," he says.

"I get that all the time," I say.

"That's a good thing, isn't it?"

"It's annoying at times. Don't get me wrong, I appreciate good genes, but I have to go above and beyond at times, to convince people I have something up here," I say, pointing to my head. "I think that's what motivated me to go into journalism. You have to know your stuff, current events, politics, economics, you have to be well-rounded. I like learning new things, and I love writing and reporting the news."

"Has there been anyone who's influenced you?" he asks.

The waiter returns before I have a chance to answer. He sets the food on the table and Sam digs in.

"Outside of my mother, I have to say, Barbara Walters, of course. I also love Diane Sawyer, Oprah Winfrey, and Christiane Amanpour from CNN. How's the food?"

"Try some, he says," handing me his fork.

I take a piece of rib, put it in my mouth, and slowly chew, savoring the tender tasty meat. I feel the heat of Sam's gaze. I hand him the fork and take a sip of the water the waiter left.

"How is it?"

"Delicious," I say.

"Forgive me for saying so, but you are beautiful, Maddie and smart."

"You're not so bad yourself," I say.

Ⅱ

Standing in the hallway of my apartment, Sam thanks me again for going on the date. Then he clears his throat and says, "Maddie, I'm a straight up guy. I pretty much tell it like it is. Right to the point. I like you. I like you a lot. In fact, I haven't stopped thinking about you since you showed up at the station looking like you had just stepped out of Vogue Magazine. Now I'm not sure if you like me, but that's okay. I needed you to hear that. One more thing—in case you were wondering, I've never been married, I have no kids, and I'm straight. Yes, I have been in love if you count my fifth grade teacher. I had such a big crush on her, I almost failed elementary school."

"I like you, too, Sam, but I need to take it slow. There's a lot going on. My new job, trying to find Melissa. I'm not sure if I can handle a relationship, and I've been hurt in the past."

"I understand. Tell me, you'll go out with me again. Just be my friend."

"I can do that," I say.

"Good. Well, I better let you go."

"Yeah, it's getting late and I have work tomorrow."

He walks me to the elevator, and I turn and kiss him on the cheek. "Good night, Sam."

"Good night," he says, touching his face.

We share a smile and then I go into my apartment.

Ⅱ

"How was your date?"

"Ruby, what are you still doing up," I ask, setting my purse on the coffee table.

"I made the mistake of bringing work home. This crazy program I'm working on is driving me nuts. I'm obsessed," she says, tinkering with her laptop computer. "How was your date?"

"Sweet," I say.

"How sweet?"

"It was nice. I told you, I'm taking it slow. You know, Sam's grandfather was a cop and he was killed in the line of duty."

"Sorry to hear that."

"That's something else to think about. God forbid, but the same thing could happen to —"

"Stop looking for excuses to shut him out, Maddie."

"It's not an excuse, it's a reality." I sit on the sofa and remove my shoes. Pepper enters the room and sniffs them. Then he sits at my feet. "Hey boy, no hugs and kisses? What's wrong with you? Are you mad at me because I went out with Sam? Don't be jealous." I pat him on the head and notice a box in the corner of the living room. "What's that?"

"I thought that was some of your stuff?" Ruby says, getting up from the floor to take a closer look.

"I've unpacked everything," I say. I go to the box and open it.

"What's in there?" Ruby asks.

I thrust my hand into the box and yank out a fistful of newspaper. Pepper walks over and sniffs it. I dig in deeper and stop when my hand touches something soft. "What's this?" I ask, pulling out...a jacket. A child's jacket with fur around the collar — a blue jacket. My jacket. "Ruby, I think you may have taken this box out of my parents' garage when you got the books."

"Ooops," she says.

"This is the jacket I was talking about. This is the jacket I was wearing the day my mother got carjacked. This is the one I see in my dreams. I used to love this jacket. My mother said it was the only way she could get Melissa to stop crying so that she could take us to our doctor's appointment. Melissa wore her jacket, I wore mine, and my mother wore a jacket."

Ruby and I turn to the box when Pepper grabs it with his teeth and rips and tears it. "No, Pepper, don't boy. What's the matter? Are you mad at the box now?" I say, laughing. I try to pull it out of his mouth and it comes apart, revealing another jacket. A red jacket, Melissa's jacket. I stand here wondering, how and why Melissa's jacket is in the box when she had it on in the car. She was wearing the jacket when she was kidnapped.

"What's wrong?" Ruby asks.

"This is Melissa's jacket. My mother said Melissa was wearing it the day of the carjacking. What is it doing here?"

"Good question," Ruby says.

I grab my phone off of the coffee table. I hit speed dial and wait for my mother to answer. I put it on speaker.

"Hey, kiddo, it's late. Shouldn't you be in bed? I was thinking about you. I was thinking about how I'm going to make it up to you for the boneheaded stunt I pulled. I hope you're not still mad at me."

"I'm getting over it, Dad. There is something you can do to make up for it."

"What?"

"As you know, the station's doing a feature story on Melissa and me and they need some footage at the house.

I'm not ready to tell mom about what I'm doing and I know you're not either. So if you could get her away from the house on the day we shoot, that would be helpful."

"So, you're still going forward with the feature story?"

"Dad, I never said I wasn't going to do it."

"I don't get you, Maddie. Don't you care about your mother's feelings?"

"Dad, you know I do, but think about how happy mom's going to be when I find Melissa. It's going to be worth it."

Ruby gives me thumbs up and I wait for my father to respond.

"Dad?"

"I heard you."

"Can you get mom away from the house? I'll give you advance notice."

"I'll see what I can do, Maddie. I can't make any promises. Is that all?"

Ruby points to the jacket and I remember why I called. "Is mom there? I need to ask her something."

"What do you want to ask her?"

"It's nothing serious."

"Maddie, please don't upset your mother."

"I'm not. Can you ask her to come to the phone?"

"Millicent, pick up. Maddie's on the phone."

"Maddie?"

"Hi, Mom."

"Alvin, you can hang up. I have it."

After a second or two there's a click and my mother continues. "What are you still doing up, Maddie? You're going to be falling asleep at work."

"Mom, it's a little after eleven. I'll be fine."

"Are you coming home for dinner this weekend?"

"Not this weekend. I have some errands to run. Mom, remember when you told me Melissa wouldn't stop crying because she wanted to wear her red jacket with the fur the day you were carjacked." There's silence and I lock eyes with Ruby, hoping this conversation goes well. "Mom?"

"I heard you. Why are you asking me about a jacket from the past? Shouldn't you be focused on writing news stories?"

"Mom, you said Melissa was wearing her jacket that day. If she was, why did I find it in a box with mine?"

"What box? Have you been going through my things in the garage? Your father doesn't want you going through things in the garage. Why are you picking on me, Madeline?"

"Mom, I need to know about the coat. You said she was wearing it. If she was, why is it in the box with mine?" I ask, my voice escalating a bit. Ruby approaches, signaling me to tone it down.

"Why are you screaming at me, Maddie? What is wrong with you?"

"Answer me, Mom. Why is Melissa's coat— Hello? Hello? She hung up on me."

Chapter 16

"Hello! Hello! Listen up, people. Hello!"

I look toward the sky, using my hand to shield my eyes from the sun, while Ruby, armed with a bullhorn, tries to get the attention of the crowd. We're at McArthur Park. It's a park in the Westlake neighborhood of Los Angeles, named after General Douglas MacArthur. I wish he was alive and here, so that he could get this army of people in order. Ruby put the call out on all our social media sites that we would be distributing fliers today. When we got here an hour ago, we thought there was a bomb threat and that the crowd gathered here were residents of the neighborhood. But we soon learned they were here for Melissa.

I look out at the street filled with our supporters consisting of people from all walks of life, including numerous sets of twins, holding banners, balloons, and wearing buttons, and I'm moved and overwhelmed.

FIND MELISSA NOW!

MELISSA, WHERE ARE YOU?
MADDIE LOVES MELISSA!
MADDIE ABOUT MELISSA!
LONG LIVE MELISSA!

It's like a movement — The Melissa Movement. Thinking about it makes me a little weak in the knees. I started this. What if it gets out of control? Feeling parched, my eyes scan the park. *Where is our cooler?*

"Are you okay?"

I give the middle-aged woman, wearing a long blonde wig, a grateful smile. "Just a little thirsty," I say. "I'm trying to find my cooler."

"It's over by that tree," she says, pointing. "By the way, my name's Angie. My friends and I have been following you on the Internet." She points to three women wearing long blonde wigs. They smile and wave with wonder in their eyes. They remind me of myself the first time I saw Justin Timberlake in concert. "We're so excited to be here, to be a part of this. We came all the way from Dallas. There's a group there passing out fliers, too, but we wanted to be in L.A. We wanted to meet you."

I tilt my head and say, "Did you say they're passing out fliers in Dallas?"

"That's right. Didn't you know? It's happening all over the country." She points to a stack of boxes filled with fliers. "We had those made."

I go to the cooler, grab a bottle of water, and drink up. *That's better.* I wonder does Ruby know what's going on. I look around, contemplating making an escape, but all eyes are on me. I make my way back to the bench where Ruby's standing and pull her by the arm for a sidebar.

"What's up?"

"Did you know there are groups all over the country

passing out fliers?"

"I heard something like that was going on, but I wasn't sure."

"Those ladies over there confirmed it. They came here all the way from Dallas."

The women smile and wave at Ruby.

"Get the hell out. This thing is huge, Maddie."

"I know. I really need to get to Dancing Hills to talk to my mother."

"You haven't reached her yet?"

"No, she's dodging my calls. And my father's helping her. I have to get her to tell me why Melissa's jacket was in that box."

"She probably got things mixed up," Ruby says, surveying the throngs of people, with a spark of pride in her gaze. "I can't believe how effective the campaign is."

"Ruby, what do you mean 'she got things mixed up?' There's more to it than that. Whatever happened to your doubts?"

"Maddie, look at all these people. They believe in this. They believe Melissa's alive and I do, too. Now let's start passing these fliers out."

Ruby leaves me and jumps onto the bench. She puts the bullhorn up to her mouth and addresses the crowd. "Does everyone have fliers?"

"YES!!"

"Let's get busy people!"

In a matter of seconds, what appeared to be chaos moments before, turns into complete order. Over a dozen groups of ten take off in various directions with fliers in tow. Ruby and I high-five, get into her jeep, and start making the rounds.

♊

Sitting in a downtown burger joint, I scroll through my messages and stop when I come to Sam's. *Hrd about crwd@park. Hope yr ok.*

"Who's that?" Ruby asks, looking up from her plate of pasta.

"Sam. He said he heard about the crowd."

Thanks 4checkingn. Things rgon well. I set my phone down on the table and bite into my burger. "Passing out fliers is hard work," I say.

"Tell me about it. But people seem really receptive," Ruby says.

"I know."

"Too receptive. If I had a dollar for every guy that has tried to get your phone number, I'd be rich," Ruby says.

"You're one to talk. What about tall, dark, and handsome on Olympic?" I ask.

"Speaking of tall, dark, and handsome, I have to pick Clay up from the airport tomorrow. He gets in at noon. And no, he's not staying with us. I told him he needs to get a room."

"I don't mind," I say.

"I do," Ruby says, looking over my shoulder.

"Excuse us, but have you seen this young woman? She was abducted in a carjacking nineteen years ago when she was three. She would be twenty-two now and she would look like this. She's an identical twin. She was last seen in Dancing Hills, California."

Ruby, grinning, points to me and I turn around.

The two young girls, a brunette and a blonde, turn fire

engine red and burst into girlish giggles. "OMG! It's you. We found her. We found her, everybody!" the blonde says.

"No, I'm Maddie. I was at the rally. I'm the other twin," I say.

Seemingly dispirited, they quiet down and give me curious looks. "Right. Okay, well we're going to keep on passing out fliers," the brunette says.

I get out of my seat and give them hugs. "Thank you so much. I really appreciate what you're doing."

They pull out of our embrace, with bright eyes, and renewed energy. "You're welcome and don't worry, we're going to find her," the blonde says.

My eyes burn with tears of gratitude and guilt while I watch them flounce out of the door, thinking about what they might be doing on this sunny Saturday if I had listened to my father. Maybe shopping at the mall or catching a good movie. But instead, they're in downtown Los Angeles, going from stranger to stranger, asking those strangers if they know another stranger, who was kidnapped by strangers. It can't get any stranger than this. I'm the manufacturer of all this strangeness. I flop down in my seat, drained.

"What's wrong, Maddie?" Ruby asks with her elbows on the table.

"I'm having so many mixed emotions. One part of me is grateful for all of this support and then there's another part of me that feels guilty. What if I'm wasting everyone's time? What if this is all about nothing? And next week The Special on KYON airs. It's going to really get crazy then."

"Maddie, you have to stop doubting. I know what's bothering you."

"What?" I ask.

"You haven't had any more dreams."

"What did you say?"

"You haven't had any more dreams."

"But...but I did. I did have a dream last night or this morning. I forgot all about it."

"Was it about Melissa?"

"Yes."

"What did she say?"

"She didn't say anything. That's probably why I didn't remember it. She was swinging on our swing set. She was grown up, but the seat was big enough for an adult. She was kicking her bare feet and waving at me. She kept swinging higher and higher. I remember reaching for her, afraid she was going to fall. She was wearing this red chiffon dress and it was flying up, covering her face. Then she fell down into the dirt and the earth sucked her up. I dropped to my knees in the dream and I started digging, trying to save her. And a large hand reached down and pushed me out of the way, and grabbed her. Then the hand brought her up out of the ground and then I woke up."

"Girl, that dream gives me chills," Ruby says.

"It frightened me, but then I felt better when the man showed up. The *man*. There's the man again. The one who saved her."

"Maybe it's the hand of God. Maybe we're taking it too literal," Ruby adds. "Maybe the man pushing you out of the way is God saying, 'I have this. Stop worrying. Let me handle this. Get out of my way.'"

"You have a point. That's definitely a possibility. Anyway, we better get back to passing out fliers."

"Let's go," she says, leaving a tip.

♊

Sitting at my computer, with Pepper at my feet, I read messages from people all over the country who passed out fliers yesterday. There's all kind of photos, selfies, and photo bombs. I laugh out loud at the four women from Dallas. They took a photo pulling their wigs off. Pepper, hearing my laughter, gets up and thrusts his nose onto the keyboard. "Do you want to type something?" I ask. He lifts his ears and yawns. "I guess not," I say, chuckling. "Pepper, mommie still needs to clean your ears and give you a good brushing. Where are you going, Pepper? Come back here."

"Hello, we're here."

I follow Pepper to the front door and greet Ruby.

"Pepper, guess who's here. Uncle Clay is here to see you," Ruby says.

Pepper jumps up and licks Clay and Clay recoils. "Ruby, get him off of me. He's going to ruin my suit."

"Stop whining, Clay. He loves you."

"Come on, boy, let Uncle Clay breathe," I say, nudging Pepper toward the other side of the room.

"I'm sorry, I don't mean to be a grouch, but not everybody is a dog-lover, I mean, they're nice and all, but..."

"Careful, Clay," Ruby says, giving him a cautious glare.

"How are you doing, Maddie?" He walks to me and gives me a warm hug.

"I'm hanging in there."

"I can imagine," he says, rubbing his goatee. "Your story about Melissa is all over the Internet, and a girl handed me a flier when I was on my way to Langdell Hall at Harvard yesterday."

"It's a movement," Ruby says.

"I hope something comes of it, that it's not all a waste of

time," I say.

Clay clasps his hands and rears back, shaking his head. "Maddie, how long have you known the woman of my dreams?"

"Since the fourth grade," I say.

"And she hasn't rubbed off on you yet? Positivity is her middle name. You have to think positive. Think it, see it, believe it, and it'll be yours. How do you think a little boy raised in the projects made it out alive, graduated second in his high school, graduated undergrad with honors, and got accepted into Harvard Law School? I saw it, I believed it, and it happened. Of course I had to do the footwork, and you're doing that."

"That's what I keep trying to tell her, Clay."

"You guys are right," I say.

"Why don't I take you two ladies out to dinner? Let's celebrate you getting closer to finding Melissa."

"Why don't we make it a foursome," Ruby suggests.

"Excuse me," Clay says, with knitted brows.

"Sam's probably busy. He does have other cases he's working on," I say, kind of excited about the possibility of seeing him.

"Call him and see if he'll meet us," Ruby says.

"Who's Sam?" Clay asks.

"Maddie's new beau," Ruby says.

"He's just a friend," I say, rolling my eyes at Ruby. "By the way, where are you taking us?" I ask.

"I'm not that familiar with the restaurants out here. Now if we were back east, I'd take you to —"

"No worries, Clay. I have just the right place," Ruby says.

♊

Sitting on the patio of Moonshadows Malibu restaurant, I take in the breathtaking panoramic view of the ocean, wondering why Ruby never told me about this gem.

"What do you think?" Ruby asks.

"Girl, this place is amazing and really romantic. It might be *too* romantic," I say, chuckling.

"Shhh, the guys are coming," she whispers.

"What's so funny?" Clay asks, sitting next to Ruby.

"Nothing," Ruby says.

"Clay, I think we may have been the topic of their conversation," Sam says, sitting next to me.

"We were talking about how incredible the view is," I say, casting a knowing look Ruby's way.

"You're wrong, Maddie. I have the most incredible view in the house," Clay says, gazing at Ruby.

"Clay, stop. You're embarrassing me."

"It's true," Clay says. "Sam, this woman right here is my heart and she doesn't want to accept it, but she's the only woman for me. She's smart, beautiful, kind. I can go on and on."

"You'll get no arguments from me," Sam says.

"So how did you and Maddie meet?" Clay asks.

"The case brought us together," Sam says.

"So you didn't know her before that?" Clay asks.

"A friend of Sam's partner was at my birthday party and through him, I ended up meeting Sam," I say, shifting in my chair.

"You guys make a nice couple," Clay says.

"Thanks," Sam says.

Thanks?

"Ouch," Clay says, reaching down under the table. He turns toward Ruby and grimaces.

"We're just friends," I say. The waiter approaches and I breathe a sigh of relief.

"Here you are," he says, setting the food before us. "Black cod, Salmon with spinach and potatoes, Chilean Sea Bass, and Vegetable Salad."

"It looks delicious," Clay says.

"Will there be anything else?" the waiter asks.

"Ladies," Sam says.

"I'm good," I say.

"Me too," Ruby says.

"Clay?"

"It's all good. Thanks."

The waiter leaves and we attack our plates.

"How do you like the champagne?" Clay asks.

"It's good," we all say.

"You sure you don't want anymore?" Sam asks, eyeing my nearly full flute.

"Not right now," I say.

I look around at everyone eating, and get a good feeling inside. It seems so right, the four of us. If I didn't know us, I'd swear we were all married and best friends. Clay must read my mind.

"This is so cool. I love this restaurant and the company. We have to do this again."

"It is nice," Ruby says.

"Good choice, babe," he says, passing his hand over Ruby's cheek. "I love you, woman. I really do and I'm not afraid to tell the world."

Ruby tries to keep from laughing but she loses the battle and falls over, chuckling. I can tell she's impressed.

"You don't believe me?" he asks.

"Clay, sit down. What are you doing?" Ruby asks.

Sam and I watch with wide eyes when Clay gets up from his seat and goes to the center of the dining area.

"Excuse me, everyone, but I have an announcement to make. Forgive me for disturbing your meals, but I can't help myself. You see that beautiful woman over there, the one sitting by the window, I am madly in love with her, and I need her like I need air to breathe. I want to marry her, but she told me she doesn't want to be in a long-distance relationship, so I'm shaping plans to relocate to California. I got to have that woman."

The patrons give him a standing ovation. Ruby, with her mouth open, and tears streaming down her face, grabs my hand.

"I can't believe he did that," she says.

Sam, red in the face, is grinning from ear-to-ear.

"Thank you, everyone," Clay says, returning to the table.

"Clay, you are...you are...amazing," Ruby says, hugging him.

"Anything for you, babe," he says.

Sam and I exchange nervous glances, and resume eating, while Ruby and Clay gape at each other.

II

"Sitting in Sam's car in the parking lot of our apartment complex, I peer out the windshield, wondering how Ruby and Clay are doing. Barely able to keep their hands off of each other, they left the restaurant thirty minutes before we did. I can only imagine what they're up to and I guess I'm a little envious. It's been a while since I've made love to someone I care about. I try not to think about it, and when I do, I shut my raging hormones down with a cold shower. Masturbation has never really been my thing, and I'm not into sex toys.

"You okay?" Sam asks.

"Yeah," I say. "What about you?"

"I'm good. I'm still thinking about what Clay did. That was wild. I guess sometimes when you want something really badly you have to go all out, make a fool of yourself."

"What?"

"I don't mean it like that. I didn't mean to say Clay was a fool."

"Well, that's what it sounded like."

"What's wrong with you, Maddie?"

"What do you mean what's wrong with me?"

"You've been acting really standoffish."

"Maybe it has something to do with you acting like we're a couple."

"What?"

"When Clay said we make a nice couple, you said 'Thank you.'"

"Are you kidding me? This is so childish and petty."

"So Clay is a fool and I'm childish and petty."

"You know that's not what I meant."

"Then why don't you try saying what you mean for a change."

"You know what, why don't I walk you to your apartment and leave before this little discussion escalates."

"Don't bother. I can walk myself," I say, getting out of the car. I slam the door and I don't look back.

"Maddie, Maddie," wait, he says, running behind me.

I rush into the building and enter the elevator. Just as the door is about to close, he pushes it open with his foot.

"What is it?" I ask.

The door shuts and he gets in my personal space. "What's really going on? Talk to me. You can't be mad at me because of that couple thing."

"Sam…Sam…I…I'm scared."

"Of what?"

"Of us, of falling for you, getting hurt. What if we don't work out? What if you're killed in the line of duty? I've already lost a sister; I couldn't deal with losing you."

"Maddie, in life there are no guarantees. I wish I could tell you that if we got into a relationship it's going to last forever. I wish I could tell you, I'm Superman and bullets can't harm me. But I'm not, I'm human. I want a chance. Don't shut me out."

We gaze into each other's eyes. Our faces come together and are lips touch ever so slightly. I let my mine part, inviting him in. I want to taste him, feel him. He gently thrusts his tongue into my mouth and I receive him full on. Heavy breathing fills the elevator, while our tongues go on an exploration. I don't think about my father or Richard or anyone in this moment. I shut my eyes and bask in the warmth and sweetness of his mouth.

We come up for air and he says, "Maddie, will you be my girlfriend?"

"Yes, Sam. We can be a couple," I say, trying to catch my breath.

Chapter 17

Standing in the shower, with the water raining down on me, I relish my anonymity, because after today, Melissa and I will probably be one of the most talked about set of twins in the country. In exactly one hour, the special Maria put together is going to air. She named it after my Facebook page, *Missing Melissa*. I grab my loofah, pour soap jell on it, and wash my size four body. I can't believe I've lost an entire dress size in just a few weeks. But I shouldn't be surprised. I've been putting in long hours at the station, dating Sam, and maintaining my social media sites.

KYON has a long reach, and I really believe the special, coupled with the flier campaign, is not only going to motivate DHPD to reopen the case, but someone is going to recognize Melissa, and then Judy will be forced to come forward. I have a good feeling about this, and if it means I'll have to be the proverbial fish in a bowl, so be it.

Today is also Clay's last day here. He got what he came

for. When I woke up to Ruby flashing her three-carat diamond engagement ring in my face this morning, the first thing that came to mind was that Clay saw himself married to Ruby, believed he would be married to Ruby, and now he's going to be married to Ruby—June 2017. I'm happy for them, and I'm glad Ruby finally gave in. Clay's good for her.

"Maddie, are you almost done? Clay and I are going to order pizza," Ruby says from the hallway.

"I'll be out in a minute," I say, turning off the water.

I step out of the shower, dry myself off, and peer in the mirror. I put my face close to the glass, checking for premature wrinkles. I'd be lucky if I could look half as good as my mother at her age. Grandma Patterson looks good, too. I grab my robe off of the bathroom door, put it on, and attack my walk-in closet. I decide to wear a dress in honor of Ruby's engagement.

"Hey, Maddie," Ruby says, entering my bedroom, wriggling her fingers.

I lift my hand over my eyes and fall onto the bed, feigning a fainting spell. "You're blinding me, Ruby. Get it out of here."

"I can't believe it. I'm going to be Mrs. Clayton Grant Towers. Why are you looking at me like that?" she asks.

"I'm so happy for you," I say. "Love looks good on you."

"It looks good on you, too," Ruby says.

"What?"

"You're falling for Sam."

"I am not 'falling for Sam.'"

"Is that why your face looks like the tomatoes your grandmother likes to eat when she's painting. The very red tomatoes she says inspire her."

"Ruby, you are not right."

"By the way, she's here."

"She's here already?"

"Clay's keeping her company."

"I better get dressed before Sam gets here. I'm so nervous about this special; I don't know what to do with myself. What if Maria has pulled another fast one? You know she never got over not being able to film at my parents' house. She ended up using green screen."

"What's green screen?"

"It's a green background that can later be filled in with images. I was filmed in front of the screen."

"That's the doorbell," Ruby says. "Get dressed and put on your face. That's probably Sam."

"Okay, see you in a few. And congratulations, again."

"Thanks, sweetness and light," Ruby says.

♊

Sitting on the sofa, next to Sam, I hold his hand while my grandmother shows Clay how to do the Electric Slide. She says it's basically line dancing. Clay, a dance virtuoso, is being gracious and humors her.

"You're an expert," he tells her, moving from side to side. She steps on his foot and he gasps, but maintains his cool.

"I'm sorry, Cassius Clay, I mean, Muhammad Ali. You know you used to be called Cassius Clay."

"Grandma, his name is Clayton Grant Towers," I say.

"It's all good, Maddie. Don't bother her. She's having fun," Clay says.

Ruby, shaking her head, is laughing so hard, she ends up running to the restroom. Needless to say, Grandma has had a little too much "medicine." Ruby's going to spend the night with Clay at his hotel, and has already agreed to let my grandmother sleep in her bed tonight. Thank goodness. In her state, I wouldn't even be comfortable with her taking a taxi home.

"Turn up the music, Ruby!" My grandmother says, stumbling to the sofa. Sam breaks her fall and helps her sit.

"Grandma, Ruby's in the restroom, and there is no music playing."

"There is in my head," she says, singing out of tune.

"You okay?" Sam asks.

"I'm wonderful. When are you going to propose to my granddaughter, like Cassius proposed to Ruby?"

"Uh…" Sam looks toward me for help.

"Grandma, I'm going to make you some coffee. Get comfortable. Missing Melissa is coming on soon."

"I miss Melissa, too. Maddie, are you going to find her?"

"Yes, Grandma, I am." I go to the kitchen with Sam on my heels.

"Does she get like this often?"

"She's never been one to shy away from a Martini or a Bloody Mary…or —"

"I get it," he says.

"But lately, she's really been overdoing it."

We're silent while I finish making the coffee. I break the silence with a confession.

"I actually feel guilty because it seems as if her drinking started to intensify right around the time I told my family I wanted to reopen the case."

"I see. Oh, speaking of which, I heard back from my

source. The last known address for Judy is in San Francisco. Caroline was right. By the end of the week, I have a hunch we'll catch up to her."

"That's good news!" I say. "And I'm sorry about the proposal thing. I know she put you on the spot."

"I agree with Clay. It's all good." With one dazzling smile from Sam, all my anxiousness and nervousness about my life right now slips away.

"Maddie, Sam, the show's starting."

"We're coming, Ruby."

♊

Sam winks at me when my face fills our wide screen television. My grandmother sips on her coffee and dabs at tears trickling down her face. Clay and Ruby sit on the love seat, snuggling. During the commercials, Clay plants kisses on Ruby's cheek. I get tingly all over witnessing his love for her. She deserves a man like Clay.

I glance at my phone I'm holding in a death grip, wondering if my father's going to call. He said he was going to keep my mother away from the television. In a way, I want her to see this, so I don't have to hide anymore. I stiffen when we come to part two of the special. Sam notices and offers me some pizza, but I'm too on edge to eat.

"I love her. I mean I used to love her," Ruby says when the camera zooms in on Maria.

"Madeline, nineteen years ago your mother and father experienced every parents' worst nightmare — their child was abducted and as we discussed earlier, that lost took a huge toll on them. But what people fail to realize is that you have gone through a great deal yourself. Albeit, you were three at the time, but as a twin, there was a strong emotional attachment to Melissa. What has it been like for you these past nineteen years?"

"It hasn't been easy, Maria. I still have vivid memories of us as toddlers. We had our own language, and we loved for our father to push us in our swings. Her favorite color is red and mine is blue. Over the years, I've always had this feeling that some part of me is missing."

"Is it safe to assume that what happened impacted you mentally?"

"Yes, it has. It's had an effect on me mentally, emotionally, and spiritually."

"Can you elaborate?"

"I've always had a sense of guilt, especially when experiencing milestones, like turning sixteen, getting my driver's license, driving for the first time, going to the prom. I wonder about Melissa, I wonder if she had the opportunity to experience those things. I've also struggled with my belief in God, wondering why he would let something like this happen. But over the years, I've gained a better understanding about how things work spiritually, thanks to my best friend's parents."

Ruby, smiling, gives me thumbs up.

"There's a segment of the population who believe Melissa is no longer with us because so much time has passed and she's never surfaced. What do you have to say to those people?"

"I say that we don't know. There were people who thought Elizabeth Smart was dead, Jaycee Dugard, and the three women in Cleveland. I believe my sister is still alive, and I pray someone will see this program and call in with information regarding her whereabouts."

"What makes you so sure she's alive, Maddie?"

"Twins are connected and Melissa comes to me in dreams, and I believe she's guiding me, leading me."

"To her?"

"Yes."

"Good answer," Ruby says.

"On that note, we'll take a commercial break, and when we return, we'll take a closer look at some of your accomplishments and your plans for the future."

II

I stand in the doorway of Ruby's bedroom, watching over my grandmother. She finally sobered up and went to bed about an hour ago. Ruby, Clay, and Sam left right after the special. We all agreed it was done tastefully and hope it brings in some *substantial* leads. Tomorrow is Sunday, and I plan to pay a visit to my parents' house. I need to talk to both of them about the special, and I need to fill my mother in on what I'm doing. No more hiding. I also need to talk to her about Melissa's jacket. It's really nagging me and with all the speculation and doubts lately, I need to get closure. I know my mother's innocent, but I need to prove to the rest of the world that she is.

"What are you doing standing in the dark like that?" My grandmother sits up and beckons me to join her.

"I'm watching over you," I say, sitting on the bed.

"I should be watching *over you*. I used to watch you and Melissa when you were little."

"I know."

"I should have been watching you the day your mother took you to the doctor, but I had that damn art show. I've never talked about this before, but your mother called me that day. She called me out of the blue and asked me if I could help with you and Melissa. I was so caught up, I didn't have time. It was all ego. I was going to be a famous artist and that show was my one big chance. And what did it get me? I didn't get discovered and I lost a granddaughter in the process. I wish I could take that day back."

"Is that why you rarely paint anymore?"

She nods.

"Is that why you drink so much?"

She nods again.

"Grandma, I'm concerned about you. First of all, don't blame yourself for what happened to Melissa. You had every right to attend that art show."

"But your mother was a bumbling mess and Melissa was having one of her tantrums. I could hear her in the background. It's been almost twenty years and I can still hear her shrill, eardrum-bursting screams. She was the crier. She cried about everything. You on the other hand would sit and look, like you were taking it all in."

I stare at my grandmother while she grapples with her guilt, wishing I could ease her pain, but I only have words and hugs. "Don't be so hard on yourself, Grandma."

"I need to be hard on myself, and I acted a fool in front of your company. Please extend my apologies to Ruby. Her fiancé must think I'm a raving lunatic. And Sam, on Lord, I hope I haven't ruined it for you."

"Grandma, stop it! Stop it right now. Calm down. You're going to drive yourself crazy worrying."

She grabs the pillow off of the bed and puts it over her face. I breathe a sigh of relief when I hear the muffled laughter. I snatch the pillow.

"I see you're feeling better."

"A little. You know I love you forever, right?"
"I love you, too, Grandma."

II

Lying in bed, I turn toward the window, bracing myself for my close encounter with my parents today. I pray it goes well and that I have a good day. I get out of bed wondering where Pepper is. He usually greets me with wet kisses. Maybe he's hanging out with Grandma. I go to my restroom and grab my robe off of the back door. It was so hot last night, I slept in the buff. "Grandma? Pepper? Hmm. Where is everybody?" I make my way to Ruby's room and the bed is made. I squint when I notice a note on the pillow.

Thank you for encouraging an old lady last night. I felt so much better this morning and decided to head home. Don't worry about me, and if I haven't told you lately, I am extremely proud of you. Love, Grandma Patterson.

I slip the note into my robe pocket and go on my hunt for Pepper. "Pepper?" He's not in the kitchen or bathrooms. Okay, I'm getting a little worried. I hope my grandmother didn't let him out. I grab my phone off of the coffee table, turn it on, and hit speed dial. "Grandma, are you okay?"

"Yes, I left about forty minutes ago. I hope I didn't wake you?"

"No, you didn't, but, I can't find Pepper."

"You can't find Pepper?"

"No, he's not here."

"He was there when I left."

"Where exactly was he?"

"In the kitchen eating. I fed him before I left."

"Well, he's not there now," I say, trying not to panic.

"Oh, goodness. Let me come back and help you find him."

"No, no. You get home. I'll find him. He might be hiding. He does that sometimes," I say.

"You call me the moment you find him."

"I will," I say. I hang up the phone and notice text messages — dozens of text messages and voicemail. I run to the computer and turn it on. I go to my social media sites and website and I can't access anything. "What the hell is going on?"

Chapter 18

The house phone rings and I nearly jump out of my skin. Who calls on the landline? I hesitate and then answer the phone in case it's important.

"Hello?"

"Maddie?"

"Yes. This is she. Who is this?"

"It's George from KYON."

"George? What's...uh...what's going on?" I ask, pressing on my stomach that's now in knots. I hope he isn't the one who drew the shortest straw when they were trying to figure out who would be the person to tell me I no longer have a job at KYON.

"I'm sorry for calling you at home, but I tried your cell and you didn't answer and your voicemail is full."

My voicemail is full? "What's going on?"

"I wanted to be the first to congratulate you."

"About what?"

"The numbers for your show last night are in the stratosphere. The entire news department is talking about it. And I overhead Curt talking to the news director about possibly putting you on the air. Creating some kind of show about missing kids and teens. He says the camera loves you and so does the audience. The phones have been ringing nonstop. It all started right after the show. And get this; a lot of leads have come in about your sister. Sightings in Phoenix, Dallas, New York, San Francisco. We've been directing them to DHPD—"

"Just a minute, George. I have a call coming in. Hello."

"Maddie, it's Sam. I've been trying to call you."

"I just got up and my cell phone was off."

"I'm at the station and the hotline is blowing up. We're also getting calls from KYON. There have been at least ten strong leads and sightings. Can you meet me down here?"

"Of course. I need to stop by my parents' house. I definitely need to get this news to them. This is great. Sam, I'm sorry, I have George on the other line."

"Who's George?"

"He's the researcher at KYON."

"Okay, hurry. I can't wait to see you. And by the way, the Chief has given me the go ahead to reopen the case. But that's not public information yet."

"That's excellent, Sam. I can't wait to see you, too."

I click over to George. "I'm sorry. I have to go. I'll be in first thing in the morning. And thank you for calling me. I really appreciate you helping me get my story out there, George."

"Anything for a fellow Bruin. You take care, sweetie. And I'll see you tomorrow."

I hang up the phone, thrilled about the news. People have seen Melissa. "Thank you, God!" Then it hits me — Pepper's still missing. How ironic, we're about to find Melissa and now Pepper's gone. I rush to my room, throw on my sweats, and head out to do a quick search of the neighborhood. By the time I get out the front door, Pepper and Ruby are heading my way.

"When did you get home? I thought my grandmother had let him get out."

"I got here right after your grandmother left. I tried to flag her down in the parking lot, but I don't think she saw me. As soon as I got here, Pepper was all over me wanting to use the restroom and stretch his legs."

"Hey, Pepper," I say, hugging and kissing him. "Ruby, I have to get going. I have to meet Sam at DHPD, but first I have to go by my parents' hou — "

"Excuse me, but weren't you on KYON last night? You're the twin right?" Ruby and I exchange knowing looks, and then turn our attention to the middle-aged man holding out a piece of paper and a pen. "Can I get your autograph? And I hope you find your sister."

"Thank you," I say, scribbling my name on the paper.

"No, *thank you.*"

Before Ruby and I can continue, more people jam us up, inquiring about the interview, asking for my autograph. Pepper, nervous, howls and rears up, sending everyone running for cover, giving us enough time to make our getaway. The three of us, out of breath, run into the house. I shut and lock the door.

"What is going on?" Ruby asks.

"Everything is going on. George and Sam called me and told me they're getting tons of calls about the interview and that there have been Melissa sightings all over the place. And the ratings went through the roof and Curt wants me to have my own show."

"Shut the hell up," Ruby says.

"Have you been on the sites today? I couldn't access anything," I say.

Ruby sits at my computer and checks out my website and other accounts. "The website crashed. Too many people were trying to get on at the same time. Don't worry. I'll take care of it. You get ready and go see your parents so you can follow-up on the leads with Sam."

"Right," I say, rushing off to the shower.

♊

I slip out of the apartment with my shades on, a pair of jeans, and a comfy blue t-shirt. Right as I'm about to get in the car, the man who asked for my autograph points to me from across the street and motions to other people. They head my way, but I get in the car and take off before they can catch up to me. This is absolutely insane. Now I know how celebrities feel and I'm a nobody.

It's a beautiful day outside, and I feel beautiful inside — happy like I did the day I had the first dream about Melissa. I can't wait to see my mother's face when I tell her there have been Melissa sightings. I get on the ten freeway east, making good time. When I get close to Dancing Hills, my phone rings. "Answer," I say into my Bluetooth. "Grandma, I'm sorry I was supposed to call you when I found Pepper. Ruby had him and I have a lot of other good news. Grandma, are you there?"

"I'm here. I'm glad you found Pepper because now I'm lost."

"Lost? I thought you'd be home by now."

"I thought so, too, but I'm all turned around, and I'm about to run out of gas."

"Grandma, use the GPS on your phone."

"Maddie, I don't know how to work that darn thing."

"Just hit—"

"I've tried that and…and…"

I hope she's not drinking and driving again. "Grandma, you haven't taken any of your 'medicine' since you left the house have you?"

There's silence and I take a deep breath. "Grandma?"

"Maybe a little."

"I want you to stop right now and park the car and tell me what street you're on."

"Maddie, I see a bus that says Dancing Hills Shopping Mall and Medical Plaza. That's not far from the house. I'm going to get on the…the…bus. Yep. The bus."

"Grandma, wait. Wait. Hello? Hello?" *Wow, I can't believe this.*

Thank God I'm not too far away. I should call my parents, but my grandmother would never forgive me. I speak into my Bluetooth. "Call Ruby."

"Hey, Maddie. What's going on?"

"My grandmother is at it again."

"Don't tell me she's drinking and driving."

"She's supposed to be on a bus. Do you remember the route of the bus that goes to the mall?"

"Yeah. Where are you?"

"I just passed Birdsview."

"Get off on the next exit. Valley Boulevard. All the buses going that way go to the mall."

"Thanks. I'm going to try to call her again."

"Be careful, Maddie."

"Will do," I say, hanging up.

"Call Grandma." I continue onto the exit listening to my grandmother's phone ringing. "Where is she?"

I get off of the freeway and drive south along the bus route, craning my neck, still searching, thinking about the intervention I'm going to orchestrate. She needs help and it would be totally irresponsible of us not to make sure she gets it. Maybe if someone had been there for Judy, she wouldn't have ended up in the streets and losing my mother.

I rubberneck when I spot a bus in my rearview mirror that says, MALL/MEDICAL PLAZA. I drive ahead of it, park, and get out of the car. I flag the bus down. The driver's eyes bug out. Shaking his head, he points forward. I look up and the bus now says OUT OF SERVICE. He stops at a red light, and I go to the door and knock. He opens it and gives me the once-over.

"I'm sorry, but do you think you can help me? My grandmother is ill and she told me she got on a bus going to the mall. Is there any way you can call dispatch and see if word can be sent to the other drivers to look out for her? I would really appreciate it."

He grimaces, picks up a sheet of paper from his console, and stares at me. I start to repeat my request, but he speaks first. "It's you. You, you the one. Right here, on this flier, and on the TV. I saw you last night. My goodness, I can't believe my eyes. I'm seeing you," he says with a thick African accent. "I get excited when I see that program, because I remember when I first worked here. Almost twenty years ago. I was a younger man. I was going home, back to Nigeria the day I see you. Not you now, but you small." He extends his hand in attempt to show me how tall I was. "So you're found now."

"No, the girl on the picture is my missing twin. I was the girl on the TV program talking about my missing twin."

"So your sister was the girl on the bus?"

"What bus?"

"This one, not this same one, but the bus I was driving that day. Just like now, I was off duty, and there was a lady. She look like you, but a little older. And she had a little girl. She ran out in front of my bus. I almost hit her and the girl. It frightened me. She was crying, upset, her and the girl. She said she had been carjacked. She asked me to call the police. I let her on the bus with the girl, with you, and I called in her situation. I'll never forget that girl, this girl, you. Beautiful golden hair and blue eyes. I always wanted to know what happened, but I was away in my country. When I came back a year later, I forgot about it. Now all these years, I see it all on TV and fliers."

"Are you telling me you saw my mother upset and crying?"

"Yes."

"What's your name?"

"Babatunde. Babatunde Eka."

"Babatunde, I was that little girl. I was crying."

"I'm sorry. I hope you are better."

"I am. Babtunde, did you see a car, an SUV? Was my mother driving a car?"

"No, this lady was on foot, her and the little girl...you. They were hysertics...how do you say it?"

"Hysterical."

"Right. Yes. She didn't have a car, but I saw a car, a black SUV speed past me, driving crazy. It caught my eye, because I noticed a sign on the bumper that said *Twins on Board*. I remember wondering who would drive like that with children in the car."

"That was my mother's car. Did you see who was driving?"

"No, I'm sorry. But I did help your mother as much as I can. She was so upset and it scared me. She scared me. Then she grabbed the girl...you, and jumped off the bus. I was scared for her and myself, because at the time I was not here legally. I'm ashamed to say I didn't have my paperwork together, but today I am a proud citizen," he says, beaming.

"Con...congratulations," I say, wanting to stay on track. "Babatunde, what happened after my mother got off of the bus?"

"I see her going around in circles, running here and there. And then she goes to a phone booth and then more people come. Then I hear sirens and I see police cars from a distance, then I leave. Didn't want trouble, you know."

"Babatunde, thank you so much. You're the first person and only person to have seen my mother after she was carjacked, well, to have seen her car."

"My God. I still wonder who would do something to such a beautiful woman with her child."

"Do you have a phone number?" He reaches into his pocket and hands me a business card. "Thank you so much. I'll be in touch. Oh, can you also put the word out about my Grandmother? Her name is Alicia Patterson."

"I will do that for you."

II

Pulling into my parents' house, I feel like the heavens have opened and poured every blessing available right into my lap. My grandmother was found and is safely home now. I rush out of the car, so full of excitement; I feel like I'm going to detonate. Letting myself in, I holler, "Mom, Dad, where are you? I need to talk to you."

My father comes to the foyer with his index finger over his mouth. "Shhh, I finally got your mother to go to sleep?"

"What's wrong with her?"

"She saw the show, kiddo. I tried to keep it from her, but one of the neighbors came over. She's seen the fliers, too. She knows what's going on. She hasn't been to sleep all night. I told you, Maddie. I told you this would happen."

My father's words cause my face to drop, and I stand here contemplating my next move. "Dad, I need to see mom. I have so much good news I want to burst. First off, there have been Melissa sightings all over the place, and I met the bus driver who saw mom after the carjacking. He said mom was crying and upset and so was I. He saw the carjackers in the car. Finally, there's a witness, Dad. Mom was carjacked."

We turn toward the stairs when my mother approaches. "Millicent, go back to bed, sweetie."

"No, Alvin, I'm not going back to bed."

I brush past my father and meet my mother at the bottom of the stairs. I hug her tight; wanting to make her past and all her suffering go away. I take her to the living room and sit her down. My father follows us.

She looks up at me with tear-filled eyes. "Why did you do it, Maddie? After I told you not to."

"Do what?" I say, sitting next to her.

"Why did you start this search, this three-ring circus, all over again?"

"Mom, it's okay. The show I did yesterday got people talking. We've been getting all kinds of tips about Melissa. So much has happened; I haven't been able to tell you about. I went to see your parents, but I met Caroline."

"You met Caroline?" she asks.

"Yes and she told me everything. About the Darcys and

what they did to you."

She rises and walks to the window in the living room, peering out, trembling. I go to her and put my arms around her. "Mom, it's okay. And guess what, Ruby and — "

"Ruby?"

"Yes, Ruby's been helping me. We found a letter from your mother to you. I have a copy in my purse. Mom, she loves you. She didn't mean to give you away. I have it right here."

I run to my purse, grab the letter, and thrust it into my mother's hand. She holds it without looking at it.

"And it gets better. Today I met the bus driver who helped us. He saw the TV program and the fliers and he remembers us. Mom, he remembers us. He saw you crying. He saw the carjackers speeding away in our car. There were people who didn't believe you. Now this proves you were telling the truth."

I stand here waiting for her to come away from the window, to hug me, and to tell me how proud she is. She walks to me and I extend my arms to her. She walks past me and rips the letter into pieces. I let my arms drop to my sides while I stand with my mouth open, watching the shreds of paper fall to the floor. I snap out of my stupor and go to her.

"Mom, I'm sorry. I didn't know it would upset you like this. Didn't you hear me? People have seen Melissa. She's alive."

"Why do you insist on doing this, Maddie? Melissa is not alive."

"She is, Mom. You have to have faith. You have to believe."

"I said she is not alive!"

"How do you know? You don't know that."

"I do!" she screams.

"How can you be so sure?"

"Because I killed her!"

While I stand before my mother, with a quivering face, I watch her stumble to the sofa and sit. My father joins her. He caresses her back while she weeps. I want to move, but my feet are glued to the Berber carpet. Tears well up in my eyes and I force my feet to go forward. Now standing over my parents I say, "What do you mean you killed Melissa?" My heart is racing, and I'm hoping and praying that's not what she said, that I heard her wrong.

"I killed her, Maddie. In my mind she's dead. I had to kill her in my mind," she says, pressing on her head. "That was my baby—my precious little girl. She was a miracle. You both were. So many doctors told me I would never conceive, never have a child after that monster in Long Beach destroyed my insides, but God saw different. Not only did I have a child, but I had two children. The day we found out we were pregnant was the happiest day of our lives," she says, gazing at my father.

"Yes, it was," my father says.

"Maddie, she can't be alive, because if I let myself believe she's alive, then I have to wonder if she's okay. If she's alive, then she's vulnerable, and your father and I can't be there to keep her safe, to protect her. It's the only way I've survived all these years. It's the only way I've been able to be here for you. Because if I allow myself for even an instant to believe she's alive, then my mind will be flooded with the unimaginable, horrible things, things that make me want to die. So I keep telling myself she's no more. She's no longer here with us. Just her Spirit is here. No one can hurt her Spirit."

I sit on the other side of my mother and hold her hand. "It's okay, Mom. I'm so sorry."

"No, I'm sorry," she says. "I should have been a better mother."

"You're a great mother," I say, squeezing her hand.

"Listen to her, Millicent. She's right. You're a great mother," my father says.

"I haven't always been a 'great mother.' As much as I loved having you and Melissa, sometimes it was too much. I didn't always have it together, Maddie. I was so nervous —

so all over the place. My hormones were doing strange things and Melissa used to cry, she cried a lot. I keep thinking about that day, wondering what I could have done differently. Maybe if I had canceled the doctor's appointment. Maybe if I had gone down another street. Maybe if I had been paying attention more. Blame, blame, blame. It's all my fault."

"Stop, Millicent. Stop saying that," my father says.

"If only I could take that day back," my mother says, her blue eyes shifting from me to my father.

"What happened, Mom?"

Chapter 19

My mother looks at me, almost through me, and takes my hand. "Maddie, I was so young and unprepared. I didn't know how to be a mother. I never had a good example. Mother Gardner, Mother Darcy, Mother Patterson—they all had their struggles. The day I took you and Melissa to the doctor, I was at a loss. I remember asking myself that day, 'What would Mother Teresa do?' What would she do if she had to take her twins to the doctor, but every time she reaches for the oldest, she's spat on, scratched, and kicked? What would she do when she tries to sing to her, but instead of enjoying her singing, the child cries and screams unmercifully?"

"Grandma Patterson told me Melissa cried a lot," I say.

"Your mother did her best," my father says, wringing his hands.

"I begged your sister to stop crying that day, but she wouldn't. 'Melissa, please, please stop crying. Please stop crying for, Mommie.' That's what I told her, but she looked at me, laughed, and screamed even louder. It was like she was taunting me. Then I said, 'Melissa, look at Maddie. Look how sweet she is. She's not crying. She's a big girl. See what a big girl Maddie is?'"

"Did she stop after that?" I ask.

"No, but you were so cute. You tried to get her to stop crying. I remember it like it was yesterday. 'No cry, Missy. No cry.' You didn't know how to pronounce her name yet."

"We thought it was so adorable," my father says, grinning and rocking.

"Then she got quiet. The silence was more than golden. I felt a sense of relief, because I had already missed three appointments in a row and I didn't want to miss a fourth one. Then she started wailing again. At that point I couldn't take it, so I went to the medicine cabinet and got cotton balls. I stuffed my ears."

"Wow," I say.

"From the bathroom, I could hear you both crying now. I ran back to your bedroom and the two of you were a sight—twisted red faces, red eyes, and runny noses. 'You're supposed to be big girls. Look at the big girl spreads and pillows Grandma Patterson bought you.' I was hoping that would calm you down. Then Melissa asked for her pillow."

"The pillow from my dream."

"I grabbed it and put it in her arms. She squeezed it and tumbled over. I helped her stand up right. It seemed to do the trick. I removed the cotton from my ears and prepared to leave, but the moment I touched my purse, Melissa turned on her screaming machine. That's when I knew I needed help. I called Grandma Patterson. It was the last thing I should have done, because she made me feel like the worst mother in the world and she refused to help me. Said she had her art show."

"Kiddo, your grandmother had issues back then. She's changed a lot."

"That's a matter of opinion, Alvin," my mother says.

"Grandma told me about not helping you, Mom, and she really feels badly about that. She says that's why she drinks so much."

"Well, I needed her that day. She did tell me to put you all in your jackets, and for me to wear one, and that did help to a point. I mean, I was able to get you two into the car. On the way out, Melissa started asking for her pillow, so I gave it to her, and I hurried to the garage through the kitchen. I was praying the fat guy across the street wasn't watching."

"The Renter," I say.

"The who?" my mother asks.

"Maddie and Ruby named the stalker The Renter," my father says.

"I found out about him when I was doing my investigation, Mom. I believe your mother hired him."

Frowning, my mother looks at me and says, "I could believe that. My mother was worse than Grandma Patterson. Anyway, I got you and Melissa into your car seats and I sped off. Unfortunately, when I drove over the speed bump at the end of the block, it set Melissa off. She threw the pillow and started yanking on her hair. In the rearview mirror I could see her flailing her arms, and I also spotted Mr. Fatso in his nondescript car following us. I came to a stop sign and ran through it, trying to escape him. My eyes scanned the road, looking for some place to ditch him. I swung a quick left into the construction site — the never ending construction site. Melissa screamed louder and my head started to pound. My eyes stung, thinking about what a horrible mother I had, what a horrible adopted mother I had, and what a horrible mother I was. The crying pierced my insides; every sniffle ripped me in two. The floodgates opened and I sobbed so hard my whole body shook. Blinded by my tears, I struggled to climb to the back seat where you and Melissa were, and I gave her the pillow, but she knocked it out of my hand.

Then she said she had wet her pants. I had just changed her. I took her out of her car seat, removed her jacket, and checked her Pull-Ups. They were bone dry. She laughed at me. Then before I had a chance to pull them up, she let me have it. Pee went down her leg, onto the car seat, and onto the floor. I started wiping it up while I gritted my teeth and frowned. Melissa, mimicking me, raised her eyebrows and grinned widely. I couldn't help but laugh. Then she giggled and you joined us. Soon the car was filled with laughter. The noise died down and then some of the sweetest words I've ever heard filled the car.

"'I love you, Mommy.' That's what your sister said to me. Maddie, it was so precious. I stopped wiping and swallowed hard. In that moment, hearing Melissa tell me she loved me for the first time, my heart got so full, and I no longer thought about how much she cried or how much she seemed to fuss all the time. I thought about how blessed I was to have my beautiful twin girls."

"That's so sweet, Mom," I say. "Then what happened?"

"After that brief moment of gratitude, I got you both settled in and I got back on the road. Feeling like the best mother in the whole world, I headed toward the main boulevard. I peered into the rear view mirror, hoping Mr. Fatso was nowhere in sight. I was in luck. There was a car behind me, but it wasn't his. I noticed you and Melissa in the back, drifting off to sleep. I also noticed the clock and that we were running late. I drove a little faster and made my way to Valley Boulevard. Scanning the block, I winced at the sight of the construction. The businesses were blocked off and there were signs and arrows pointing to alternative routes. I loved living in a new development, but the only downside was that there was so much construction. I guess that's the price of progress. The area seemed deserted with the exception of a few cars and buses. I came to a stop sign. Tempted to roll through it again, I thought about you and Melissa and decided not to push my luck. I came to a full stop. Out of nowhere a young man jumped in front of my car with newspaper in one hand and a bottle of some kind of blue solution in the other. He grinned at me revealing two front gold-looking teeth. He was about seventeen or eighteen years old."

I stiffen and brace myself while my mother continues.

"I told him I didn't need my windows washed. Then there was a hard knock on the driver side window. I turned to my left and my eyes widen when they met the barrel of the gun being pointed at me. I started to press on the gas, but I remembered the window washer, who had ignored my request. Oblivious to the gunman, he sprayed and wiped. I looked over my shoulder at you and Melissa and you were both asleep. The banging on the window started and I couldn't move or speak. I froze. I always wondered how I'd react if I was ever attacked. Would I be a fighter? I always thought I would, but I was paralyzed with fear. Within milliseconds a series of thoughts went through my mind. If I drive off, will he open with gunfire, killing us all? My thoughts were interrupted by his voice.

"'Lady, open this door right now or I'm gonna blow your fuckin' head off.' He said something close to that."

My father puts his arms around my mother's shoulders.

"I'm sorry, Mom," I say, holding her hand.

"I wish I would have been there," my father says, his face red.

"Trembling, I unlocked the door, and he snatched it open. He yanked me out of the car, and put the gun to my head. I begged him not to hurt us. I told him he could take my purse, the car, but don't hurt my girls. That's what I told him, Maddie. He told me to shut up. His eyes were wild and bloodshot. He said he didn't need my pocket change. He was young, too. Then the window washer started yelling at him, telling him they needed to get out of there."

"They were working together," I say.

"Right," my mother says. "The boy took the gun away from my head and pointed it at my chest."

"Jesus," I say.

"I knew he was going to pull the trigger, but he didn't. He told the window washer something about not getting enough money. I couldn't figure it out. I was too terrified. I begged him again to let me get you and Melissa. He told me I had two seconds. I scrambled and got you out of your car seat. You both were still sleep. I couldn't believe you were sleeping with all that was going on, but I was grateful that you were. You woke up and started holding onto my neck, Maddie. By the time I got you down and reached for Melissa, I could hear distant sirens. I thought maybe someone had seen what was happening and had called the police. They must have thought the same thing because they cursed, jumped into the SUV, and told me my time was up. I was grabbing Melissa and the car started moving. I got a hold of her jacket and fell away from the car without her. My heart was in my throat and a wave of fear took over my entire being. The car door was open and I was running after it, praying Melissa wouldn't fall out. The window washer closed it from the inside and they sped away. I screamed and yelled and continued to run after the car. I tripped over an orange cone in the road, and further up the street I noticed two teenage girls approaching. I ran to them, crying, sobbing, pointing at the direction my car was going. But it was no longer in sight."

"'Help me! Please help me! I've been carjacked. They took my little girl. My little girl was in the car,' I screamed. Failing my arms, I got in their faces and pulled on them both, trying to make them understand the gravity of the situation. They told me to calm down and they pointed to you and said you were okay. I told them Melissa was the daughter I was referring to and that she had been taken in my car. Then they told me to be careful, because you might get hit. I was so caught up, I didn't realize you were walking aimlessly in the middle of the street, Maddie. I grabbed you and flagged down the bus. He almost hit us. But he didn't."

"The man from Nigeria?"

"Yes. I was out of breath, sweaty, and desperate. I stood in the street with you in my arms, looking up at the bus driver's contorted face. He scolded me for jumping in front of the bus. I ignored that and asked him to call the police. I told him I had been carjacked. He told me to get on the bus. We got on and you started crying for Melissa and that made me cry. We were both a mess. He made contact with dispatch and told them what had happened. His accent was so thick, I wasn't sure if they understood him. That made me more nervous. The bus driver asked me what had happened and when I told him about the car he told me he had seen it speed by him and that he saw the *Twins on Board* bumper sticker. Then thoughts about Melissa being in the car and what might happen to her flooded my head, and I threw up breakfast right there on the floor of the bus. I apologized but he said it was okay. Then I started panicking because the police were still nowhere in sight. I grabbed you, got off the bus, and searched for a phone booth. I could hear the bus driver calling after us, but I shut him out. I had to get help. Talking through sobs, I told the 911 operator what had happened. People started to arrive, opening up their businesses, and they noticed me. Passersby started gathering while I was on the phone. Then the air filled with sirens. The bus driver took off and the whispering and mumbling of the group surrounding us resonated in my head. People were asking one another if I was okay? Were you my daughter? Was I on drugs? Stuff like that. Then I heard a familiar voice. It was Mrs. Brown. A horrified look crossed her face when she saw me. She scooped you into her arms and asked me what had happened. I told her we had been carjacked. She said she would call your father. Then I thought about how I would face him and Grandma Patterson and my legs went out from under me, and I sank to the ground. She tried to help me up. You screamed and then several police cars pulled up and an officer jumped out of a black and white and approached me. I collapsed in his arms. When I came to, I was in an ambulance and your father was sitting next to me with one hand holding mine and the other holding Melissa's jacket."

"Now I understand about the jacket," I say.

My father nods and says, "Your mother looked into my eyes and told me she was sorry. I told her the police were looking for our car. I told her to be strong and to tell the police what had happened. I asked her if she could describe the perpetrators. She told me it was a teenage boy with a gun and that he was Hispanic. Then she said there were actually two boys—a Hispanic guy with a gun and a black guy washing the window."

"Then I told your father I really wasn't sure, but that the boy who had the gun may have been white. I was in shock."

"I told your mother to calm down and to keep a clear mind. I told her she needed to tell the police everything she could remember. An officer approached us and your mother and I held onto each other, knowing we were going to have to be strong to get through this ordeal."

"And Maddie, that's when the madness began," my mother says.

My parents and I form a tight group hug, reeling from my mother's account of what had happened the day of the carjacking. I think about all the tragedy my mother has endured, starting with her mother and then her adoptive mother. And I know the pain I feel hearing about what happened to Melissa can't compare to what she felt the day it happened. A pang of guilt sucker punches me, and I turn away from my parents. I walk to the mantel and my eyes scan the family photos. I wonder if my search for Melissa has been worth it and even with all the sightings and leads, will we find her. Has this all been for nothing? Have I caused my parents all of this turmoil for no reason?

A hand on my shoulder startles me and I jump. "I'm sorry, Maddie. I didn't mean to frighten you," my mother says. "I know you meant well. I know you thought you could find her and that you miss her. It's okay."

I turn and face her. "Mom, if you want me to stop looking I will. Sam's waiting for me at DHPD. He says there have been a lot of calls. I don't have to go. I can let it go. I don't want to cause you any more pain."

She looks at me and I try to read her eyes, but I can't. "What do you want to do?" she asks.

"It's not about me, Mom. Dad's right. I need to consider how you feel."

"Maddie, if you want to continue looking you can. Just...just...don't talk to me about it. It's the only way I can keep it together. Do you understand? I can't get my hopes up. I can't let my imagination start getting the best of me."

"I understand, Mom. Dad, are you okay?" I ask.

"Kiddo, I'm good. You're like your old man, stubborn as an ox."

"Mom, are you going to be okay?"

"Yes. Will you come have dinner with us soon?"

"Of course," I say. "I have a meeting with Sam."

"Speaking of Sam, why don't you bring him to dinner the next time you come?"

"Okay, Mom. I think I will," I say.

Chapter 20

I pull into the parking lot at DHPD, thinking about my mother. She deserves some happiness in this life. I pray I can find Melissa. A smile wipes out the frown on my face when I imagine finding her and surprising my mother. My phone rings and S-A-M flashes across the screen.

"I'm here. I'm in the parking lot," I say.

"Okay. I was worried about you."

"I'm sorry. I should have called. I had a long talk with my parents."

"Why don't you come in? I'll meet you in the lobby."

"I'm on my way," I say, clicking the phone off.

I make haste to the entrance and stop when a police woman pushes the door open. I wait for her to pass and then I enter. Sam waves and approaches. He glances around at the few people and officers passing by and gives me a halfhearted hug. I can't help but think about our first kiss and if he's lost interest already. *Let me stop tripping. The man is at work. Putting his tongue down my throat wouldn't actually be appropriate.*

"Maddie?"

"I'm sorry?"

"Are you okay? I was saying we can meet in my office. I want to bring you up to date."

"Sure," I say, following him.

He takes me to the same interview room as before. I sit and watch him pace. He yanks his blue tie. Sleeves rolled up and a furrowed brow, I wonder what's on his mind. He sits across from me and smiles. "How are you?"

"I'm good," I say, maintaining a professional posture.

He squints and says, "What's wrong?"

"Nothing. I'm anxious about moving forward."

"You sounded so excited this morning..."

"I was until I got to my parents' house. My mother was really disturbed by the special KYON aired. This is all really too much for her. I even told her I would stop looking if she wanted me to."

He rears back and shakes his head. "You've come so far and I have some real solid leads, Maddie. You can't give up now."

"I know. She didn't ask me to, but she did tell me to keep it to myself."

"That's understandable," he says, looking at his watch.

"She told me what happened the day of the carjacking in detail. Now everything makes sense. She was carjacked, Sam."

"I believe you, especially after hearing from a witness today."

"What's going on?"

"I'm meeting with a woman in a few minutes. Here at

the station."

"Who is she?" I ask.

"She saw the special and she saw the fliers posted. She says she has some information that might help our investigation. She didn't want to tell me anything over the phone, but she did hint at her brother possibly being involved. I'd like you to be a part of the interview. You don't have to sit in. You'll be on the other side of a one-way mirror."

I give him a curious look, not sure I'm comfortable with the setup.

"If you prefer not to, that's okay, too."

"No, I want to hear what she has to say, it's a little different, eavesdropping."

"It's police work and she said she didn't mind talking to you. She actually wants to meet you, but I suggested she and I talk first. She'll be less self-conscious, and we'll get more info out of her."

"Okay—"

"The door opens and a middle-aged man with pepper and salt hair steps into the room."

"Hey, David, this is Maddie."

"Right. I saw the show," he says, approaching me, extending his hand.

"Nice to meet you," I say, reciprocating.

"David was the one who told me about Vanessa Fernandez," Sam says.

"By the way, she's here. I put her in the interrogation room," David says.

"Great," Sam says.

"I'll circle back later," David says. "And it's good meeting you."

"You, too," I say.

Sam and I exchange curious looks and then he locks the door. "Come here, you," he says, pulling me toward him. "I missed you."

"Do you? I wasn't sure when I first got here. You hugged me like I was your grandmother."

"I'm sorry. The guys around here like to find anything to rib each other about, and I don't want our relationship to be food for the fodder. It's too special for that."

"You think so?" I ask.

"I know so," he says, sprinkling my hand with soft kisses.

I get a little weak in the knees and my face fills with heat. "We better go to the interview."

"Yeah, you're right. We better go, because I might end up attacking you, Miss Patterson."

"I hope not. I'll have to call the cops," I say, laughing.

He unlocks the door and motions for me to go ahead of him. I get focused. We enter a small room, and I peer at the profile of the rail thin woman sitting on the other side of the one-way mirror. She turns her head toward the glass and runs her fingers through her long black hair with blonde highlights.

"You sure she can't see me?"

"No, she can't," he says. "I'm gonna go in. You okay?"

"I'm fine," I say. Sam leaves the room and I sit on my sweaty hands. The forty-something woman rises and walks to the glass. She examines her jeans and straightens her purple knit top. I notice a tattoo of a skull on her hand. She returns to her seat and fishes in her purse. I look closely. She pulls out a tube of lipstick and puckers her lips, looking at the mirror. She dabs her mouth and then jerks her head forward when the door opens. Tossing her lipstick into her bag, her eyes follow Sam entering the room. They shake hands. She gives him the once-over when he turns to shut the door.

"Would you like some water?" he asks.

"Nah, I'm all good. Like I was tellin' your partner, I don't know for sure if what I have is anything important. I mean, but I think it might be."

I scoot closer to the glass, anxious to hear what she has to say.

"Why don't you start from the beginning," Sam says. I notice his eyes shift toward the mirror and then he gives Vanessa his undivided attention.

"My brother, John. God rest his soul." She makes the sign of a cross. "He was no saint, but he wasn't a devil either. He had a conscience. He wouldn't kill nobody. Especially a baby. You couldn't pay him to do that. No amount of money."

Sam gives her a questioning look.

"Well, I think he may have had something to do with that carjacking."

Sam sits up straight and pulls on his tie.

"What makes you think he had something to do with the carjacking?"

"I said he *may have* had something to do with it."

"Okay, why 'may have' and why are you just now coming forward with this 'may have' after almost two decades?"

Vanessa recoils and runs her fingers through her hair. "I'm not sure if I like the tone of your voice."

"I'm sorry. Forgive me. I appreciate you coming in. We've been fielding calls all day, hundreds of calls and I'm...there's no excuse. Continue," he says.

"It's all good. No worries. Anyway, I think he may have had something to do with it, because I found some papers in his things. Notes, stuff like that. It has information on it. Like directions, instructions. It said something about a black SUV and Valley Boulevard. There was a description of a woman. It said she was pretty, blonde. I don't remember everything, but it kind of gave me the chills. And I also remember my brother coming into some money around the time of the carjacking. I remember, because we talked about the reward money and he said he had more money than the reward money under his mattress. I thought he was bluffing, but then I started seeing him with new things. Like Nike's, a motorcycle and stuff like that. He told me he was putting in a lot of overtime on the docks. Out at San Pedro. Then he disappeared. Word on the street back then was that he was living in Mexico. Then a year later he came back, broke and strung out."

"Vanessa, do you have these papers?"

"Yep. I have them in a safe deposit box."

"When did your brother pass away?"

"Two weeks ago," she says, rubbing her eyes.

"I'm sorry," Sam says.

"It's okay. He had been sick for a while. John Fernandez Junior. He was the apple of my father's eye."

"J.F."

"Huh?" Vanessa says.

"If you don't mind me asking, how did your brother die?"

"Complications of AIDS. It was a terrible way to go. He used to laugh and say he was glad he was already skinny, so you know, it wouldn't look so bad when he was losing the weight, you know people wouldn't be able to tell. He wasn't gay or anything. Not that that's a bad thing. He was into needles and stuff. Drugs."

Sam shakes his head and offers his condolences again. "Vanessa I'd like to see those papers. Actually, I'm going to need those papers. You can turn them over voluntarily or I can get a warrant."

"No, you don't have to do that. That's why I came in. I saw that special about those twins. The little girl who was taken was so pretty, and I saw the other twin you know being interviewed. It broke my heart hearing her talk about how she felt like she was missing a part of herself. That's how I felt about my brother. We were close. Then I remembered cleaning up his apartment and the papers that I had put away. I pray my brother didn't have anything to do with that carjacking. But if he did..."

"I'd like to talk to you some more if that's possible. I need to know about your brother's friends, homies, associates. Who did he run with?"

"Most of 'em or in jail, strung out, locked up, or dead, like John" she says, shrugging.

"I understand, but I still want to get a run down. When can you get the papers?"

"When the bank opens in the morning."

"I'd like to meet you there."

"What time?" she asks.

"How much stuff is it?" he asks.

"A lot."

"Let's meet at ten. David's going to come in and ask you a few more questions. You can give him the bank info. I really appreciate you coming out and again, I'm sorry about your brother."

"Thank you. If I'm able to help with this, it'll mean my brother's life wasn't in vain. I know whatever happened, he didn't hurt that little girl. My brother would never do that."

"I pray you know your brother," Sam says.

I watch him leave and Vanessa rises and paces. David enters with a bottle of water and sets it on the table. She opens it and sips. I turn my attention to Sam when he enters.

"Did you hear it all?" he asks.

"Yeah. I did. Wow, it sounds like her brother may have been involved."

"I agree and it sounds like he had been paid."

"But if he was motivated by money, why didn't he take my mother's purse."

"This guy was motivated by big money."

"Do you think my Grandmother, Judy Gardner, paid him?"

"I don't know. Hopefully, I'll know more after I meet with Vanessa tomorrow." He looks at his watch and says, "It's getting late. I want to go over the Melissa sightings with you. Maybe we can do it over dinner."

"That works. I am hungry, but I have to get home soon. I have to go to work in the morning, and according to George, I'm the talk of KYON. I have to get mentally ready to face everyone."

"Don't worry. I won't keep you out late," he says, flashing me a mischievous smile.

II

The music fills the downtown supper club and couples take to the floor. I look across the table at Sam who's singing along with the voluptuous songstress that's surrounded by a quartet.

"I didn't know you could sing. You have a nice voice."

"I didn't know I could sing either," he says.

"No, really, your tone is great."

"Maybe I'll try out for American Idol," he says, sipping on his wine. We turn our attention to the couples on the floor and then I feel his hand on mine. "Would you dance with me?"

I take a moment before answering.

"Don't take too long. I have to be at Vanessa's bank by ten and like you reminded me, you have to go into the station."

"Mr. Warren, we're going to have to stop meeting like this. We need to start scheduling our rendezvous for the weekend. But I'm glad you talked me into coming out. I felt so drained after I left my parents' house. Drained, but relieved, and now I'm feeling relaxed. The wine is helping," I say, taking a sip.

"I'm glad you're feeling better, and I'm happy you mentioned the weekend. One of the officers at DHPD is giving his wife a surprise birthday party Saturday. Will you be my date?"

"Let me see if you can dance first," I say.

He takes my hand and leads me to the dance floor. His timing is perfect. The singer belts out Adele's "Someone Like You," one of my favorite songs.

"I love Adele" he says, pulling me in close.

"I do, too. I'm a huge fan."

"What's the name of her first album?"

"Am I going to be graded?" I ask.

"Maybe. Do you know?"

"I do. It's called 19."

Sam and I exchange knowing looks. "Wow," we both say at the same time.

"What an eerie coincidence," Sam says.

"I know. It's like the color red."

"What do you mean?"

"It's nothing. But yeah, that was the name of her first album — 19."

"I think that's a good sign, Maddie. I know none of the sightings panned out, but you have to keep hoping."

"I am," I say. "Okay, my turn. What's the name of her second album?"

"21," he says.

He places his hand on the small of my back, and I lay my head against his chest, closing my eyes, breathing in his intoxicating scent. We move easily, without effort.

"You feel nice," he says.

"So do you."

I look up at him and he plants a soft kiss on my mouth and moisture materializes between my legs. I shiver and put a little distance between us.

"Are you okay?" he asks.

"I'm *too* okay."

"You want to sit?"

"I think we probably should go. We both have early days tomorrow."

"You're right he says," making a little manly adjustment.

I look away and head to the exit, with him following.

♊

"Ruby, Pepper?" I set my purse on the table in the foyer. A rustling sound gives me pause. I turn on the light and make my way into the living room. "Ruby. Girl, you need to go to bed."

"What time is it?" she asks, lifting her head from the computer keyboard.

"Time for you to hit the sack. What are you doing?"

"I was making some changes to the Facebook page and the other sites. Then I started reading all the comments about the interview. That led me to the blogs, the columns, the editorials. Girl, you should read some of the conspiracy theories. There are people out there that actually believe you, your mother, and Melissa were abducted by aliens and Melissa's on another planet and you and your mother are clones."

I sit on the sofa and remove my shoes. Rubbing my feet, I listen to Ruby, one part of me glad she's staying on top of things and another part of me feeling guilty that the Melissa Movement is taking up so much of her time. "That's wild."

"What's going on with you?"

"A lot," I say, stretching on the sofa.

"How'd it go with your parents?"

"It was a tearfest. My mother found out about everything and was really messed up. I think I understand her a whole lot better now. She's buried Melissa mentally. She says if she allows herself to believe Melissa's alive, it would be too painful."

"I don't get it," Ruby says.

"If she's alive, that means she's out there in the big evil world and anything can be happening to her."

"I get it," Ruby says.

"Anyway, I'm going to keep things to myself from here on out. I also met Sam at the station, and I got to sit in on a really important interview. There's this lady who thinks her brother may have been involved with the carjacking. She has documents in a safe deposit box. Notes and instructions. We were right. It doesn't look like the carjacking was random. It definitely may have been planned."

"Do you think your grandmother Judy is behind it?"

"I don't know, but I do know I can't wait to hear from Sam tomorrow. Where's Pep?"

"Sleep in your bed."

"That boy is so spoiled."

"Like they say, the fruit doesn't fall far from the tree," Ruby says, chuckling. "You must be exhausted physically and emotionally."

"I am, but it's a good tired. You know, finally going over everything with my mother, her sharing her story, we have a break in the case, and Sam and I went over some Melissa sightings."

"How'd that go?"

"It was a wash. But dinner and dancing were great."

"You guys went out?"

"Yep."

"Wow…can he dance?"

"We slow danced and it got really hot. Ruby, hmm…he had me going. I had to cut it short. I think it was a bit much for him, too. I'm not trying to get in between the sheets with Sam…not right now."

"I think you're doing the right thing. Keep getting to know him."

"Don't worry. That's my plan," I say, heading to the kitchen. I stop in my tracks when I notice a massive vase filled with over a dozen red roses. *I see Clay's at it again.* "These are even prettier than the other ones," I say.

"What are you talking about?" Ruby asks from the living room.

"The roses Clay sent you."

"Those aren't for me. Those were at the door when I got home. They're for you," she says.

"For me?"

"Yeah. The card should be right next to it. I forgot to tell you," she says.

Smiling, I grab the small envelope and read the card. *Long stemmed roses to brighten up your very long day. You stay on my mind, lady. Sam.*

"They're beautiful," Ruby says, entering. "From Sam?"

"Yes," I say, feasting my eyes on the gorgeous arrangement.

"He did good," Ruby adds.

"Real good," I say.

Chapter 21

Sitting at my cubicle at KYON, I make the final edits to the afternoon news copy. I can't believe how slow the morning's going by. I feel like I've been working for a week. *No more late night dinners with Mr. Warren.*

"Maddie?"

I look up at Tina, happy to tell her I've finished editing the stories she gave me.

"I'm done."

"Great. I see you're learning me," she says. "I love it when you're three steps ahead."

"I do, too," I say.

"By the way, congrats on your new show."

"Is that final? I thought it was in the discussion phase."

"Curt has a lot of pull. If he wants this show to happen, it's going to happen. The discussions are a formality."

"I like the sound of that."

"I better get back. You can send that copy to my printer," she says. "Send me a soft copy, too."

"Will do," I say.

I cup my face with my hands, giddy about the possibility of having my own show. Things are really starting to look up. I take a minute and check my email. I made contact with ten different people in three states who said they had seen Melissa. One in San Francisco looks pretty promising. A text message from Sam comes in and I stop to read it. I've been waiting to hear from him all day.

Hope urhvg a good day. Safedepositbox a goldmine. Need2talk. Interesting developments. Glad you luv the roses.

I stare at the message wondering what Sam has discovered and hoping it's going to put us closer to getting answers. My phone rings. Restricted flashes across the screen. It's not Kaitlin because she's in my contacts now. I answer, thinking it may be one of the people I reached out to today.

"Hello."

"Is this Madeline Patterson?"

"Yes, it is," I say, looking around, hoping no one is within the sound of my voice. "Who is this?"

"I'm the lady in San Francisco. I saw the show Saturday night."

"Right. Thank you for returning my call. You said there's someone on your block who could be my sister."

"Yes. If she's not your sister, she's a dead ringer. Only thing...she has dark hair. But you know it could be dyed. Whoever took her could have changed her identity. Poor girl probably doesn't even know she was abducted."

"You're right. When do you think you can send me a photo?"

"I just did," she says.

"Oh...okay. Let me look."

"Madeline." I toss my phone into my top drawer and sit at attention when Tina enters. "I thought you were going to send me the copy. When I got back to my desk, Curt and Maria were waiting for it. I told them I had it and it wasn't there and it still isn't. Whatever happened to being three steps ahead of me? Please send me the copy and take your phone out of your desk drawer before you end up leaving it and I have to contact you after hours. Then I'll really be pissed when I can't reach you."

I give her a sheepish look and say, "Right. I'm sorry. I'll send it right now." I bring up the copy and send it immediately. One minute I'm a star reporter and the next I'm a screw up. I really need to focus, and I really need to see that picture.

II

I pull into the DHPD parking lot, beginning to feel like this is my second home. Traffic was horrendous and I'm exhausted. I wish Sam would have been willing to meet in L.A., but he called me later in the day and said it was important that I meet him at the station. I look into my rearview mirror at my weary eyes. I feel like I'm on a rollercoaster and can't get off. I didn't like the sound of his voice, and I'm really anxious about what he discovered when he met with Vanessa at the bank today. I grab my phone and pull up the photo the lady in San Francisco sent me. I stare at the face of the blue-eyed beauty with long black hair. The lady's right, this girl looks a lot like Melissa and me, but it's not Melissa. The shape of her nose and mouth are all wrong. I sigh and check for more emails. I notice the message Sam sent me earlier and decide to head in. There's a part of me that wants to go back to L.A., back to my pretty loft, and my big dog, and forget all about this crazy case that's driving me even crazier. But I suck it up, put my phone in my pocket, and go inside DHPD.

⚏

"You look tired," Sam says, entering his office with two cups of coffee. "How was work?" He sits and places one of the cups in front of me.

"Busy and I got busted for being on the phone and not turning in an assignment."

"Sorry," he says.

I shift in my seat, take a sip of the coffee, then my gaze locks onto the elephant in the room—a large gold envelope sitting on the desk in front of us. "So how'd it go with Vanessa?"

Sam, silent, averts his eyes.

"What's wrong?" I ask.

"How much do you know about your father's business?"

I shrug and say, "Not a lot, but I know he's one of the most successful dentists in the area. Why?"

"Well, once upon a time, he almost lost his practice," Sam says.

"I know."

"You know?"

"My grandmother mentioned it when they had that fight about her drinking. She said he almost lost his practice and his license because of what happened to Melissa. He was doing a lot of drinking."

"This happened a few months before Melissa went missing. Your father was default on several loans."

"How do you know this?"

"Maddie, I told you what your father did at Oliver's really didn't sit well with me. I started checking into his background."

"Remember he was a person of interest, but he was cleared because he had an alibi during the time of the carjacking," I say.

"Yes, I know this. But..."

"But what?"

"There's new evidence pointing to your father, Maddie. I'm sorry. It's very compelling evidence."

"What do you have?"

"Your father was struggling back then. He was way over his head with the house, the practice, and a couple of other business deals he was juggling. Not only that, but he took out a half a million dollar life insurance policy on your mother a few months before the carjacking."

My eyes widen and I feel heat rising to my face. "What else?"

"What kind of relationship would you say your parents have?" he asks.

"They have a great relationship. It's not perfect, no relationship is, but they love each other. They met in middle school, lost touch after high school, and then got together again. My mother told me once my father said he would die for her and I believe he would. They're really close. Why are you asking?"

Sam dumps the contents of the envelope onto the table. He goes through the items and shows me a wrinkled piece of faded paper. He points to what looks like scribbling. I look more closely and I see my parents address listed, the doctor's office, the appointment time, the make and model of the SUV, and a description of my mother. I don't recognize the handwriting. It's childlike, but legible. It's written in black marker. Many of the words are misspelled. There are other scraps of paper with dollar amounts ranging from five to ten-thousand dollars. There are various numerical calculations. Then he shows me another piece of paper that says TAKE THE MOTHER OUT, DON'T TOUCH THE TWINS. A. PATTERSON.

I sit here, feeling like I've been gutted. We don't say anything. I don't know what to say and it appears he doesn't either. He finally breaks the awkward silence.

"I hate to say this, but I'm in the process of having a warrant issued for your father's arrest. A lot of this evidence is circumstantial, but it's still pretty damning. It appears as if this was never about you or Melissa, but about your mother. Your father wanted your mother out of the picture. He hired those carjackers, but fortunately for your mother, for some reason or another they didn't kill her. They probably got paid in advance, got cold feet, and decided to take the car not knowing Melissa was still in the backseat. They may have told your father they were going to kill your mother, but I have a gut feeling they never intended to. It was about the money for them. I believe Vanessa's brother was one of the carjackers. He had recently turned eighteen and she said he bragged about having come into a windfall. Said he wasn't violent. I have David looking into who he hung out with back then, and as you know, he died recently, so unfortunately we have limited information."

"What do you think they did with Melissa and the car?"

"I wish I knew the answer to that question, Maddie."

"You know that's almost how my mother described what happened. It's so hard to believe my father would pay someone to kill my mother. If he hated her that much, why did he stay with her? It doesn't make sense."

"Maddie, as a cop, I see it all. People do crazy things when they're desperate, when they're under financial stress. Who knows what your father's state of mind was at the time. Again, I'm not attempting to try and convict him, we have to let the justice system do its job, but again, with the insurance policy, his financial woes, and the notes, it's not a good look."

"When are you going to bring him in?"

"David and I need to have a conversation with the Chief. I'll give you a heads-up, and I need you to promise me that you won't talk to him about any of this."

"I won't, but I do need to talk to my grandmother. She needs to be warned. This is going to destroy her. She's already drinking too much." I clench my fist and force back the tears burning my eyes. I'm determined not to cry. I'm going to be strong for my mother, for my grandmother.

Why don't I take you home, back to L.A.? I don't want you driving."

"I'll be okay. I'm going to see my grandmother. I'll stay at her place tonight. I'll call Ruby and I'm going to call in sick. I can't go to work tomorrow. I just can't. I appreciate everything you've done, Sam. I have to go."

II

Sitting in my car, in my grandmother's driveway, I muster as much courage as I can. The last thing I want to do is cause her to drink any more than she already does. Emerging from the car, I look around at the quaint street that's walking distance from my parents' house. I approach my grandmother's pink and white cottage and the memories of my grandfather playing with me in the front yard lift my spirits. I miss him and wish he was here to straighten this mess out. I ring the doorbell, shifting my weight from foot-to-foot, hoping she answers the door sooner than later. After a few beats, I let myself in with the key to her house I've had since I was a little girl.

"Grandma? It's me, Maddie." The house is dark with the exception of a light on in the kitchen. I pause when I hear music coming from the television. I go to the family room. An episode of Dancing with the Stars is on the screen — my grandmother's favorite show. "Grandma? Are you in here?"

"Maddie...Mad...Maddie. What are you doing here?" I walk to the sofa and stand over her. She squints and attempts to sit up. "Oh my head. My aching head," she says, pressing on her skull. "Maddie, the room is spinning. What's happening?"

I look down at the beer cans and whiskey bottles on the floor and say, "Grandma, you're having a bad hangover."

"A what?"

"You've been drinking again!" I pick up the bottles and cans and make a beeline for the kitchen. "I'm going to make you some coffee."

"Make it hot. Real hot," she says. "What are you doing here?"

"I came to check on you."

"All the way from L.A.? Don't you have to go to work tomorrow?"

"I'm taking the day off," I say, making the coffee.

Shaking my head, I run hot water over the stack of dishes in the sink. The stove is covered in dried tomato sauce and there's a pot on the floor filled with old stuck-on rice. My grandmother needs help, and I'm going to make sure she gets it. After the coffee is ready, I pour her a large cup and go back to the family room. I pause, surprised she's no longer on the sofa. I set the brew on the wooden coffee table and walk around looking for her.

"Grandma, what are you searching for?" I ask. She moves away from the hall closet and we both jump at the sound of the bottle of vodka, she was holding in her hand, crashing to the floor. Clear liquid flows down the hallway. She tries to clean up the mess.

"Stop. You're going to cut yourself. What are you doing? You're going to kill yourself with all this drinking."

"I can't help it," she says, sobbing.

I help her to the sofa, and I put the mug up to her mouth. "Drink this. Drink it right now."

"Ouch, its' hot," she whines.

Once I have her settled, I leave her there and start my intervention. I grab a garbage bag from the utility closet in the kitchen. Then I go to her room and attack the bed. I pull the covers off and start pushing on the mattress. Out of breath, I give it one last shove. I search for bottles and find two. I drop them in the garbage bag. I go through her dresser drawers, her closets, and I look under the bed. I dump three more bottles in the garbage bag. I thoroughly search her bathroom, and to my surprise, I don't find anything. From there I move on to the den and the living room. Then I go to her painting room.

"Maddie, where are you?"

"Don't worry about me. Just drink that coffee. I'm taking you to A.A. tomorrow."

"You have to go to work tomorrow."

"I told you, I'm not going to work. Drink the coffee."

Opening the door to her painting room, I stop and breathe in the smell of paint, fresh paint? I walk to the easel that's in the corner of the room. I study the picture of my grandmother holding Melissa and me. It's the same photo my father has on his office desk. From the look of it, she recently painted it. It's beautiful with vivid shades of red and blue. I notice a large red tomato sitting on a saucer and chuckle. I wonder how many my grandmother had to eat to finish this work of art. I stop oohing and ahhing and get back to my mission.

When I open the closet door, I'm greeted by an avalanche of towels, pillows, and clothes. It all tumbles onto the floor. "What a mess." I pick up the items and place them to the side. *She's probably hiding a brewery in here.* I enter and search the shelves and floor. Just when I'm about to give up, I notice a cardboard box in the corner. *The mother lode.* My grandmother likes to collect those little bottles of liquor and this box is the perfect hiding place. I take the box out of the closet. It's heavier than what I expect. I sit on the floor and open it. I close it and open it again, thinking I'm seeing things. I take one of the towels that fell out of the closet and lift a large hand gun out of the box. I set it to the side. I didn't know my grandmother had a gun. It's most likely my grandfather's. She said she never worried about him working on the docks because he had a piece. I remember my father trying to talk my grandfather into coming to work with him at the dental office because there was an incident where someone had been stabbed. My father thought there were too many unsavory characters working on the docks. But my grandfather was fearless.

Curious, I rifle through the paperwork. There are birthday cards, grocery lists, recipes, old receipts, bills, and bank statements. There's also a list of names. The one that makes the fear of God sweep through me is J-O-H-N F-E-R-N-A-N-D-E-Z. It's staring at me, taunting me. It's written in my grandmother's handwriting. Underneath the name there are other notations. And then I see my mother's name listed a dozen times. And each time it's crossed out. I keep reading and searching. There are photos—my parents wedding photos. My mother is crossed out in each of the pictures. There's a notepad with dollar amounts ranging from two-thousand to five-thousand dollars. I grab the envelopes with the bank statements. I check every envelope but they only go back ten years. My hands shaking, I look at the name again. I turn the paper over and there's doodling and more writing. K-I-L-L. K-I-L-L. *Alvin & Sylvia Patterson* is written a dozen times with hearts next to each name. *Who the hell is Sylvia?* Then I see John's name again and next to it, T-Y-R-O-N-E J-A-C-K-S-O-N. Next to each name is $5,000. Sylvia? Then I remember what my mother had said: *Grandma Patterson wanted him to marry a girl named Sylvia. She lived on their street when they lived in Long Beach. Her parents had money. She thought Sylvia was perfect.*

The name on the note John Fernandez left behind was A. Patterson. We assumed it was my father—Alvin Patterson. The other Patterson never crossed my mind. "Alicia Patterson."

"Maddie, what are you doing?"

Chapter 22

I rise and face my grandmother who's standing in the doorway. She gives me a shaky smile. "Why are you going through my things, Maddie?" She walks to the pile of towels and clothes and begins folding them. She gives the gun and paperwork a gander but says nothing.

"Grandma, you asked me why I came over. I'm here because I wanted to warn you."

"Warn me about what?"

"Dad's going to be brought up on charges."

Her eyes widen and she says, "Charges. What charges?"

"He's being charged with attempted murder and kidnapping."

"Murdering and kidnapping who?"

"My mother and Melissa."

She rears back and laughs. "Alvin wouldn't hurt a cockroach."

"What about you, Grandma?"

"What about me?"

"Could you...would you hurt someone?"

She looks through me with tears filling her eyes. "You know I love you forever right."

"It was you, wasn't it? You paid those boys to carjack and kill Mom. It's all here, Grandma. Don't deny it. John Fernandez was one of the carjackers. His sister came forward with information and A. Patterson was on a piece of paper along with information about my mother. It was you?"

Tears streaming down her face, she slumps to the floor, wailing, shaking. "Yes, yes, it was me. It was me, Maddie. I'm guilty. I tried to stop it. I tried, Maddie. Believe me. I was crazy back then!"

I grab one of the towels and hand it to her. She wipes her face and babbles. "Slow down, Grandma. I can't understand you. What happened? Why did you do this?" I sit on the floor next to her.

"Maddie, I was obsessed with becoming someone. I wanted to live the good life. I wanted status. I came from nothing, and I wanted more for myself and for your father. I was the one who motivated and pushed him to go to school and to get into dentistry. Your grandfather didn't care about any of those things. He felt that if you had a good job that was enough. He scoffed at me because of my ambition, but when Alvin made it, your grandfather couldn't stop talking about his son the dentist. Then when we moved to Dancing Hills, I felt like somebody for the first time in my life. The women here gravitated toward me. They were impressed with my talent as an artist. I got invited to the join the Country Club. The women talked about their perfect lives and their perfect children and their perfect in-laws. I got drunk on their conversations, not literally but figuratively. I felt perfect...but then there was your mother and her mother and all their filth."

"You knew about Judy?"

"Of course. Not in the beginning. If I had, I never would have let your father marry into that family," she says with venom. "Your mother and her mother were the two pieces of my life I couldn't escape. I don't know what came over me. I don't know why I thought killing your mother would be the panacea to all that plagued me. I wanted Alvin to marry a debutante—Sylvia Oleander," she says, with a faraway look. "It was the hair, your mother's hair that got to him."

I sit here while my grandmother stares into nowhere, realizing that's she's mentally disturbed or worse—a sociopath. "Grandma, talk to me. Tell me what you did, how you did it." I remove my phone from my pocket. I put it on record without her seeing me.

"You promise me it'll be our secret."

"Yes, it'll be our secret."

"I found John on the docks. Sometimes I would drive out there and have lunch with your grandfather. I'd see all kind of weird characters down there. So when I got the idea, I thought about him. He didn't work directly with your grandfather, but he worked there. I could tell he was lost and desperate, hungry for money. We met and I told him what I wanted done and that I needed him to get someone to help him. I also told him not to hurt you or Melissa. He seemed eager to do the job. We set it up for the day of you and Melissa's doctor's appointment. I paid him up front. He demanded that."

"How much?"

"Five thousand for him and his partner."

"That was a lot of money for you." I say.

"He wanted more than that, but I wouldn't give him more. I wasn't too worried because I had talked your father into taking out a huge insurance policy on your mother. So I figured we would all be set once Millicent was out of the picture."

"Did you know dad was struggling financially?"

"Yes. I think I pressured him too much. He was taking on more than he could handle. But I knew we would be coming into money soon, so I told him everything would be okay."

"Did he know what you were planning?"

"Oh God no. He loves your mother. He would die for her."

"Then what happened?" I ask, choking back a mixture of rage, anger, and sadness.

"Well, the day of the carjacking things went crazy. First off, your mother called me asking me to come and help her with Melissa."

"Yeah, you told me that before. You said you felt guilty about not being there for her."

"Right. Well, now you know the truth. I was beside myself because she was throwing the schedule off. Then something happened. I heard Melissa crying in the background and something came over me."

"What?"

"A feeling of remorse, fear. All of sudden, I became human again, and I realized what I was doing was more than wrong, it was evil. As soon as I hung up with your mother, I tried finding John. That's why my art show wasn't a success. I never made it there. I was running around trying to find that little punk I had hired, hoping and praying somehow some way he wouldn't go through with it. I never found him. When your father called and told us Millicent had been carjacked, I almost passed out. The only thing that kept me from going under was learning Millicent hadn't been killed. But then the news about Melissa was beyond devastating. The guilt was excruciating. I struggled with what to do. Do I keep it to myself or do I tell my husband — the love of my life, and my only child, and his wife, that I was behind it all? But I wanted Melissa to be found, so I needed to tell them what I knew. But how do I do that without implicating myself?"

"So you didn't say anything? You let everyone go crazy with grief knowing you had the information back then that the police needed to find the carjackers?"

"I'm evil, Maddie. I'm evil and I don't deserve to live."

My God, she's a sociopath.

"What happened to the carjackers? Did you ever talk to them again?"

"No, I went down on the docks, but I couldn't find John, and I had never met his friend. He disappeared right along with the SUV and Melissa."

"Grandma, were you ever going to tell the truth?"

"I wanted to, Maddie. I think that's why I never destroyed the notes. Deep down, I wanted to be found out. Do you hate me?"

"I feel sorry for you."

"You should hate me. Because I hate me."

I lean over to get my phone and when I turn back to my grandmother she's smiling at me, but her eyes are flooded with sadness. "Are you really going to take me to A.A.?"

"Yes."

"Do you think they'll accept me?"

"Anybody is welcome who's willing to go, Grandma."

"Can you do me a favor?"

"What?'

"Can I have one more drink?"

"I've thrown everything out. There are no more drinks," I say.

"In the garage. I have a stash. There's a box next to the freezer."

"Grandma, don't."

"Please, Maddie. Just this last time."

"Okay," I say. I give her a look of disappointment and leave her there, thinking about her confession. Thinking about and wondering what's going to happen to her. When I get to the door leading to the garage, a tingly sensation comes over me and the hairs on the back of my neck rise. I turn and rush back to the room. Before I can get there, a loud blast stops me cold. "Grandma! Grandma!" I scream, running back to the room. When I get to the door, she's lying on the floor, the gun still in her hand, and blood pouring from her head. I grab towels and press on her wound to try to stop the bleeding. Then I call 911 and sit with her, watching her life soak the towel and spill out onto the hardwood floor.

"I love you forever, Maddie."

Ⅱ

Ruby puts her arm around me while we stand in my grandmother's front yard. I nervously tug on the t-shirt and jeans she brought me from home. The blue pants suit I wore to work today is covered in my grandmother's blood. I threw it away.

The coroner approaches my parents and Sam. After a few minutes, the coroner and other police officers leave the scene. My father and mother join Ruby and me in a group hug. Sam looks on while my grandmother's neighbors make their way back to their homes, some crying, others shaking their heads.

"I can't believe it," my father says, moving out of our embrace.

"She tried to stop the carjacking, Dad. She really did," I say, trying to gauge my mother's reaction. "She was sorry, Mom."

My mother, red in the face, looks at me. "She knew. She knew all this time and she never said anything. I've never had any luck with mothers." She walks away and gets in my father's Range Rover.

"Give her time," my father says.

"Of course," I say.

"Are you going to be okay? Why don't you come and stay with your mother and me tonight?" my father asks.

"That's okay, Dad. I'm going back home with Ruby."

He blinks rapidly and swallows deep. "Sure."

"Dad, I'm sorry about Grandma Patterson," Ruby says.

"I am, too, Ruby." He blinks back tears and then looks away. "I better get your mother home."

"Dad, I'll call you tomorrow. I'm not going in. I had actually planned to take...to take...Grandma to A.A. tomorrow." I get a glimpse of my father's tear-streaked face and tremble. Sam approaches and I curl over bawling. The three of them try to console me, but I'm inconsolable. Thoughts about every ugly thing my mother endured as a child and a woman invade my head. I think about my father and how devastated he is. Now both of his parents are gone. I think about my grandmother and her illness and suicide. Thoughts about Melissa take over and I fall to my knees, feeling empty and lost.

"Hold on Maddie, hold on," Sam says, lifting me into his arms.

My father and Ruby stand by seemingly more helpless than I am. Only God knows when and how we're going to get through this.

Chapter 23

I can't believe a month has passed since we buried my grandmother. A bittersweet smile creeps over my face when I think about her lying in peace next to my grandfather. A lot has happened in the last thirty days. There was a huge explosion in social media about my grandmother, and the station did a special follow-up story, covering her confession and suicide. I didn't want them to, but my father felt we owed it to the public because of all the support we had received during our Search for Melissa Campaign. Many of the people from the Missing Melissa Rally showed up at my grandmother's funeral and a small group is here at the cemetery today, including the women from Dallas and the two girls who thought I was Melissa.

Maria and I worked on the story the station did about my grandmother. I suggested we interview mental healthcare and substance abuse experts, so we were able to shed some much needed light on alcoholism and mental illness as well. I really believe my grandmother would have been proud of the piece.

I'm learning second by second, and minute by minute to get used to being whole without Melissa. I set a rose next to the three headstones here at Dancing Hills Memorial Park—one for my grandfather, one for my grandmother, and one for Melissa. Today my grandmother would have turned sixty-four. We all agreed it was a good idea to pay her a visit.

My parents, Ruby's parents, Ruby, Clay, Sam, Ted, Kaitlin, Tina, George, Curt, Maria, and I hold hands while Ruby's mother leads us in prayer. Afterwards, I greet the supporters, expressing my gratitude for their ongoing encouragement and for being there for my family and me. Then everyone disperses and my family and I head to our cars.

Ruby's mother has prepared a soul food spread at our place fit for kings and queens. Sam stops in midstride and claps his hands. We all give him a curious look. "What is it?" I ask.

"It's Mitch. I forgot to tell you, he called me yesterday and wanted to know if we could come by."

"Who's Mitch?" Clay asks.

"My partner," he says, staring at his phone.

"What does he want?" I ask.

"I'm not sure. Why don't you ride over with me and we can meet everyone else at your place later."

"Ruby—"

"No worries. Go ahead, Maddie. Dinner will be waiting for you all."

"Thanks. I guess I'll follow you," I say to Sam.

"Put this address in your phone," he says. "3451 Ivescrest Street."

"That's not too far from here," I say. "I've seen that

street before."

The others wave goodbye and Sam and I make our way to Ivescrest.

♊

Sam pulls into the driveway and I park behind him. "Is this where he lives?" I ask.

"No, unless he moved," Sam says, looking at the brown and white house with a manicured lawn and lots of colorful flowers in the yard.

We approach the front of the house and before we have a chance to ring the bell, Mitch flings the door open. He grabs Sam in a bear hug and squeezes a grunt out of him.

"It's good to see you, fat ass," Sam says, moving out of their embrace.

Mitch laughs and says to me, "I told you he's a work in progress." He motions for us to enter and we do so.

We step into the living room that's smartly decorated with a green satin sectional sofa and mosaic inlay coffee table.

"Have a seat," Mitch says.

We all sit and Sam goes for the jugular. "So what the hell is going on? I miss you. David is okay, but he's not you. Is everything okay? You mentioned it was family-related, but you didn't get into specifics and when did you move?"

"I didn't actually move. This is my father's place. I'm taking care of him."

"Is he ill?"

"He has diabetes and recently lost his right foot."

"I'm sorry," Sam says.

"Thanks," he says. He looks toward me and says, "I'm sorry about everything that happened with your grandmother."

"Thanks. Today's her birthday. We just left the cemetery."

"I'm sorry. If I had known, I would have canceled the meeting."

Sam gives him a curious look.

"I have someone I think Maddie needs to meet."

"Who is it?" I ask.

"Come with me," Mitch says. Breathing heavily, he holds onto the arm of the chair he's sitting in to rise. After a couple of beats, he's on his feet and leading us to a room in the back of the house.

I stretch my neck, curious about where we're going and who we're meeting. Sam puts his hand on the small of my back. We come to a door, Mitch knocks, and a man's voice can be heard saying, "Come in. It's open."

We step into the room and I gasp. Every inch of the walls are covered in photos of my mother, Melissa, and me at various stages in our lives. I also notice photos of a brunette, who I suspect is my grandmother— Judy Gardner. Mesmerized, I study the pictures. Mitch breaks the spell.

"Sam, Maddie, this is my father, James Faulkner."

I grab Sam's hand when Kaitlin's text comes back to me: *J.F. That's what was on the faded piece of paper my father found in storage. Sorry, wish we could have found more.* "J.F. James Faulkner. You're J.F? You're The Renter?" I ask, eyeballing the obese man sitting before us.

"Yes, I'm The Renter."

"Mitch, did you know?" Sam asks.

"No. I found out when The Special aired on KYON. My

father was watching the program, and that's when he broke down and told me about his relationship with Judy."

"You had a relationship with my grandmother?" I ask. "Is she the pretty brunette?"

James nods and says, "Please sit down, both of you."

Sam and I exchange inquisitive looks and then sit in the two folding chairs across from The Renter.

"I first met Judy when I busted her for prostitution in L.A. I couldn't believe someone as beautiful as she was, was out on the streets. On the way to the station, she told me how she had run away from home when she was sixteen after her mother's boyfriend molested her and that she had been living on the streets. She also told me about how she had gotten involved with this real nasty pimp. She ended up having a baby for him."

I share knowing looks with Sam.

"You guessed right. That baby is your mother. By the way, your mother, Millicent, gets her blonde hair from her father, your grandfather," James says. "He's doing time in San Quentin." He continues with, "At that time, Millicent was in a foster home, and Judy was trying to straighten up her act so that she could regain custody."

"Did she?" I ask.

"Yeah, for a while. Then she messed up again and got evicted. I was keeping tabs on her the whole time. I have to admit, I was sprung. I was in love with her. I had recently divorced Mitch's mother so that intensified things for me. Judy and I lost touch and then a few years later I heard she had lost Millicent. She says she was tricked into giving Millicent up for adoption. She had me track down Jean and Jerome Darcy and she had me basically staking out the place. I've followed your mother for a long time. The last time was the house your parents now live in."

"I know. Kaitlin Burhenn told me. She told me you were

there and my mother told me you were following her the day she was carjacked."

"Judy was obsessed with Millicent, but she was too afraid to approach her, afraid of rejection. After Millicent got married and had you and Melissa, Judy became obsessed with the two of you."

"My friend and I thought Judy had paid you to take Melissa from my mother," I say.

"Judy wouldn't have done that. Actually the way things worked out..."

"What do you mean 'the way things worked out?'" Sam asks.

Mitch gets up and goes to his father. "Are you okay, Dad? You don't have to say anything. You can call your lawyer first."

"Why would he need a lawyer?" I ask.

"Because I did something very stupid out of love. I would have done anything for Judy. I would have married her and taken her off the streets. But she didn't want an overweight ogre like me."

"Don't, Dad," Mitch says.

"It's true," James says. "I was there the day your mother left the house with you and Melissa. I followed her. She tried to ditch me by going to the construction site, but I parked and on foot, I found her. I was big, but not as large as I am now. But I was also quick and stealthy. I watched her while she sat in the car, apparently waiting for me to get lost. After about ten minutes she pulled off. I kept my distance, and ended up losing her. I was pissed, because I had promised Judy I would never let her out of my sight. Then I got lucky. She sped right by me. I was taken aback by how fast she was going. She was driving erratically. I followed her for about forty minutes, wondering where she was going. We ended up near the mountains. I kept my distance and used my binoculars to keep tabs. For the hell of me I couldn't figure out what she was doing out there with you and Melissa. Then I saw these two kids get out of the SUV. They weren't actually kids, but they couldn't have been more than sixteen or seventeen years old. A couple of punks. I tell ya, those two were a piece of work. Screaming and cussing at each other. I had my gun ready, figuring they had done something to Millicent, you, and Melissa. I knew the license plate and I could see the *Twins on Board* bumper sticker. I found a strategic location and moved in on foot, close enough to hear and see everything going down. I had my gun cocked and ready."

Sam and I exchange surprised looks. I scoot to the edge of my chair, waiting to hear more. James glances down at his right leg, sighs and says, "I'll never forget that day."

"I remember the Hispanic kid calling the black kid an asshole. He was complaining that the black kid didn't have his back. Tyrone, yeah...the black kid was Tyrone and the Hispanic boy was John. At least that's what they called each other. Tyrone felt John was grandstanding back at the carjacking and that's why they ended up with Melissa still in the back seat. Then they talked about an old lady wanting your mother dead."

"The old lady was my grandmother," I say.

"John said he never had planned on killing your mother. Said he didn't kill babies or ladies. Tyrone reminded him he had told your grandmother he was going to take your mother out. But he admitted to Tyrone he was lying the whole time and he would have said anything for 5Gs. Then they started arguing over what they were going to do with Melissa. John said they had to take her back. Tyrone wanted to leave her there and head to Mexico. That's when I stepped in with my piece drawn, ready to take them both out if I had to. I noticed John's eyes shift toward the car, so I figured that's where his gun was. I told them to put their hands up. They nearly shit their pants wondering where I had come from."

"I checked on Melissa and she was in the back seat playing with her toes, oblivious to everything. Gorgeous little girl."

"Then what happened?" I ask.

"They started calling me fat ass, and all kind of names, but it didn't matter to me. I had them cornered. I told them to get amnesia and to get the hell out of town."

"Amnesia?" I ask.

"He wanted them to forget everything that had gone down, including the carjacking," Sam says.

"Right," James says. "But before that, I made them strip down to their birthday suits, and then I shot my gun up in the air. Those two fools ran out of there like horses coming out of the starting gate. The blast scared Melissa and she started crying. I got her out of her car seat and rocked her until she started making sweet toddler sounds. Then I put in a call to Judy. I arranged for the SUV to be destroyed. I dyed Melissa's hair black and hired a driver to take me to San Francisco where I turned Melissa over to Judy."

"You're the man Melissa talked about in the dream — the man who saved her."

"I guess I am the man," James says, smiling.

"Where's Melissa now. Is she still with Judy?" I ask.

"Yes," he says, dropping his head.

"What's wrong?" Sam asks.

"What I did was wrong. I should have turned Melissa over to the authorities. I committed a crime I have to pay for."

Sam nods and runs his hand through his hair. "We'll

talk about that later," he says. "Right now I need you tell us how to get in touch with Judy."

"I can't do that," James says.

"What do you mean?" Sam says.

"Judy passed away early June. She had stage four ovarian cancer. But I can put you in touch with Melissa. Maddie, Judy had cleaned up her act. She gave Melissa a good life. A healthy life."

"Where is she?" Sam and I ask at the same time.

"San Francisco," he says.

She's alive. All this time I was right. My God, my sister is alive. I fight to keep it together and I ask, "Does Melissa know what happened?"

"She didn't until Judy became ill. Judy raised her as her own daughter. She named her Millicent Gardner. She paid her connections to put paperwork together. So Melissa aka Millicent has a birth certificate with Judy as her mother, father unknown."

"Does Melissa know about her other family?" I ask.

"Yes, she does," he says. "Judy told her and she left a bunch of journals."

"I wonder why she hasn't tried to reach out to us," I say.

"You have to imagine that this is all a big shock to her, finding out her mother is her grandmother, then losing the only mother she's ever known to cancer. This all just happened. She's trying to process it all."

"Are you in contact with her?" Sam asks.

"Yes," James says.

"Can you coordinate a meeting?" Sam asks.

"I think that's possible."

"He can as long as he's given immunity," Mitch says.

"I can't make any promises like that," Sam says. "What I

will do is give you a few days to turn yourself in."

"I appreciate that," James says. "And I'll get back to you regarding Melissa."

♊

I put the key in the lock at my apartment and open the door with Sam behind me. I'm nearly knocked over by Pepper when I step into the foyer. "I love you, too, Pepper. Where is everybody?" I ask.

"Stuffing our faces," my father says, biting on a piece of fried chicken. "Did you see your friend?" he asks Sam.

"Yep. I'm hungry," Sam says, going to the kitchen.

"Wash your hands, sweetie," I say.

"Yes, mother," he says, doing an about-face and padding to the bathroom.

I follow him, shove him in, and shut the door. "Hey you," I say, pushing up on him.

"Hey you yourself, pretty lady." He leans down and plants a succulent kiss on my mouth and I receive it wholeheartedly. "Wow. Careful. We're not alone," he whispers.

"Samuel Gregory Warren, thank you for coming into my life."

His face turns bright red and he smiles, showing off his deep dimples. "The pleasure's all mine. You know what?"

"What?" I ask.

"I knew you were something special the first time I saw you sitting in the lobby at DHPD with that shocked look on your face. The look everybody who Googles Mitchell Faulkner gets when they meet Mitch in person. And then after you got over the shock, you sat there. I was trying to get a really good look at you, but I couldn't get around Mitch. And then when I did see all of you, I started having shortness of breath, and I was perspiring. I thought I was going to pass out," he says, curling over in laughter. "You looked so sweet, so vulnerable, so delicious,"

"I love how free you are with your emotions. Don't ever change," I say.

Loud knocking on the door brings our conversation and Sam's laughter to a halt.

"Hey, you two, I have to use the restroom," Clay says.

"We'll be right out," Sam says.

We wash our hands and then open the door. Clay, with an accusing look on his face, shakes his head. "I'm not mad at you," he says, chuckling.

We go to the living room and join the others. I greet everyone there and in the kitchen. Before Sam and I prepare our plates, I ask them all to gather in the living room.

"What's going on?" Clay asks, returning.

"I want to take a moment to thank all of you for your support this past month."

My gaze goes to Ted, who's licking his freckled fingers. His eyes lock with mine and he sets the plate of greens he's eating on the coffee table. "Ted, thank you for showing up at my house on my birthday. You were the beginning of something beautiful."

He grins, grabs his plate, and resumes eating.

"Kaitlin, thank you for being an inquisitive ten-year-old, and thank you for never forgetting The Renter." She clasps her hands over her tear-stained face and nudges Ted.

"Ruby, my girl, my sister. Thank you for helping me. Being there for me."

She comes to me and gives me a deep hug. Her parents

join her.

"Mom and Dad Flowers, thank you. Clay, thank you for loving my girl and for making her an honest woman. Mom and Dad, I will love you forever." I blow them a kiss. My father catches it and falls down onto the sofa. My mother giggles and messes up his hair. He grabs her and pulls her down onto his lap. It's good to see them being playful. I want so badly to tell them Melissa's alive, but Sam and I agreed that it'll be better to wait until things are confirmed and then I want to surprise them.

"And my KYON family, you have given me more support than I deserve."

"It's been our pleasure," George says, stuffing his face with sweet potato pie.

"You're a member of the family," Curt says. Tina and Maria nod.

Chapter 24

Ruby, covered in green paint, climbs the ladder in the middle of our kitchen, looking over her shoulder.

"What are you looking for?" I ask.

"I was trying to see how much more is left to do. I think we're going to run out of paint."

"That's because you're wearing half of it. You need to go to paint school, Ruby," I say, laughing.

"What time does Melissa's flight get in tomorrow?"

"Six," I say, painting the area behind the refrigerator.

"Are you nervous?"

"No, Pepper, don't. Ruby get him, he's about to turn over the paint."

Ruby jumps to the floor and pushes Pepper toward the living room.

"Thanks. That was close. Yes, to your question. Yes, I'm nervous."

"How does she sound over the phone?"

"Like me. It's like talking to myself. We have the same voice."

"Did she seem nice?"

"Yes. I mean, it was somewhat awkward. We almost Skyped, but we decided to wait and see each other in person."

"That's a good idea."

"Speaking of paint, she paints," I say.

"Houses?"

"No, she paints like Grandma Patterson. Maybe that's where she gets her talent and she works at a museum."

"She sounds interesting?"

"Hmm," I say.

Ruby stops painting and glares at me.

"What? Why are you looking at me like that?"

"Because something's off about you," she says.

I lay my paint brush on the tray on the floor and flop down at the breakfast nook. "I guess I'm feeling a little blue today."

"But that's your color," she says, trying to cheer me up.

"Stop, Ruby."

"Why do you feel blue?"

"I guess there's a part of me that's afraid of the unknown. I've gone through a lot, my parents have, too, and things are starting to settle down. I have you. Sam and I are getting along really well, my parents are doing better."

"How is Melissa visiting going to change that?"

"I don't know her. What if she doesn't end up liking our parents?"

"Maddie, you've been through so much. It's

understandable you're a little nervous about her coming into your life, but like my mother always says, you're going to have to let go and let God."

"I don't know how to do that. Before I found out what my grandmother did, it was easy to trust. Now I feel like the moment I'm not in control, everything is going to go haywire."

Ruby pulls me to her and grabs me by my shoulders. "Look at me. Nothing is going to go haywire. You've been waiting a lifetime for this moment. You, Melissa, and your parents deserve to be together. Both your grandmother's would want that—Grandma Patterson *and* Grandma Gardner. I can't believe you haven't told your parents Melissa's alive. I couldn't keep a secret like that."

"We want to surprise them."

"More like give them heart attacks," Ruby says.

"Don't say that."

"I'm sorry. Why don't you go take a hot bubble bath and get ready for your date with Sam? Pepper and I will finish up in here. And Maddie."

"What?"

"Thanks for letting the kitchen be green."

"My pleasure, Rubik's Cube. And Ruby, I know I've told you before, but I can't help myself. If you hadn't believed in me and worked with me, I never would have found Melissa. You were my rock. Starting with what you did with the computer, the social media, your ideas, being there for me, not giving up. None of this would have happened without you or Ted, Kaitlin, Sam. I feel like I really didn't do much."

"I appreciate you thanking me, but Maddie you were the driving force. And I think you would have made it happen somehow with or without me, the dreams, Ted, Kaitlin, Sam, somehow you would have made it happen."

♊

Pulling up to Sam's condo, I glance at the address on the paper sitting on the console to make sure I'm at the right building. I can't believe I'm just now getting a chance to see where he lives. He's only a few miles from my grandmother's house. Why did I think of that? I get the jitters thinking about her old house. I repel the image of her lying on the floor, bleeding profusely. *Okay, shake it off, Maddie.*

I turn the engine off, and look in my rearview mirror to make sure all is well. Getting out of the car, I check out the block that's lined with apartment buildings and condos. Rumor has it this part of town is called Single Alley, because mainly single people live in the apartments and condos. I smooth my dress down and toss my hair over my shoulder. *Ready or not, here I come.*

Approaching the white building, I zoom in on the call box, trying to locate his apartment number. Before I have a chance to go through the process, the door buzzes and I enter.

"Maddie, I'm up here," Sam says. "Don't get on the elevator. It's not working."

"Okay," I say, climbing the stairs to the second level. He meets me and takes my hand, pulling me into his man cave. He shuts and locks the door and then holds me. I lay my head on his chest and he runs his fingers through my hair. "I love your hair," he says.

"Hair can't make you and hair can't break you," I say.

"Let me guess, Ruby said that."

"How'd you know?"

"Lucky guess." He steps back and his eyes trace the

shape of my body. "You are radiant this evening."

"Thank you, Mr. Warren and you look pretty good yourself. I like you in brown. It brings out your eyes."

"Come here you." He grabs me and lifts me off of the floor, swinging me around, sprinkling my neck with warm kisses. I giggle like a school girl and then he sets me back on my feet.

"I'm dizzy," I say.

"Now you know how I feel."

"Why are you dizzy?"

"Have you looked at yourself in the mirror lately?" he asks.

"Flattery will get you everywhere," I say.

"Is that a promise?"

"You are too funny, Mr. Warren. So take me on a tour." I stretch my neck, trying to check out his digs.

"Why don't we start in the living room," he says. "This is my grandfather," he says, pointing to an oversized silver frame on the mantel.

"I see good looks run in your family. He seems like he was a really proud man."

"He was. And that's my family at my sister, Susan's graduation from NYU."

"You, your uncle, and your mother favor."

"That's what everyone says. Susan and my father could be twins, with their blonde hair and blue eyes."

"Great pictures," I say. "You have nice taste," I add, taking in his modern art deco furniture.

"Over here is the kitchen," he says, nudging me forward.

"Smells good." I walk to the black and white stove where he has pasta and spaghetti sauce marinating in a large pot.

"Do you like garlic bread?" He opens the oven door and the smell of garlic wafts up my nose.

"You're making me hungry."

"And I made a fresh salad," he says, opening the refrigerator.

"You've out done yourself." I sneak up behind him and take a gander, wondering if he has the typical bachelor frig—no food and all booze. I'm surprised to see fresh fruit, some juice, cheese, bread, and lunch meat.

"Are you checking my frig out?"

"No, not at all," I lie.

"This is my way of celebrating Melissa coming home."

Upon hearing his announcement, the excitement I felt moments before dissipates.

"What's wrong?" he asks.

"Nothing."

"I can tell something's bothering you, Maddie."

"I'm a little jittery about Melissa coming and if we'll hit it off. When I thought she had gotten kidnapped and she was out of my life, I couldn't wait to get her back in my life, and now that she's coming, I don't know how to act."

"Come and sit down."

I sit with Sam on his sofa, hoping he can convince me that I have absolutely nothing to worry about.

"Maddie, it's okay to have the emotions that you're having. You have been through a lot in the past few months. I don't even know if I could handle all you've been through. Relax about Melissa coming. You have me, Ruby, your parents, and Pepper. We're going to protect you. Nothing bad is going to happen." He takes my hand and kisses it.

"You are so sweet, Sam."

"You're easy to love, Maddie."

"Love?"

"Don't be mad at me. Yeah, I'm falling for you. I can't help myself."

"But—"

"Please don't make more out of it than what it is. I said, I'm falling. I'm not going to pressure you, so take it easy."

"Can you do me a favor?" I ask.

"What?"

"Hold me?" He takes me in his arms and cuddles me. I feel safe, like I belong here.

"How's that?" he asks.

"Great."

"You know I'd like to do more than hold you."

"What did you have in mind?" I ask.

"What do you want?"

"Surprise me," I say.

He looks at me dreamily and says, "Your wish is my command."

♊

Sitting at my computer, I read the email I just finished writing to Melissa. I want to make sure I said everything I had planned on saying.

Dear Melissa, it was really nice speaking to you on the phone the other day. It was a little strange because it sounded like I was speaking to myself. We sound so much alike. I wanted to send you this email in preparation for your visit tomorrow. I have to admit, I'm really nervous and I wonder if you are, too. Maybe we should have Skyped. But then again, I like that we're going to wait until we see each other at the airport. While I'm writing this email, I feel like I'm having an out-of-body experience, like this is a dream. I don't know if you remember any of our childhood, but I do have some memories. I remember when our father would push us in our swings. I remember how we had our own language. Oh, by the way, I am going to have to show you the special, the TV station where I work did about us. They also want to do a show on us finally coming together. That's only if you're comfortable with it. I've only been working there a few months, but everyone is really great to work with and they've been really supportive. I'd love for them to meet you even if we don't do the special. I hope you like my place. My roommate and I (Ruby) painted so that it would be nice for you. We also finally got around to decorating. We turned our den into a guestroom, so you'll have your own room. I'm not sure if you're a clothes and shoes horse like I am, but feel free to bring whatever you want. I'll make room in my closets for you. I'm a size four. I used to be a size five. I wouldn't be surprised if we're the same size.

You'll love Ruby. She is smart (computer geek) and funny and can't wait to meet you. I have all your flight info, and I'll be at the bottom of the escalator waiting for you. I would love to hear more about Grandma Gardner and one day maybe I'll get a chance to read the journals.

Well, I'm going to end this email now. Sorry for being so long-winded. See you tomorrow.

Love,

Your twin, Maddie!

P.S. I hope you're not allergic to dogs. I have a tan mastiff named Pepper. I named him that because his former groomers used a powder that made me sneeze.

Satisfied, I hit send and spend time catching up with all my supporters and followers.

After about an hour, I notice an email in my inbox from Melissa. Excited, I promptly open it.

Dear Madeline, I just finished reading your email. I wasn't expecting it and it was a nice surprise. It's weird that you sent it, because I spent the past hour Googling you and checking out your Facebook page and all your other accounts. I can't believe I didn't run across the Missing Melissa Page. It's bananas. I'm really impressed with you. You're smart as hell. I wish I had you around when I was going to San Francisco State. I struggled, but I made it through thanks to Grandma Gardner. I graduated with a B.A. in art. It's taken me a minute, but I'm starting to get the hang of calling myself Melissa and Mama Gardner, Grandmother Gardner. Lol. I think we sounded alike on the phone, too. Sorry I couldn't talk that long. I can't believe I missed the big search for me and the rally. I saw all the pictures. Those ladies from Dallas are a trip with the wigs and stuff.

As you know, Grandma Gardner passed away around the time your campaign was going on, so I was spending most of my days at the hospital. You would have really loved her. She turned her life around and really did good by me. I mean, we aren't rich or anything, but she made some pretty good investments. We own the duplex I live in with my roommate Reba. Shut up about your roommate being named Ruby! That's crazy. When I saw that, Reba and I fell out laughing, and when I got to the end of your email and saw that you have a mastiff, I almost fell out of my chair. I have a mastiff. He's black, and sit down because his name is going to make you fall down. His name is SALT!!! SALT!! I'm not lying. I got him the same time Angelina Jolie's movie Salt came out. She's one of my favorite actresses and I loved that movie, so I decided to name my new dog Salt. I wonder if they'll get along. They probably will. Next time I'll have to bring him. Isn't that crazy?

I'm glad you have memories of our childhood. I don't have a lot of memories. But I learned a lot by reading the journals. Grandma Gardner used to spy on our mother and she had people spying on us, like James Faulkner. He told me you call him The Renter. It's so sad that he lost his foot. Anyways, he has always loved Grandma Gardner. And as you know, I owe him my life. I feel bad for him because he wasn't able to come to her funeral. And between me and you, he always thought Grandma Gardner didn't want him because of his weight. That was so not the case. She didn't feel she was good enough for him. I probably should tell him.

I'm sorry you had to go through so much. People would think I've gone through a lot because of being kidnapped, but I don't remember any of it. All in all, I've had a good life. It would have been nice to have had a father, I mean, I know I have a father, but I didn't grow up with him. I can't wait to surprise Mom and Dad. It feels strange saying Mom and Dad. I'd love to do the TV special. Maybe they could showcase my artwork. Anyway, I am talking way too much. I'm so excited. I think I love you already, little sis!

I look forward to seeing you tomorrow!

Love, your twin, Melissa.

"She wrote a book. That's your sister alright," Ruby says, looking over my shoulder.

"She said she loved me already, Ruby."

"I'm not surprised. What's not to love? I can't wait for her to get here. Lord, how am I going to deal with two Maddies!" I rise and go to Ruby and hug her. "What's that for?"

"For being you. For being here. For loving me."

"I feel the same way. I'm glad you'll have Melissa. You know we can't live together forever. I am getting married in a few years and if my hunch is right, you might be getting hitched, one day, too."

"What?"

"Don't what me!"

II

Standing at the bottom of the escalator at LAX, I shift my weight from one foot to the other while I wait for Melissa. Ruby and Sam wanted to come with me to the airport, but I felt like I should do this alone. I can't help but think about us being one egg. We were one. And then we were fertilized by our father's sperm. Then came the split, from one to two. Two individuals, but exactly the same.

My phone rings and my stomach flutters when I see M-E-L-I-S-S-A flash across the screen. *Please don't tell me she isn't coming or she missed her flight.* "Melissa, are you okay?"

"I'm fine. I just got off of the plane and I'm headed to baggage claim. I wanted you to know I'll be there in a minute. I sensed you were nervous."

"You sensed right. Why don't you stay on the phone, until we see each other," I say.

"That's a good idea," she says. "I like the airport here. It's easy to get around."

"I'm going to have to visit you in San Francisco," I say.

"I can see the escalator sign," she says.

I stand on my tip toes, gripping the phone.

"Are you there, Maddie?"

"Yeah, I'm wearing a blue sundress. What do you have on?"

"I'm at the top of the escalator. I can see you."

I disconnect the phone and look up. My eyes sting while I watch Melissa descend the escalator in a red sundress, the exact sundress I'm wearing, but red. Her blonde hair is cut short, making her vibrant blue eyes stand out. Her smile is blinding. My feet take off on their own and the next thing I know, we're squeezing and hugging each other, oblivious to everyone and everything around us. We pull out of our embrace, looking at each other, touching each other, tears streaming down our faces.

"You look like me," she says.

"You look like me, too," I say. "And we're the same size."

"I'm actually a size five," Melissa says.

We curl over in laughter. It's like we've never been apart.

"I feel like we've never been separated," we say at the same time.

"Look at that, we said the same thing at the same time," we say again in unison

More laughter.

"Are you twins?" an elderly lady asks.

"Yes," we say.

"You even talk together," the lady says, chuckling as she goes on her way.

"Let's get your bags," I say.

I notice all eyes on us as we head to the carousel. People tend to look at twins because they're rare and only occur in two percent of all pregnancies and out of that, thirty percent are identical. The other seventy percent are non-identical, or fraternal.

"Maddie, I see my bag over there," Melissa says, pointing.

"You only have one bag?" I ask.

"I'm not that into clothes, but I do love purses," she says, tapping her Louis Vuitton.

I grab her bag and we head out to the parking lot. Crossing the street, I notice her looking up at the sky. "Is it true it never rains in Southern California," she asks.

"It rains, but not a lot. I'm right there." I point to my car. We put her bag in the trunk and leave the airport.

"I like your car. I drive a Honda."

"Dad bought it for my twenty-first birthday." Melissa looks away, and I put my hand on hers that's resting on the console. "Are you okay?"

"I'm alright. I wasn't expecting what you said to make me feel that way."

"How did it make you feel?"

"Like I missed out."

"I'm sorry, Melissa."

"It's not your fault," she says. "I can't wait to see them."

I smile at Melissa, excited for her but also nervous. *Maybe it's not a good idea to surprise my parents. What if they don't react well? What if they go into shock?*

"What are you thinking, Maddie? You got really quiet on me."

"I'm starting to have second thoughts about surprising Mom and Dad."

Melissa's face turns crimson and tears well up in her eyes. I reach over for tissue and hand it to her. "I don't know why I'm crying. It's like all these emotions are coming up that I didn't expect. Reba asked me before I left why I was so nonchalant. I told her what happened was a long time ago and that I don't remember any of it. Even when I read about it, it didn't affect me. It was like reading a good book or watching a good movie. I did have dreams about the stuff I read, but it was like somebody else's life, but when we talk about it, it's real."

"I was connecting with your dreams, Melissa."

"I believe that," she says.

I grip the steering wheel, now wishing I would have let the members of Team Maddie come with me to the airport. *Melissa and I are identical twins, but we've led separate lives, we've had different experiences. I grew up with both our parents. She grew up with our maternal grandmother. Melissa may have resentments that she's not even aware of.*

"There you go again."

"What?" I ask.

"Getting quiet on me."

"I'm sorry, Melissa. I was thinking about our situation, about mom and dad and if it's a good idea to surprise them. Who knows how you'll react or how they'll react. I think we should really spend some time thinking about it. It might even be a good idea to call and talk to them over the phone before going out in person."

She stares at me, giving me an uncertain look. "You're right, Maddie. Let's think about it."

Chapter 25

"Ruby, Pepper, we're here," I say, entering my apartment. Pepper jumps on both of us, looking from Melissa to me. "Pepper, this is Aunt Melissa."

"Hi, Pepper," Melissa says, reaching out to pat him.

He barks and runs to the other room.

"He's huge," she says.

I set my purse on the wall shelf and motion for Melissa to leave her bag at the door. She does so and then she takes my hand and squeezes it. We stare at each other and then she smiles and releases my hand. I turn to go into the living room, but she stops me. I wait to see what she wants, hoping she's okay with everything.

"I still can't believe I'm in Los Angeles with you, Maddie. All my life, I was a single person. I didn't know there was someone out there that was my other half. When Grandma Gardner was diagnosed with cancer she told me there were some things she needed to share with me. I had no idea she was going to drop the twin bomb on me. In the beginning, I was angry with her. I felt she had robbed me of my life, but when I heard the entire story, I realized in a way, she had saved my life. If she hadn't had James watching, no telling where I'd be today."

"I'm glad James was there, too, Melissa. And I'm glad you're here with me now. I want you to meet Ruby. I'm not sure where she is," I say, stepping into the living room.

"SURPRISE!"

I stand back and take in the look of shock on Melissa's face. She waves at Ruby, Clay, and Sam and says, "Thank you."

I link my arm through hers and take her to meet Ruby. "Ruby, this is my sister, Melissa."

Melissa extends her hand, and instead of shaking it, Ruby pulls her in and gives her a warm hug. "We *hug* around here," Ruby says, smiling. It's a smile that goes beyond her eyes; it's deep in her inner parts. "It's so good to finally meet you, Melissa. Maddie was determined to find you and I'm so glad she did. She always believed that you were...you..." Her voice trails off and she averts her eyes.

"That I was still alive?" Melissa asks.

I cringe and Ruby and I share a knowing look.

"It's okay. It really is," Melissa, says. "You remind me of my best friend back home named Reba. And thank you for all you did to help find me. Maddie told me about how hard you worked."

"It was my pleasure and Maddie told me about Reba," Ruby says, beaming. Clay joins us and Ruby pulls him to her side. "Oh, this is my fiancé, Clay. He came back to L.A. to welcome you."

Clay extends his arms and then hugs Melissa. I notice her stiffen a bit. "Thanks for the welcome," Melissa says.

"It's my pleasure. Except for the short hair, I can't tell you and Maddie apart," he says.

Melissa nods and grins. I notice her look toward Sam. Melissa and I haven't had a chance to bring each other up to speed on our love lives. She did mention she also dated a guy named Richard and like my Richard, he cheated on her.

"Melissa, come," I say, pulling her toward Sam. "This is my boyfriend, Sam. He's a detective with DHPD and he's Mitch's partner."

"It's nice to meet you, Sam. Maddie didn't tell me she had a boyfriend."

"It's nice to finally meet you, too. You don't know how monumental this day is. Your sister has wanted to see this day for a very long time."

"Speech! Speech!" We all turn toward Ruby who's now in the center of the room. "Speech. Well, if no one will, I will," she says. "I want to welcome Melissa to our home, to our city, and I want her to know she's already loved. This is a day we've all been waiting and praying for."

I wait for Melissa to say something, but she's quiet. "Melissa, are you okay?"

"I don't feel well," she says. "Where's the restroom?"

"Around the corner near the front door. I'll take you."

"That's okay. I can find it," she says.

I follow her anyway and she goes into the restroom, slamming the door in my face.

"Melissa, are you okay?" I ask, knocking.

"I'm okay. Give me a minute."

"Are you sure?"

"Yes," she says, sniffling.

I stand at the bathroom door wondering why she's crying. Was it because of what Ruby said? The party's probably too much. Once again, I listened to Ruby. I'm going to have to stop listening to Ruby and follow my first mind. My first mind told me to keep it simple — to keep it between Melissa and me. She doesn't know these people. She's probably mad at me. I leave her and join the others in the living room.

"Is she okay?" Sam asks.

"I'm not sure. I think the party's too much."

"How's Melissa?" Ruby asks, sidling up next to me.

"She was crying in the bathroom. I think — "

"Excuse me, Maddie. Can I talk to you alone?" Melissa asks.

Surprised she's back so soon I say, "Of course. Let's go to your room."

I take her to the old den Ruby and I turned into a guestroom. I turn on the light and she smiles, seemingly admiring our baby pictures on the wall and the red and white comforter set and pillows. "This is nice. Did you do this?" she asks.

"Ruby and I."

"Maddie, I appreciate everything you've done, but I can't stay. I have to go. I don't feel well."

"Do you need to see a doctor?"

"I'm not sick in that way. I'm overwhelmed."

"I shouldn't have thrown the party. It was too much," I say.

"It's all too much, Maddie. The party, the only mother I knew dying, finding out our father's mother wanted to kill mom. This is your life. I have a life in San Francisco and I need to heal. I need to grieve. I'm not ready to meet our real parents yet. It was a mistake coming. I'm glad we got to see each other and I do love you, but I need time. I hope you understand."

"I do and I'm sorry for rushing things."

"We were both excited."

"When do you want to go back home?"

"Now," she says.

"I'll let Sam know I'm going to take you back to the airport."

"No, I need to be alone. I'll take a cab."

"Are you sure?"

"Yes, Maddie. I'm sure."

Ⅱ

It was great coming home to your email, Melissa. I look forward to your emails, your texts, Skyping. Can you believe it's been six months since you first stepped foot in L.A. Thank you for not giving up on me. I know I've said it a million times, but I'm sorry again about giving you that surprise party. It was so unfair and really selfish on my part.

I hope you had a good day at the museum. Work for me was really busy. Anyways, I am beside myself that you want to come and visit. And yes, to your question about mom and dad. I did as you requested and told them last week you're alive and well and that we've been talking to each other. I wish I could have taken a picture of their reaction. They are beyond ecstatic. I don't really think it's hit them fully, but it will when you're standing before them. They told me to let you know they'll pay for your trip whenever you come, so don't worry about that. This is all so miraculous. Well, I better go. Please let me know when you want to make the trip out here. Mom and Dad want to plan something special and we all talked about coming to San Francisco to visit you, too.

Love, love, love, you so much.

Your twin Maddie.

P.S. James doesn't have to do time, because the statute of limitations had passed.

♊

Maddie, good news. I want to come next weekend and I hope it's okay, with you and mom, and dad, but I'd like to bring Reba with me this time. She's so excited and she wants to meet Ruby. Please book the flights for next weekend. Any time in the morning. WE CAN'T WAIT!!! Thanks for sharing the good news about James. Maybe I'll get to see him, too.

Love you more, Melissa

♊

Sitting next to Sam in his customized Corvette, I turn to the back of the car, all smiles and giggles. Seeing Melissa sandwiched between Ruby and Reba is surreal. Her hair has grown out and it's like I'm looking at myself. I'm sitting next to Sam, but I'm also sitting in the back seat. Being a twin is different.

"What's so funny?" Melissa asks.

"You are, we are. I'm here but I'm there," I say.

"I know. I feel the same way," she says.

"You ladies have enough room back there?" Sam asks.

"Maddie, can you move your seat up a little?" Ruby asks.

"I keep forgetting, you have legs that go on forever," I say, adjusting my seat. "Why didn't you say something when we were back at the airport?"

"I thought I'd be okay."

"You could be a model," Reba says.

"I get that all the time," Ruby says.

"How much further to Dancing Hills?" Melissa asks.

"We're almost there. The sign says a half mile to Valley Boulevard," Sam says.

I roll the window down for a little air, thinking about my parents, wondering if they're nervous. This is the most amazing day. Sam exits on Valley and silence blankets the car. I think we're all nervous.

Sam exits the freeway. I look over my shoulder and I notice Melissa holding Reba's and Ruby's hands.

"We're almost at the house, Melissa," I say.

"Okay," she says.

Sam turns down my parents' street.

"Is this the street you grew up on?"

"Yes," I say.

"Don't worry, Melissa. We got you. You're going to be okay," Ruby says.

"I like the beautiful custom built homes with manicured yards," Melissa says.

"That's the house over there," I say, pointing.

"The large, tan and green, two-story brick house?" Melissa asks.

"That's it," I say.

"That's nice," she says. "Okay, I'm nervous as hell," she blurts out.

The car fills with knowing laughter.

"I don't blame you, Melissa. I would be too," I say.

"Ready?"

"It's now or never," she says.

We all get out of the car and Melissa takes in the yard. The grass is a bright green and there are an assortment of flowers surrounding the perimeter of the yard — daffodils, dahlias, hydrangeas, lillys.

"Somebody has a green thumb. I love flowers. This would make a great painting," she says.

"Let's go inside," I suggest. I take Melissa's hand and lead the way. The others follow.

Melissa thrusts her free hand into the pocket of her jeans while I ring the doorbell.

I hear the sound of footsteps. Melissa and I share curious looks. The door opens and my mother and father stand there with wide eyes and open mouths. They stand there staring at me and then at Melissa, as if they're trying to figure out who's who.

"Mom, Dad, Melissa's home," I say.

My mother and father grab her and pull her into the house. We all file in, observing my mother, father, and Melissa reuniting after almost two decades. They hold her and then examine her. They touch her face, her hair, her hands. My mother counts her fingers. They sprinkle her with kisses. They bring her to the living room and sit her on the sofa and sandwich her in. You can feel their love resonating throughout the room. It's overpowering and we all begin to weep. I join them and we all hug.

"I can't believe it, Alvin. Our baby is home. Our baby girl is home," my mother says.

Ruby leaves the room and returns with a box of tissue. We all take some and wipe our faces.

"Yes, she's home," my father says.

"Melissa, Maddie was determined to find you," my mother says. "Even when I begged her not to."

"I know," Melissa says. "I'm so glad she didn't give up."

"Are you okay, baby?" My father asks. "Did anybody hurt you?"

"We were so worried about you. We looked for you for a long time, Melissa. We had no idea what Alvin's mother was up to. We didn't know," my mother says.

"I know. It was a shock to me, too. But I had a good life, Mom. Your mother, Mama Gardner took care of me. She loved me."

"I'm so glad to hear that, Melissa. I wish things could have been different. I hate that you didn't get to grow up with Maddie," my mother says.

"It's okay, Mom. Let's not dwell on that. I thought about that a lot when I first came here six months ago, but I've gotten over it. I try to think about the positive side of all of this. I think about James finding me. Imagine where I'd be today if Grandma Gardner didn't have James following you."

My mother nods and says, "You're so right, baby. I never thought of that. That man who used to make me so mad is the reason you're here with us today."

"It's funny how things work out," my father says.

"We have a lot of catching up to do," I say.

"We sure do," Melissa says.

My mother looks at Melissa, and she squints. "You cut your hair?"

"Yes, it was shorter than this. It's grown out. I cut it all off to show support for Grandma Gardner when she was going through chemo."

"That must have been really hard on you," my mother says.

"It was. She loved you, Mom. I know she should have given me back, but she did the best she could at the time."

"It's okay. The important thing is that we're back together. We're a family again," my mother says.

"Right," I say.

My parents look toward Reba and share curious looks.

Reba flips her long black dreadlocks over her shoulder and smiles. "Hi, everybody."

"Mom, this is my best friend, Reba," Melissa says.

"Hi, Reba," they say.

My father, noticing Sam standing in the background, gets up from the sofa and gives him a hug. "Thanks, man for everything you did to make this day possible."

"It was, Maddie, Mr. Patterson. Ruby and Maddie."

"Yeah, it was," my father says, casting a proud look our way.

Chapter 26

The studio at KYON is packed to the rafters. It reminds me of the day we had the rally at McArthur Park. Only this time, the crowd isn't here to find Melissa, but to meet her. It's been three months since my parents and Melissa reunited and it seems as if she had never been taken. She sold her duplex in San Francisco and she and Reba moved to our apartment building and are sharing a loft. Melissa got a job at the Museum of Contemporary Art, and Ruby helped Reba land a job at her company. Clay relocated to Los Angeles and transferred to USC and is attending law school there. He has his own place that Ruby stays at more than she does ours. I'm waiting for her to tell me she's moving in with him any day now. Sam and I are doing well and we finally took our relationship to the next level and boy did he surprise me! As Clay would say, it's all good. Salt and Pepper get along fabulously and have formed a curious bond with the neighbor's cat and her kittens. My father finally got them from up under the house. Speaking of my father, he and my mother are happy and closer than ever.

I save my latest journal entry and shut down my laptop.

I wave at the Dallas Dames and the two girls who thought I was Melissa. Sitting in the front row, they grin and chat.

"You're a little shiny," the makeup artist says, dabbing my face with powder.

"Thanks, Gladis," I say.

"Maddie, you look stunning," Curt says, approaching.

"Are my parents and Melissa here?"

"They're in the green room. They're good. I love the idea of the live studio audience," he says.

"I thought it would be nice to have some of our supporters here."

"You're right," Curt says. He reaches into his pocket and hands me a few index cards. "Just some bullet points. I want to make sure you don't miss the highlights we talked about in the production meeting. I have great hopes for MISSING. I think your show could win an Emmy. George told me you're already working on your next installment."

"Yes, I am. It's called Missing Michael."

"I'm sure it's going to be a winner. Well, it's that time. Let me get out of your way. Break a leg."

"Thank you, Curt." He leaves, I skim the cards, the stage manager does the countdown, and then I look into the camera and say:

"Good evening. My name is Madeline Patterson. Welcome to Missing. We have a very special show for you. It's unlike anything you have seen or will ever see. Many of you are familiar with my story, but I'm sure there are countless others who may not be aware of what happened to my family twenty years ago. On a hot June in 1995 my mother was carjacked while taking my twin sister and me to the doctor..."

After I give an overview of the story, the studio is filled

with loud applause. Then quiet blankets the room when I introduce Melissa and my parents. My eyes follow Melissa, flanked by my mother and father. I motion for them to sit on the studio sofa, adjacent to my chair. The audience rises to their feet and there's applause and cheers. I take tissue off of my desk and hand it to my mother.

"Thank you, ladies and gentlemen. This is my family and thank you Melissa, and Mom, and Dad for being a part of my show."

"It's our pleasure," my father says.

"Melissa, please tell the audience what it was like when you first learned Judy Gardner was not your mother, but your grandmother."

Melissa shifts in her seat and clears her throat. "That was one of the most difficult days of my life. As you know, Judy had been diagnosed with ovarian cancer and she was fighting to stay alive. I was struggling with the thought of losing her. The last thing I expected was for her to tell me she was my grandmother and that a man she had following me, took me from the carjackers. At first I thought she was delirious from the medication. But she told me where her journals were and after reading them, I realized she was telling the truth."

"How did you react when you learned you were an identical twin?"

My parents grab Melissa's hands and the three of them smile.

"I thought it was a trip," she says.

The audience laughs.

"They say we all have a double, but to be an identical twin. That's crazy. Once I got to talk to you and see you, it was great. I mean it took me a while to adjust to everything."

"Mom, Dad, how has this experience been for you?"

My father nods at my mother and says, "You first, Millicent."

"This whole experience has been life-changing. The most astounding thing is the determination you displayed, Maddie." She turns toward the audience and says, "I didn't believe Maddie in the beginning. I couldn't let myself go down that road only to be disappointed. So much time had passed. It's been a rollercoaster, with Alicia committing suicide. I didn't know how we were going to get through it all. And then the day our doorbell rang and I opened the door, and there Melissa was. Words can't describe it."

The audience applauds.

"I feel the same way," my father says to the audience. "It's been excruciating at times. I made a lot of mistakes. I was against Maddie using social media. I was afraid for my daughter, but if it wasn't for the Internet, KYON, and you all, we may never have found Melissa."

"Melissa, how do you deal with the lost time? Does that bother you at all?" I ask.

"Not anymore. I had a life for nineteen years. Judy was a good mother. I went to college. And it's funny how things worked out. My mother died of cancer, but she didn't leave me alone. She left me with another family, my real family."

"You're right," I say. "On that note, we're going to take a commercial break."

The audience claps and cheers and the red camera light goes dark.

"This is absolutely brilliant," Curt says, approaching.

"Maddie, you're so good at this," Melissa says.

"Thanks."

The KYON photographer approaches and I notice Sam, Ruby, and Clay in the audience. They wave. "Let's get some shots," he says.

We all go out to the audience and greet everyone and then the photographer positions us for photos.

"Let's get a shot of the family," he says, motioning for my parents, Melissa, and me to get together. "That's good. Right there," he says.

"Did you get it?" I ask.

"Sure did," he says.

We move out of the pose and fall into a group hug. "I love you guys," I say.

"We love you more," they say to me.

The End